T0129436

MARK OF AARON

Mark of Aaron
The Fight to Build the Temple of Solomon in the California Desert

Stephen "Pops" Cohen

MARK OF AARON
THE FIGHT TO BUILD THE TEMPLE OF SOLOMON IN THE CALIFORNIA DESERT

iUniverse books may be ordered through booksellers or by contacting:

iUniverse
1663 Liberty Drive
Bloomington, IN 47403
www.iuniverse.com
1-800-Authors (1-800-288-4677)

ISBN: 978-1-5320-4437-3 (sc)
ISBN: 978-1-5320-4438-0 (e)

Print information available on the last page.

iUniverse rev. date: 02/27/2018

Dedicated to the Descendants of the Tribe of Levi
Joshua, Gabriel, Andrew, Stephanie, Harrison and West

Contents

PROLOGUE

Generations after the time of the Patriarchs, Abraham, Isaac, and Jacob,

Aaron and Moses came upon the Earth
And were of the Tribe of Levi

Moses came to Egypt and Aaron and Miriam to Goshen
God brought them together to free the People of the Word
Aaron spoke for Moses, performed magic before the Pharaoh,
Brought plagues
Together they traveled into the wilderness with his people
Moses went to Sinai with Joshua and received the Commandments,
Aaron remained with the people and could not persuade them to not
create the Golden Calf. When Moses returned, he held his brother,
and forgave him the transgression.
Aaron cried a single tear, that
collected upon his cheek and left a scar below his right eye.
Aaron become the keeper of the tabernacle in the desert,
and maintained an eternal light outside the tent that housed the Arc of

the Covenant

Aaron became the first Kohen, who as Priest would command generations
of his progeny to lead the People in prayer and his flock of Levi to attend to
the Arc and the Temple. After 40 years, Moses took his brother to a cave at
Mount Hor, where he entered a wall of rock that opened to reveal a resting
place surrounded by the angels of God. And the descendants of Aaron became
the Priests and
the keeper of the Temples.
When the Temples fell, they awaited their reclamation by another who
had the Mark of Aaron,
who would rebuild them.

From Rebbe Nachman of Breslov's THE HIDDEN BOOK

CHAPTER I

❖❖❖

ON THE DAY OF ATONEMENT

SANTA MONICA MOUNTAINS

There is some comfort in moving slowly up a familiar trail. The autumn sun warms the spot between my shoulder blades, old legs find a slow gait to take me to a refuge that I have hidden off the path to an overlook of the bay.

Every year, on the occasion of Yom Kippur, I leave the Temple service, and trek up here. The year's when I could afford to belong to the Wilshire Boulevard Temple, I could attempt to repent surrounded by hundreds of others, appearing for a holy week service. Surrounded by the murals depicting the events of the Old Testament, funded by film mogul, Irving Thalberg. I was always struck by the image of Moses, imagined by Michelangelo with his fingers parted to form a V, index and middle, and then ring and pinky, with thumbs extended. It was the two handed blessing of the great priest, Kohen Gadol, over the assembled. First used by Moses over the Jews in the Exodus, but come to be known, in popular culture, as the salute of a Vulcan, played by Leonard Nimoy, who adapted it for his character from his memory of iconic gestures in his own upbringing.

As each service ended, I drove to this place, and began the walk of consideration of the year behind, the current dilemmas, and what hope I might have for the future. I thought it arduous enough to symbolically tie me to the meaning of the day. I often thought, if I could bring the entire congregation to the same sweaty, kinetic agitation of spirit, they would find themselves hardened, and more resolute in their dedication to a new beginning. Sweat might purify them all.

I rarely saw another soul. One year a darkly tanned runner, all of 5"3", ran alongside on the uphills, and told me of his running tours to Machu Pichu. Two days of trekking followed by a 26 mile jaunt to the site on the final day. He offered my water and a gob of some corn mash paste he had in his pouch. It was the energy potion of the legendary Tarahumara runner's of Mexico. I declined with a brief explanation of the fast of the day, which he seemed to understand, only as an ancient, if bizarre ritual.

But, he told me we would meet in some distant place, on a trail again.

He could have been Don Genaro, the Yaqui sorcerer and spirit guide, to my Carlos Castenada, I was always ready for an epiphany. No peyote buttons, or mushrooms, only scrub grass, and cactus on this path. Perhaps, an empty stomach and the ancient texts of the synagogue would bring the mystic mix required to alter my consciousness. None came.

I was faced with the same reality this year as every other. At the top of this path was a pile of rocks. Each rock, a year since I had lost a son to the simple fate of a car accident. One rock for each year alive, one for each year gone. 19 and 19. Some years they were in a neat pile as I had left them, others scattered, as if by a maddened hiker, who could not stand order, or reverence. No one piles rocks without a purpose, rarely for pure artistry. I have seen these piles everywhere, often exactly where people expire. Along the lava flows in Kona, across mountain roads in Colorado, near crossroads deep in the Sinai, in front of a school, or on a grey marker in a cemetery under a freshly planted dogwood.

Half together this year, the rest to be gathered. I came upon them slowly, wary of the occasional rattlesnake, out to absorb the midday warmth. Run enough mountain trails, you seem them, thick and long. Here I saw one stretched out to look like a long staff, and I thought it a stick, the year I placed rock 21 on the pile. I looked for it every year since, afraid of it, unable to shake it's presence, even after all these years gone. Some memory buried in the limbic system, there without reinforcement or reoccurrence.

I took my time on the mound, pretending it was more than it was. I'd recite what I could remember of the mourner's Kaddish, which is a prayer that praises God, and deals not at all with the soul gone. When my son died, I had journeyed to a local Rabbi, who I did not know. I had paid to go to his services, but little else. He offered me a brief, review of the meaning of the prayer, and did nothing to console me, or offer any Talmudic advice. He was everything I hated about the faith, it's attention to fund raising, the men's club and those devoted to the Temple. The rest of us, were entitled to a few ceremonies and not much else.

It seems when I prayed over the stones, I became less reverential. I was always a skeptic, at times rebellious. Even as an eighth grader, I would talk to God, from my tiny room, and challenge the faith. I can remember sitting on the stairs to the bedroom, my father holding an essay I had offered to an outraged teacher. The topic was borrowed from my early reading of Marx. "Religion the Opiate of the Masses", that I had neatly handwritten four pages on why faith was destroying America. He was less angry than amused that I could cause such a stir, so early, and about Marx, no less. I was not beaten, but I was forced to agree to attend Hebrew school until I was 16, a fate from which I eventually received a pardon.

After the stones were placed, the prayer done, I continued on to the overlook to find another rock. This was the rock of atonement, that would be the size of my sins. I would identify one that was about the mass of the way I felt about my misgivings. Some years it was a small boulder, others a palm sized rock, rarely less than that. The sins were standard issue, usually of envy, detachment from family affairs, poorly chosen words, some gluttony, but not much. The real sins were not in the service; being too small, thinking but not doing, standing pat and avoiding change. Still, I found a rock of size, forced all my sins into it, faced the ocean, and threw it over the ridge.

Often, I would feel relieved. Mostly, I felt the same. Happy to be headed back to eat a meal, renew the regular life. But, now I feel more hollow, without direction. An honorable man, with some faith, more questions than answers, and no wiser or richer for all the years up this trail.

Aristotle with his skinny legs and lisp thought man at his best would search for wisdom. You might find it through some examination of your life, so it was worthwhile, if you had a life that you reviewed constantly, in the hope you would find a path that smacked of "ethics". All of this introspection may have made me smarter about any number of topics, but had not secured what you actually need besides philosophy. Like income, an owned house, or purpose. If truth was my purpose and from it some wisdom, I had some of both, but had very little of what Campbell and Meade found in Stone Age huts, that elusive ingredient of a well lived life, "happiness", pure Bliss.

It did not seem to ever have been on my life list, or anyone else in the family. If you could be "happy" in struggle, contentment from repairing the world, or what the Kabbalists called Tikkun Olam, and find bliss in that, Mazel Tov. Mostly, it seemed that work had it's own reward, homeostasis with family was close enough. But that few were pursuing it, as aggressively as they went after anything else.

The most content man I had ever met was Stuart Mishnik who taught me my Bar Mitzvah part. In an old barnlike building, along a still unpaved road, where a post war synagogue would be built, he took me through the prayers and chants. He was focused, alert and seemed filled with the joy that comes from actually doing something that starts one day, ends one other, and transformation occurs in between. He wore a brown suit, a tie twisted back upon itself, and a prayer shawl, the talis. His enthusiasm inoculated me with the idea of being a man, who could garble his way through the Torah portion. I sang in emerging baritone, "Ma- pach, pash- tau, zau- kaf, kau- tone" I mounted the 'M' chant pau -zahr, that followed the up and down of the letter. Only now, 54 year later, can I actually approximate the tone.

It was not the Haftorah or the tones. It was Mishnik's, Panglossian optimism that pushed me towards becoming a self confident young man. Voltaire let Candide find the value of optimism, it did not work out as well for Pangloss, who found he ended up on the gallows, for all his positive outlook. There was this aroma of old wood, and leather, decaying floors, and windows freshly cleaned with ammonia, that ran through my nostrils, and linger in my olfactory glands. When I chant the old tunes, I can smell that place, and Mishnik's scent, more of smaltz than Aqua Velva.

This was the best the world could be, for now, and it was better than for anyone one of us, since King David, he would say. The best of times. Mishnik was an optimist and in his way a Stoic. I sat at his "painted porch" and crooned the prayers, ate salmon and onion sandwiches, and woke up early to say morning prayers, and lay the black box of prayers on my head and wrap a leather strap around my arm, into the letters Shadai. I layed Teffilin, and was a righteous Jew for a moment.

By the next years, football, young women, fights, large finned cars and the Beatles arrived. And it all faded.

My ancestors lineage never seemed worthy of investigation. On the day of the Bar Mitzvah, the rabbi asked my grandfather, Tommy, if he would be called to the Torah as Kohanim. He angrily pulled the rabbi's ear to his mouth, and firmly shouted, "We are of Aaron, not of Moses. "A long line of Levites from the Pale of Settlement back to the Exodus, the desert and the Tabernacle. Keepers of it all, not it's Priests. My father calmed him, so attached, he was to the proper place of his progeny before the congregation.

Tough old man and his sister Ruth. They got to America, after an escape from the Tzar's pogrom of 1903. The Pale to Frankfurt, Frankfurt to Rotterdam to Castle Garden, all in steerage. My aunt Ruth, the Tante, once took me into a bathroom on Passover, took off her blouse, only to show me a long, old scar from her sternum, just below her breast, to her armpit. It was her memento of the Cossacks, who had pulled her out from under a table in their village, and slashed her with a saber as she ran away.

Before Tommy could be conscripted into the Russian Army, they fled. Being a Levite had brought him nothing, and meant less, as he quietly made a life for himself. Of the family that came here, only he and his sister stayed, the others returned to Europe before the Great War, and all died there in the years after Hitler invaded Poland.

After I was 13; football, young women, fights, large finned cars and the Beatles arrived. And, all the Judaica, it all faded.

Except for the obligatory holidays, and some rare arguments about the plight of Jews in the world, always attached to a riff on Israel, God did not enter most conversations. I lived a secular life, concerned by the vagaries of finding some direction. And later accumulated the pieces of most life mosaics; marriage, children, the usual squabbles, successes, up and downs, and enough cash to have a life firmly in the middle class of things. An unremarkable, undistinguished life.

And on this trail, on this day of being written in God's good book for another year, I would weigh the balance of my excesses and vanity against my deficiencies. Somewhere, between those polarities, I always hoped to find that had I struck some balance, some Golden Mean. Perhaps, it was the heat of the day, the smoothness of my stride, or the light headed quality that comes with an uninterrupted run, but I felt close to being balanced this year. Largely, without conflict on most things, yet, concerned that whatever mark I might have made or might yet make had not happened.

For all the good intentions, all the lists of things to do, the grand schemes. Most stayed on some yellow pad, in some drawer or folder, in a growing stack from a lifetime of collecting ideas. Few were dashed, since few were tried. That expedition to climb the Matterhorn, the summer house in the Palm desert, the movies scripts written and undone, the savings for retirement, that trip to Europe with your daughter. And, that campaign for something, important, never happened. All unexecuted ideas, vision without execution, the very definition of insanity. Was that deTocqueville who said that or was it Tom Landry?

Down a slope, around that turn, the rocks turn red, as the sun washes over them. Everything seems in it's place, as if, there was some cosmic order to any of it. Yet, if I take my mind off of the rocks, the ruts, I can trip into the crevasse, crack open my skull and have it ended. And if I am attentive, I still can be bitten by some wasp and watch my hand swell to the size of a softball. I cannot grasp what role free will plays, other than, my acts set in motion some sequence of events that create a ripple, some vibration, that alters my path somehow. So, when, I think of chaos theory, I lose my mind.

The butterfly flaps it's wings in Provincetown, a napkin blows out of the hands of a toddler in Kauai, a tsunami overtakes a Japanese shoreline. But, is not always cause and effect, not in that sequence. Sometimes the order of things plays out over a span of cosmic time, or for Buddhists in a karmic mechanism, revealed on the wheel of many lives, where there must be a consciousness to be observed, or why the karmic evolution towards enlightenment or Nirvana. In the vastness of it, every galaxy with it's own black hole, millions of suns across, billions of brown dwarfs, some planets that might sustain life, and maybe, dozens of universes, not one, where does one lukewarm Jew fit, running back to a table to break a fast.

I understand that my actions and choices shape me, or that my choices are shaped by some inner genetic soup, that is either just my soup or cooked to nuture a spirit destined to evolve into certain actions. I would not be on this journey, if I had not been beaten by some toughs from Father Judge. We'd walk down the wide boulevard, a group of boys enjoying an early summer night, only to be stopped by a younger boy, who would call us out as "Jewboys". When we would chase him to a corner, a gang of toughs in their Catholic school jackets would attack us, and beat us, until one of us screamed loudly enough to scare them away. It was the only anti-Semitism we really encountered, as much, about territory and testosterone as religious hate. But, we could fight it, and did. Eventually, we grew stronger, found the marauders and beat them; joined in squads and avenged our side of the boulevard. Something about the rush of a good defense, biting off an ear, or breaking an arm that burrows deep into your psyche.

It's certainly not the stuff of Nichomachean Ethics, more Hammurabi. Less cerebral than limbic.

Something, though, to this solitary act of repentance, always wanting to pray alone, offer up a stone of collective sin. Even when I sat on a back porch in Salt Lake City, without a family, I read through a more traditional Yom Kippur service. It outlined the service as it occurred when there was a Temple. The sacrifice of the unblemished Red Hiefer, it's blood mixed into a special brew, the retreat of the Kohen Gadol into the Holiest of Holies, 15x15 in size, where he wore white linen, and changed his garb four times after each sacrifice, and to cleanse himself in special waters. Then, on his charge, a ram with a red ribbon tied to it's horn would be sent off into the desert. Men with shofars would signal the passing of the ram, until it could be no longer be seen. All the sins of the "people" on this goats back, symbolically exiled. And the Levite would blow the final shofar call, and the New Year would begin.

Inspired by the acts, and the service, I set up Mount Olympus that afternoon, before I would break the fast. 9,000 feet of it. On any other day, a rigorous, but enjoyable hike. Without food or drink, and imbued with the ancient texts, it seemed an ordeal. It was not difficult, actually, I imagined it a trial to assist in forcing some meaning into the observance. It was a year that required a boulder to accept my ritual of pouring misgivings into a stone. I lifted it with both hands, and shoved it down the slope.

On the way back, at sundown, I drove up to the 7 Eleven to get an orange juice and a pop tart. A young couple was arguing about who would wash the car. She seemed to be winning the debate, with a toddler resting on her hip. He took off his baseball cap and wacked the front of the Ford 150, a few times, with that utter disgust and capitulation men get when they cannot prevail with the woman screaming at them. For all my hiking, reading and cosmic thoughts, the real world was right in front of me. I left the big thoughts behind, smacked into the life here for the earthbound.

Who washes the car, has the same value as the contribution of Athens or Jerusalem to our understanding of where we are in the order of things, maybe more.

The road rises more than it falls on the last miles before the Trippet Ranch. Great runners associate with their body and the pain of the effort. They become focused upon each step, their stride length and breathing. They are content to not move on to the next moment, but have the fitness level and dedication to stay exactly where they are. I could do that in the younger years, even run a New York marathon, on focus and guts, with no training. Now these last miles were a struggle. I could only disassociate the last hills. And on this day, wildly, uncoupled themes.

A woman burns to death in a Brooklyn elevator, after a black man, dressed as an exterminator sets her on fire. She is 73, lived with two sons. She owed him money.

A poet, turned statesman dies from excesses of smoking, after spending a lifetime quietly opposing Communism in the Czech Republic. He suffered greatly, after losing a lung, having his colon explode, and attempting to host the Dalai Lama at dinner before he died.

Noted critic, atheist, and consumptive personality, Christopher Hitchens goes at 62, after losing his hair, his voice, but not his dignity to cancer of his esophagus. A throng of supporters clog cyberspace with praise to his certainty that there is no God. Wonder what God thinks.

Korczak Ziolkowski fell dead at the foot of his monumental depiction of Crazy Horse, of an attack of the pancreas. The head of the Sioux warrior, finally is completed by his family, under the supervision of his wife of 82, June. Some Sioux, including Russell Means, still think it a sacrilege, this project, twenty miles from Rushmore, where Teddy Roosevelt looks out at the Black Hills.

And Quentin lays in a grave in France, where the Krauts buried him in 1914, after he took two machine gun bullets to his head, in a dog fight over the Marne. And, brave Kermit dead of his own hand in Alaska, from depression and alcohol, even after saving his father from dying along the River of Doubt.

Or what of Prokofiev, who had composed a concerto for one handed pianists, rejected by the peculiar Paul Wittgenstein, who would play Ravel's, but not, his before New York audiences.

What of them all, thoughts at the end of a fall run.

I sprint to the last turn, downhill now at full stride. Only to have a toe hit an exposed root or rooted rock. I lung forward, break my fall with an outstretched palm. But I fall on my head, and open a deep gash above my right eye. Like all head wounds it gushes, bright red, blood on the dusty trail, and pours over my right cheek. It is a boxer's gash, like a head butt or a right from Marciano to Archie Moore. I wobble to the car, assess the damage and hold a towel to my head until it stops. I press the flaps of skin together, and forget everything, the day, the atonement and the intellectual wrangling for the sense of things.

God has a way of focusing you, and it only takes a pebble or a root.

CHAPTER II

✵ ✦✦✦ ✵

THIS IS THE PLACE

BORREGO SPRINGS

There is no other sound here, between the shotgun blasts. The shells explode into the thin, hot air, in search of a round clay disk released from this rusting machine. Mostly puffs of missed shots against a cloudless desert sky, punctuated by the occasional hit, always out of practice. If I came here more than in summer, I would be better at it. I go through a hundred clays, put down the Bellini, and walk, slowly, to pick up the pieces, the shells, and savor the quiet again.

The sun zeroes in on the spot between my shoulder blades, and the warmth runs through me. It is right here, away from the courtroom, always is. Frankie has had this trailer for twenty years, I have come year almost as many, mostly alone, with no electronics, no radio waves, and without that damn phone. Connected to nothing for awhile, might reconnect me with something, besides right and wrong.

It never seemed I would be anything else, but a prosecutor. I watched my father try cases, win most of them, before anyone really cared or took much notice. His buddy Marvin, nailed some of the Manson clan in the Tate/ LaBianca case. Then, on a rainy night, his car went off the road, and he died. Of course, no one in the family thought that was what happened. Dad was convinced it was another Manson nutcase, or a paid assassin.

Some cases had a twist. Most did not. I had a 80 per cent conviction rate. Put enough gang members, angry thugs, enraged and drugged bad guys away. Was never that tough. Most juries get it right, when left to the evidence. I could put it away most nights, slept well rarely took it out on the family, but found little time for anything else. Same damn cycle of prepare, present, close, convict and then begin again.

It never seemed boring or without purpose. Everything you can imagine. A guy dresses in a pink Barbie costume and sneaks into a woman's bathroom at the Bel Aire Hotel, and rapes her. A cowboy who owes money to a refrigerator repair man, kills him, his two daughters and his wife, saws off their feet and buries them a shallow grave, and then has a dinner of green pea soup and a loaf of bread. Or, the pervert who collected pictures off the internet of women undressed for their lovers, who hated them enough to post their pictures online. And this guy posts them, and then extorts the gals to remove them. He got twenty years.

But, there were also the cases I watched, the obvious verdicts denied. The incumbent riots. The media crushing in, establishing some fake narrative that fit their needs. Rodney King begets a beaten Reginald Denny. A chopper hovers over a moke who beats him with a brick and then kicks him in the face. King walks, the cops walk, Denny bleeds.

All of it captured by a courageous helicopter pilot, Bob Tur. This guy once saved 54 people in a raging storm, and was heroic. Years later, he became Zoe, changed his sex, hormones, body parts and all the rest.

O.J. tries on a glove too small to fit. Cochran pulls a cap over his ears. Marsha and Chris are slaughtered by nuance, humor and a poorly selected jury. Simpson walks, Cochran struts, Goldman is stabbed 22 times, Nicole has her throat slashed. The condo on Bundy becomes part of the Hollywood tours.

No one got what they deserved here. Except, perhaps, for Marsha. Who parlayed her celebrity into some television deals. Founder of William Morris, Norman Brokaw sat with her at lunch at Groucho's table at the Hillcrest Country Club, and took meetings. Her good looks, wit, and inherent toughness made her a sought after "next thing".

Irving Thalberg would have gotten the irony of it, Groucho probably not.

And this year, for me, Mark Burdon, who over 32 years of teaching took his elementary kids into a room and tied them up. Then he blindfolded then and gave them samples of his semen, in tiny brightly colored cups. When he ran out of cups, he offered his samples in white plastic spoons. Of course, he documented this with photos, so he could share them with his pedophile friends around the world.

The Escape

A simple case, except for the teacher's union. Who fought to protect his rights, and paid him his salary during the trial and refused to terminate him. They knew about his activities and transferred him from place to place. Until someone saw a picture and we finally got his hard drive. Over one hundred counts of molestation, but he only went away for 20 years, with parole options.

Burdon's close friend, Bernard Stringer, tied up his girl students and teased them with a sweet confection of his sperm and honey, delivered on only blue, plastic spoons. We could only find twenty pictures, so he got 5-8 years.

They will wear ankle collars when they get out, and they will. Then, they'll live off their teacher pension, with health benefits, in a shack with shower, kitchen, and even a hot tub, in some eastern San Diego county town. The politicians will spit at the thought, and the residents will load their rimfires, but the judges will barely lift their eyes when they read the release from their overloaded dockets.

I thought I would stay a few days, but I seem to ache for more time, this year. I expect to bake like a lizard, let my skin grow dark, show off the Mediterranean in my melatonin and knock back as many cervezas I can handle. I can't run until sundown, or better at dawn, out here. The thermometer over my shoulder reads 103, and the blacktop 400 yards away would fry an egg. I need beer, shells, and some conversation.

The vintage Willy's Jeep is under the green colored tarp. Frankie bought it out here from a contractor, who converted it into a dune buggy. It was always a lucky vehicle for Frankie, he brought his model, girlfriends out here, drove them around the desert trails. They were carefree, pretty, high cheekbone types, without their make up, and, enjoyed the far away, celestial abandon of this place. Frankie married three of them, with the last one, Wendi he had four kids.

After ovarian cancer took her, he retreated out here, like me, to gaze at Argo Navis, the planetarium night sky, and pretend he was on a planet, in one of those 100 billion galaxies next to our Milky Way. The Jeep was always fueled up, and his Smith and Wesson loaded, resting in a leather holster, tied to the driver's seat. The black baseball cap was part of the ensemble, with LAPD emblazoned on it and gold scrolls on the bill of it. I felt like I was somebody, on his way to something, not just a desert rat after a six pack.

At Christmas Circle, Kittle's was the general store you would paint into desert landscape, as a way station, one or two stars better than the one Fitzgerald imagined in Gatsby, the one below the decaying billboard of some optometrist. The Kittle family started and ran the Borrego Sun, a newspaper that poked at local issues, kept track of the social calendar, and posted snapshots of any hot shots who drove into town to party with the real players, the Copley's from San Diego. The Kittle family sold off this store in the 80's, and only young Hunter Kittle applied his journalism degree to being editor of the weekly.

The proprietor was one Maqroll Sanchez, long limbed, with long hair tied with a Samurai knot and a green ribbon. Every movement seemed choreographed to appear dramatic, which fit his phrasing of the language and revealed his Spanish roots. I was approached as though I visited each day, and he extended to me the bond between men who have no need of each other except an exchange of cash for product, but hope for something more.

He shuffled through a pile of photographs, Polaroids. Put them down and pulled out two beers fused together in a block of ice. He took an ice pick and separated them, gave one to me, took the other. He then dealt me the pictures one at a time. They were all the same pose, of women, nude. They were photographed from the neck to the top of their thighs. No faces, but with breasts, pubis, rounded stomachs. He had a hundred or so. Some lean, others thick, black hair, red, blonde, Brazilian, natural, same pose, a certain promiscuity to them all. But all distant, unknown, headless Madonnas.

I followed him into a back room, where a 3x6 oil painting was framed. It was a replica of a painting I knew. L'origine du Monde, the 1866 of Courbet that famously scandalized Paris. A voluptuous, alabaster skinned subject, with black hair painted with a pornographers tastes, and erotic abandon. Maqroll had captured it. Of course, he also knew the story of Joanna Hiffernan, the likely subject, who had red hair on her head, and only in the last years did a dealer contend that he had the painting of her head, hidden by Courbet from her other lover's.

Maqroll saw the painting one time. And it became his obvious obsession.

The room was filled with renditions of it, of the women in his stack of photos. Each a different style, some mocked Gauguin, others the traditional. You could see Van Gogh here and Marcel Duchamp by the window. It was a virtual museum of headless women declaring their power to Sanchez's world.

He sold none. I asked if I might become his Khalil Bey, the rascal that bought it from Courbet, a gambler who lost it in a game. And it remained hidden, then emerged to more scandal. I told Maqroll that when it was posted on an admirers' FACEBOOK page it was taken down. Still the power of censorship, and puritanism over artistic intent.

But he would not sell me one. At least not then, he said.

And in another room, there was a single oil. A colossus. 2x5 of a naked Maja, turned to reveal a backside of perfect proportion, with no face, only black hair cascading over her back. It was Courbet reversed. Maqroll's vision of the other side of his obsession.

He had a subject coming in in a few nights to his place, where he painted and photographed. He thought I should come and witness the process. I pointed the Jeep back to the trailer, with a certain wonderment blasting through my brain. How a man, finds something so compelling that he devotes his life to it, for nothing more than satisfaction, and enjoyment. And what is it about this place, this unforgiving sand pit that makes it so.

The heat does not dissipate quickly before a desert night begins. It lingers, above the sand trails, and rises to your nostrils, so as you run towards the far away horizon, it comes into you, fills you, and you become part of it. There is rarely anyone else here, in summer, meandering from one turn to another, sweating shirtless, until the sun sinks and the darkness signals the end of another wandering.

Running towards me is a black chested man, with a small white turban on his head, a sash of white linen protecting his neck. He stops before me, revealing a darkness of skin that is like tar, a broad nose, and enormous black eyes set upon a vastness of white eyeballs. His lean body suggesting an African distance runner. He begins to run aside me on the narrow trail.

I feel lighter, as though I had just finished some meditation on being weightless, and I float with him along the trail. He is the Black Ethiopian, named Abdullah, but a Jew, a descendant of men from Zion. His story connects to nothing it seems. In Cairo, he offered advice to an Englishman, Al Crowley, who became imbued with the belief he was a guide to ancient wisdom. Even sat with someone named Noble Drew Ali, who thought he knew the high priests of Egyptian past. And, astonished I was when he claimed he had tea with Rudolph Hess, the Nazi, and claimed he told him about a great transformation that he would be part of in the 20th century.

No matter what I asked of him, he just quietly told his stories. He eventually grabbed my hand and asked that we sit by the road, on a large boulder. He reached for a jug he had left there to fill up on his long runs. I drank with him, the taste more like cold sake than fresh water. He said I was "six months late". That he had expected me earlier, and that I could not leave this place, until the 'work" was done. He would not tell me what I was to do, or why. I shook him with my hands on his skin and bone shoulders. He smiled, and suggested in perfect English that I would find "it" and what I would do would come from inside of me. But, I must stay in the desert to find it, and it was my only choice.

He had no smell of booze, seemed lucid enough. And spoke to me as if I had known him for a lifetime. I wanted to dismiss him as another desert lunatic, but, I could not. I wanted him to come back to the trailer, and explore his musings, But, he stood suddenly, gazed at the moonless light sky, rubbed his hand across my forehead, and took off back towards the horizon. I watched the sash of white linen bob against his black back, until I could not see him, as he faded into a purple haze.

I walked back mostly to the jeep, uncertain of the message. Unable to claim that it meant anything, in this desert space, where all things are out of place and perspective. The horizon seems closer, objects clearer, lines of up and down stark against a clear sky. People just who they are, but, not, perhaps, as they appear. Unlike the urban life, filled with agendas, responsibility, diversions, all there to cover your soul with enough modern debris to allow to forget your dreams, if you ever really had any.

The days did not last long enough, the nights too short. As much I tried to make the time go slowly, it did not. I shot at the clays, began to regain my aim. I ran the desert trails, night and at dawn. I saw no one, except for a couple dressed in white, with enormous cameras around their necks, from Traverse City. They had teeth capped, so large, they looked like relatives of Gary Busey. My naps were dreamless, without incident. I drooled in my sleep and awoke with a wet pillowcase. Nothing else happened.

The words of Abdullah had yielded nothing. I yearned for something, but nothing came.

Two weeks away, gone, but for another night. I drove to see Maqroll at his home, to find him photographing a monstrously large woman, named Madrid. He had her in the pose of all his other subjects, her face hidden under a red scarf. Her size and body like the statue of Gaston Lachaise, that powerful Standing Woman, that always attracted graffiti, spray canned across her breasts by errant UCLA students. I sent three of them into two year probation, and forced them to take a fine arts course for three years.

He positioned her thighs, took a few pictures. She rose, smiled warmly, and slowly walked away from us into the pool. Maqroll stopped her to take a picture of her with the turquoise water barely covering the small of her back. He held out the photos and seemed pleased with the night's work, and unmasked a large canvas that he would begin, he said, after Madrid left. He could not pint with his subjects near him.

I told him of my encounter with Abdullah and he did not seem incredulous. Instead he just gave me his phone to call my wife, and tell her to come here, so I might stay longer. And to call the District Attorney's office to extend my time off.

For District Attorney Ronnie Milstein, my need to extend my stay was hardly a problem. She knew I had not yet taken the time to grieve the murder of my brother. She and her partner, Captain Patty Ruben joined me in Manhattan to eulogize my brother, who got shot three times in the face by some con he put away twenty years ago. The DA stood with me at the grave, gave me a bear hug, and told me to take all the time I needed, which I did not. Now, she gave me a stern warning that if I failed to take the time, she would force me into retirement, or a bullshit case load.

Ruth was less forgiving. I had taken enough sojourns, some alone others with Frankie. I would find myself in a duck blind, shooting at a cloud of birds rising off the flyway in Stuttgart, or marching up the trail to Macchu Picu, hoping for some revelation, only to find a band of Chinese tourists taking pictures of each other and leaving a pile of debris behind. Often, I would be closer, swimming between the piers from Manhattan Beach to Hermosa. Still, I was often elsewhere. And, when I was there, I was not there; thinking through a case, another journey, or scheme.

She demanded a room, a day or two to talk it all out. I could not convince her it would be better to just leave me alone, to find my way back to, coming back. I think she knew what I did not. Another week or so was not what I was really after. But, for that moment, I thought it was.

The five stars places had faded away, turned to dust. The hope that Borrego Springs would become the next Palm Springs never materialized. It sits at the end of circuitous highway east of Oceanside, rests at the entrance to the stunning vistas of the Anzo Borrego desertland. Once it was populated by the San Diego elites, led by the Copley family. They developed La Casa del Zorro, that was a flashy getaway. But, it decayed, as it just seemed to far to go for most, even the Zoni's found it too far.

In it's best days, son, David Copley would drive around town with his boyfriends in a rare Voison C28. Burgundy and Cordovan in color, three times as large as an old Jaguar X150. He had the 1938, which was less rare, than the 1936, which he wanted and could not find worth millions. He would sponsor parties, and many would come from as far as the Castro District, in those pre HIV times. It might have become the moment when people settled, built a community and flourished. But, it was all transitory, whether the heat, the long trip, or the lack of purpose, drove everyone back to the cities.

Still there were memories of handsome Andrew Conanon, who brought some of his older friends from La Jolla. It was a treat to see Versace, walking through the desert trails, shirtless, effecting a bronze Adonis. Only to learn later, of how he bled out in his Miami mansion, as Conanon cowered in a houseboat, after stabbing his lover. And, the surprise of the visit of a gaggle of lesbians from West Palm Beach who knew Patti Bowman. And claimed she was raped by William Kennedy Smith, and that only the power of Roy Black and F. Lee Bailey got him off. Their friend, and prosecutor, Moria Lasch, blew the case by failing to be tough enough on Senator Ted.

17

Times of wonder. Parties that suspended judgment on any moral code, allowed for free thought, and merriment, no matter, how debauched or aberrant. Then, the desert winds came and enveloped it all, with fear of HIV, a bad economy, and the elite flight to other places.

Copley returned to a higher calling as philanthropist, art patron, and community scion. Then died slumped over his steering wheel, from a failing heart. His friend and straight confidant, Rob Shapiro, the five star plastic surgeon, announced his passing, as though Norma Desmond had passed on. And that drama was the last mark of any of it in this desert town. The del Zorro closed, only to re open under the tutelage of an equity firm that thinks 500 bucks a night will be attractive to some knucklehead from Iowa.

I made the reservation in person, so I could chat up Joey Christo.

Performance artist, Andrea Fraser, thought it would be inventive to stage a sexual encounter between her and a very handsome and fit young man. She was average in most ways and would not attract such a man, under any circumstance but a barter deal. She proceeded to stage the event, which she captured on film, called, as one would call an abstract painting UNTITLED 2004. Then a sturdy 40 years old, Joey took the role, for money, not knowing what he would have to improvise.

It turned out he performed, not a line. But, was engaged in screwing the curvy, Ms. Fraser in all the standard and non Kama Sutra ways, most of us get laid. It was less erotic than bizarre. He was appealing, stoic, and used the method training to get him through twenty minutes of ins and outs.

Fraser did not know, nor, probably care that Joey was in a committed relationship with his, to be, life partner, Seth. Seth was pleased to have the money and knew he was in no danger of losing his man. Now it was a secret they held, that I flowed out of them, when I told them I had seen the video, and thought the man looked like Joey.

He gave me a room facing a mountain range, for a cut rate. It was small, the air –conditioning was broken, but it had a hot tub on it's porch. Number 36, with a key attached to a long wooden oval, that said the "best in the desert". And there was a television, which I turned on, without any thought about what it might reveal.

Andy Griffith playing Lonesome Rhodes. The Face in the Crowd of this country bumpkin who becomes a television pundit. Until, he is revealed to be a crowd hating bastard, by Patricia O Neal. I catch the last scene, with Lonesome crying out into a blustery Manhattan night for redemption, as O Neal and Walter Matthau walk away.

How many Lonesomes, now. How many pundits, blowhards, and know it alls.

To the news, I turn, with the same mindlessness. A few murders, the standard who got shot tonight. The reporter before a yellow crime scene tape. The family behind her, holding candles, the same interview, the same grief, one night after another, in search of nothing, neither solution, nor solace. To even more horror.

The Taliban found four boys who would rather play soccer than memorize the Koran. They took them into a soccer stadium cut off their right hand and a foot. Then as they were recovering from their wounds, another Mullah comes by the oldest boy, and demands more of his leg be cut off. So they saw more of it away.

Azerbijan. Compton. Englewood.

Enough degradation of the human spirit to go around. And, I am the avenger.

But this night I go into the tub and imagine Mahler's 8th symphony being played by 1,000

Musicians, and pretend the stars will pull all the evil in men out of them, and leave us pure of heart. Breathe in, exhale deeply, breathe in….

Ruth is not about weakness. Holds grudges, endlessly. Can stop talking to her aunt for years at a time. Is loyal, protective, and warm to family and good friends alike. When, she took over her father's furniture store, when he dropped dead one afternoon, driving a forklift, she became what he always wanted, a heir to his five store, discount furniture empire.

It took us a few days to get adjusted to being together. I looked like a desert, homeless man I suspect, unshaved, uncombed and blissful. That aura that you can achieve when you finally realize the world will do fine without you, the utter chaos of it, making none of it seem worth worrying about at the moment. I expressed the simple message.

I want to stay here until, I don't.

What was Zen to me was implausible to Ruth. Why could I not stay at the house and continue my muse? Then, she would have eyes on me, I would be in contact. No one would worry. But, here, no phone, odd people, what insight or direction might I find?

Why was I was acting upon a distorted belief that this solitude would bring solace?

To her it was insanity, which was a pathway to nothing. No deeper meaning, closure, just time wasted. She would rather I build a sea worthy row boat with Frankie, or run from the Bay area to LA for AIDS research or Wounded Warriors. But, this star gazing crap seemed an endless waste, accomplishing nothing.

We did not yell, or cry into the night. I sat in the tub, with her, recalled the battles of family, finance, and life. Fell asleep through the heat of the afternoon, and one night agreed to take it all a few weeks at a time.

We shopped at Maqroll's place, and avoided his backroom. He gave her a landscape of the desert, sans woman. I put her into her Land Rover, and kissed her goodbye. She forced a cell phone into my hand, just in case, the Big One hit while I was off shooting shells into the morning sky.

I went back to Frankie's place with a week old Times in my back pocket.

Hot beans and rice fit my mood. I wanted to read the paper by the fire pit.

And I found some peace.

55 year old Manny Rackover was going to die by lethal injection in Texas that night. He had stabbed a pregnant woman and her husband to death over 15 years ago. He busted into their beachfront home, and asked for money. The nine year old boy retrieved the wallets and jewelry, then hid with his older sister. Rackover, killed the husband, raped the expectant mother, then

murdered her. The children jumped out a back window and were saved by neighbors.

That was on my watch. He was convicted, broke out of prison. In Texas, he killed two college girls, same M.O. In Texas, it was a death sentence.

Tonight, he dies. Biblical balance. Hammurabi.

There is stillness, a warm feeling that rushes through you, when justice is done. A deep soul feeling that sometimes, there is cause and effect, crime and retribution. It has it's own allure. But, it also fleeting, and debilitating.

But, tonight, alone in the night, the heat, and with these beans, it does not feel like I am surrounded by chaos.

And sleep will come, with ease and without regrets.

CHAPTER III

NOAH OF THE DESERT

MONTHS LATER

The beard emerges pure white, finally allowed to grow untouched by some cheap blade. No requirement, now, to appear before a judge, or crowded court. The only jury, myself, assessing my face in this fogged mirror. My face is browned, seared by the desert sun, and my back dark, like my father's skin tone, after a summer at the shoreline or in his pictures from Burma, bared chested, lean from fighting the Japanese. The image of that picture, that rested on the bureau in their bedroom for 50 years, is now the face I see, darker, hollow cheeks, more a man of the shifting sands than the concrete canyon.

I have spent the months with a passion for my own brand of active, indolence. Morning and evening runs and hikes through the desert trails, watching Maqroll paint a few nudes, drinking at the hotel bar, and pretending to attach to no current events, or give a good damn about anything, or anyone. Outwardly, I am without destiny, staring at nothing but sunsets, approaching no abyss, not building any bridge across a gap in my life from one thing to another.

And this is my present state, until 3 in the morning. When I rise to void, compelled by age, and drinking until midnight. It is still out back, the birds are silent under the stars, and it is the quiet that comes before you hear a scream in the distance. And the same thought arises and overcomes me. "Why are you here? What are you doing". No answer comes, and I fall back into the bed, hoping that some answer will appear, other than, "here you are".

The season change brings some cooler days. Maqroll drives me to a spot where his friend, Alberto Pando, a young Basque émigré' is building homes for other families who need a roof over their heads, and no mortgage. He commands a small troop of workers, all in red T-shirts, with the words, BUILD IT, in white on the back. I take up a hammer and become a builder. By dusk two homes have the super structure in place, and my shoulders hurt. Alberto throws me a red shirt and demands I return to finish the project.

I decide to fill a discarded tub, I found by a dump, with hot water and effect a poor man's spa. The steam of it rises towards moonless sky. Formerly a man without any depth or contemplation, I spin thoughts, I imagine of grand thinkers, of is my place amongst these stars. Nine billion light years away, a super nova explodes, five billion light years from there, a galaxy clusters, magnifies the super nova, and it can be seen. Not once but four times as the light of it reaches us, each time at a different part of the firmament. Some Norwegian predicted it, this gravitational lensing, creating, the Einstein Cross. And it shows that the universe, as we know it, has 85 %, or so dark matter and energy, unexplored. And I sit here in this tub, recovering from hammering a few nails, the only concrete act of any measure, obsessed by lack of order, purpose, and mostly, by not giving a good, god damn about any of it.

Frankie arrives in a powder blue convertible, a two door, Bentley with a tan interior, with a brunette accessory, named Tina. He appears as he always has, Lee Marvin at his peak on Carson. Tina calls him The Judge. And this he is of the Superior Court, just completing a case where he sends a Vietnamese woman and her hapless husband to jail for three years for running over a USC student. They fled the scene, after killing the boy who was the son of a lawyer, whose dad was a fellow judge. It took four years to find the couple, and only some video from a homeowner finally nailed them. Frankie had wanted to give them more time, but the Chief Judge would not allow it, concerned more about community repercussions than justice.

Tina found some ice and poured her BYO Maker's into a mug from Sea World.

Frankie staccato's a dialogue. The car comes from an ICE confiscation, from some cartel types, who made the mistake of having a safe house in Chula Vista. Tina is the current weather gal at KTLA, who gave up on dating philandering politicians for a steady date, like the Judge. He wants me to move into the hotel, so he can bliss out with her, run naked outside, and scream really loud when it strikes him. Everyone is so sensitive in Beverly Hills, now, they call the cops on him for moaning.

And as part of the ICE deal, he opens the trunk with a flourish to reveal a somewhat battered AK-47. He calls it "Cuerno de Chivo", or Ram's Horn due to the curved ammo clips it uses to dispense the 7.62x39mm round, at 60 rounds a minute. I doubt Mikhail Kalashnikov ever thought over his 94 years of life that one of his AK's would emerge from a powder blue Bentley to be used for target practice, in a California desert.

He sends Tina to Maqroll on a beer run. And proceeds to take two large pieces of dry wall out about 50 yards, and draws a few silhouettes on them. He takes off his shirt, puts an unlit cigar in his mouth and plays commando. Nothing clusters, of course. Even a skilled guerilla knows the AK kills through volume more than accuracy. Still, the release of that ammo, the nature of its lethal result, exhilarates. But, it goes quickly, and becomes commonplace, like cutting grass, attached to no great cause, but to folly, the surge of adrenalin quickly ebbs.

He pulls some clays. I pull his. We are centered upon nothing, but our aim, and the simple pleasure of actually hitting something you intend to hit.

Tina returns as we are deep into the siesta hours. I motion her to Frankie, and go to the Bentley, pull up the top and turn on the air, and nap until past sundown. By the time I return, they are dressed in white, and ready for some dark beer and corned beef at Blarney's.

Out of place is Blarney. A traditional Irish pub stuck in this desert town. It's best feature a small spiral staircase in the middle of the pub floor that winds to an opening, where you can crawl through to lean over backwards, and have your feet held so you don't fall over, and then kiss the limestone. It is for the gift of Irish gab, that one kisses the stone, to be blessed with that mix of humor, wonder, and eloquence. Here it exists to replicate the original at Blarney Castle in County Cork. This is the Night of the Tall Tale, held once a month, where patrons can climb to the stone before they tell their tales, winner gets a special Troc to wear.

And all of it is due to the lost Irishman, Donnie Herzog. He a descendant of Rabbi Yitzhak HaLevi Herzog, who was Chief Rabbi of Ireland, in Belfast. It was Donnie's great uncle, Chaim born in Cliftonpark, who became the sixth

President of Israel. Irish Jew, wanderer, and owner of this place for the last decade. And somehow, as is the way of the desert, everyone comes along, brown and black, even, the white San Diego Brahmins to tell tall tales and tap the drafts, as, his wife Doreen boils the cabbage and prepares the beef.

On the far wall away from the dart board and across from the bar, is a large picture of James Joyce and next to it another of same size of Samuel Beckett. Below that a list of the men who have been designated Saoi Aosdana, wise men in Literature, a sort of Noble Prize for the Irish. And by that list, encased in glass a golden TORC, a necklace of woven strands worn by Celtic warriors. You win the night, you get a replica made of wire and gold plate, still you wear it, as though it is a grand old relic.

Frankie tells the first tale, after kissing the stone, with Tina holding onto his legs. I have heard it before, it is neither tall tale, nor full of wonder. It finds our hero presiding over the trial of Scott Rayner who used his sniper skills to shoot a doctor who performed abortions directly in his right eye. The murdered doctor had already been shot in both arms in another incident, and had his clinic firebombed. Rayner got life, although Frankie hoped for the death penalty. The doctor had performed late term abortions, had a drug habit, and was a thoroughly unsavory person, so the jury just could not get to the death sentence. The story turns to Frankie as he gets multiple death threats, and one morning after the sentencing a man chases him with handgun drawn. Frankie gets a large tree between himself and the gunman, and manages to draw fire that hits the tree trunk. And it is all caught on tape. The video shows that the final two shots get Frankie. And, he proudly lifts his shirt to the bar crowd to reveal a healed wound above his hip bone and a healed hole, where he was shot below his left collar bone.

He receives loud hollers, and everyone raises their glass, and sings, incongruously,

"If all the young girls were like fish in the ocean, I'd be a whale and I'd show them the motion.

Oh, roll your leg over, oh roll, your leg over

Roll your leg over the man in the moon"

Donnie comes from behind the bar and offers a very tall tale, with his strong baritone, and embellishments of prose. He tells the story of the travels of Jeremiah from Israel to Ireland. He claims that one of the lost tribes came there, and the crowd laughs. He reminds them, he is a descendant of great Rabbi's, and the story has been passed through the ages from Herzog to Herzog. And, he says on a great mound near County Meath, the Ark of the Covenant, yes, that very artifact was buried there by Jeremiah and his cronies, and it rests there until the Moshiach arrives, where it will be unearthed. And because of that Ireland has always been a place to accept Jews. So, he recounts that when Pobedonestsev told the Tzar that Jews must convert or die, many fled to Ireland, and from then to today, the ark remains protected and hidden.

More roars, and more verses of the Roll your Leg, each getting more ribald as the night goes on. Tales of drug deals gone wrong, weddings wrecked by fickle suitors, and one drunken lost night in the desert, where someone heard from Christ himself.

"Roll your leg over the Man in the Moon", echoes through the small tavern. Then, from before the case that holds the Golden Troc, a slight, black man stands. On his head not a turban, but a Dodgers cap. It seems to be Abdullah, the Black Ethiopian, who came to me on a desert trail. In a voice of clarity, that rumbles through the room, he intones us to hear his tale, albeit, familiar.

Of "unveiling "he says, a tale of revelation. And he begins, and the room responds to one of the great tall tales of all time, The Apocalypse.

Abdullah transforms into some Jewish/Christian prophet on the island of Patmos, and tells his tale as though he is reading from a letter to all of us. And he ventures into the realm of what he calls, "divine mysteries". To the Church of Philadelphia he contends,

They will bear the name of God, live in the New Jerusalem, and be a pillar in the Temple of the Lord. There will be twenty four thrones and twenty four elders in them, and then Seven Seals will open. White horse, red horse, black horse. Pale horse of Death, martyrs crying for vengeance dressed in white robes. Then the earthquake comes, the earth crumbles.

We are all silent, even though, it is a story known in parts. It is never told in a fashion, as done by Abdullah, that seems immediate.

144,000 Hebrews are gathered, with marks on their foreheads. Seven angels sound their trumpets. Smoke comes out of the Abyss. Locusts with human faces, and teeth of a lion eat those not marked by God. 200 million horsemen are released to kill one third of mankind.

The holy Temple of Jerusalem is measured as nations walk round it for 3 and a half years.

The ark is revealed in heaven for all to see. A woman prepares for birth as a red, seven headed dragon, throws the stars at the earth. The child is born!

Abdullah pauses and smiles. Sips a tall, dark beer.

"You know what happens next, right"

Satan and Michael battle. The Dragon, our Satan falls from heaven. Yet, he pursues the woman. A beast of the Sea arises, and is opposed by an earthly beast, who commands all others to bear the mark of the beast or 666. The Lamb returns to Mount Zion. The forces of good and evil gather.

Armageddon.

The beast and the false prophet are cast into a lake of fire.

But, Satan returns, 1,000 years later. Only to be defeated and dispatched into a burning sulfurous lake.

Abdullah now at high fever pitch, as in trance, proclaims.

"Heaven is renewed, no more suffering, peace. And we accept and receive the Messiah"

A long pause as he slumps into a chair, looking frail from the telling of this extraordinary tale.

The pub rumbles with the screams of the crowd. Donney walks over to him, takes off his cap and brings a Golden Troc to his neck, and says something in Gaelic. Then he lifts him on his shoulders and he is applauded and dropped by me. I put my arm around him, and he whispers to me.

"You are the only one who knows what is next, and when you know, act as though you are already there. Do not hesitate"

I am incredulous. So I ask how I find what is next.

"It is already here, you must move towards it"

I tell him I have no angel to inform me. I blurt out that Moses spoke directly to God, Abraham as well, Mohammed had Gabriel and even John Smith had Moroni. Where is my guide?

"There is no one, but you, only you"

He stood up and walked into the darkness, as before. The gold troc necklace bouncing light as he walked away.

Joe put me into this Room 36 at the Zorro. It was the quietest one he had. Even the hot tub murmured more than bubbled, as I soaked hoping to process the night, unravel the Black Ethiopians charge to action. I came to this desert to lose myself for a few days, now months have taken me away to a simple routine of habits that have no purpose, unconnected to much of anything. All passions gone, objectives missing. Uncluttered mind attached to nothing.

Now flooded with thoughts of the mysterious what is next. I have no dreams to interpret, I have received no message from anyone celestial, I appear healthy, without tumor or disconnected neural connections. My right brain has not produced a vision, out of some brain chemistry gone wrong, I am not Savonarola, a Billy Graham, or later day Messiah. I am not on fire from the inside, and whatever light I possessed for justice and retribution against the damned has ebbed.

Until tonight, I was content with the uncluttered outlook. I am on no quest on some ersatz Road to Damascus, to be blinded and redeemed towards some epiphany, by a Christ spirit that could not see in me the bearer of a sword of truth.

I have no truth, as I am in retreat from meaning, hollowed out, worn out from the inside.

Still, a quiet night, to a sleep in an actual bed is solace enough for now. Joe Hyams comes to mind and that dog eared book on Zen and the fighting arts, a black and white picture of a coffee cup, a small chapter on learning Tae Kwon Do, titled Empty the Cup. Until it is empty you can add nothing, learn nothing. Empty the Cup the master said. I am empty.

I fall asleep not with that thought, but the image of his wife Elke Sommer, nude in an ancient Playboy layout.

At dawn, the desert spits it's oddballs onto the landscape. Energetic souls driven to begin the day as darkness yields to light. I'm off on a morning jog past the sculptures of Ricardo Breceda, who created massive works of sea serpents, saber tooth tigers, horses and snarling dinosaurs. 130 of them, from an artist who was crippled working construction and found that he could weld. Then, he created one for his daughter, and has not stopped since. He is unloading some parts of a giant sloth, and I can not resist the chance to talk him up, and unload some sheet metal, fashioned in his shop in Temecula, near the back of an RV park, named after the Colorado ski resort, Vail.

He has the manner of a man who has spent his days working outdoors. Confident, soft spoken, with an easy broad smile. His hands are thick, anchored to forearms of steel and his movements are deliberate and not random or wasted. He knows precisely what needs to be done, and seems in no hurry to finish. He is also not conflicted by his art or his devotion to it.

He creates them, leaves them here. Sells some to tourists and developers. It is not a living, to him, as much as what he was meant to do. And, he seems content with it.

I unload the truck with him, mostly in silence. His main topic is gratitude that he found this way, and it compels him. His favorite piece he says is, "the next one". The big red pieces of the sloth are laid out now for his crew, he calls them, sits by the rear wheel of his truck and awaits their arrival.

I wind back on the trail towards a crane that holds a boulder, wondering who would be moving such a large rock into the desert. I can hear the commands coming from beneath a purple colored, hard hat. She is small, and thick with a voice that roars above the engine of the crane. After a few waves of her hands, she orchestrates this boulder into a spot in the sand, that would seem to require much less precision than she gave its placement.

Izzy Kim is a blend of Korean and Mayan. Her father from Korea migrated to Merida on the Yucatan after the war, and her mother is pure Mayan, a long line of family back to the origins of that people. Izzy drawn to the ancient temples at Dzibilchaltun, the seven eroded "dolls" within, and spent her teens conducting tours of the ruins, bathing in the cenote at the center of the Temple, and explaining to expats the Chicxulub crater that was beneath them, formed by an asteroid with a life ending force of 100 teratons of TNT.

Here she is creating her own marker, a line of boulders to become an earth and stone marker of nothing more than a human presence over this space. An earth artist is her self definition, with a plan to lay 73 boulders off towards the horizon, one larger than the other, capped by a stone larger than the Thunderstone, that is under the Bronze Horseman is St. Petersburg. It is 1500 tons, and was carved enroute, finally brought by Korchebnikov's ship to it's resting place. The most storied stone, and Izzy tells the tale as though she lived it.

After all, she says this happens in the modern era. Mike Heizer had a truck pull a 340 ton granite rock from the Jururpa valley, on a 196 wheel transport, through Los Angeles to the museum, by the tar pits. Izzy was his field commander and logistic chief. It cost ten million to bring it to become the "Levitated Mass", but expects to attract 8 million visitors.

Monoliths in motion, art in rocks, dropped in the sand.

She parked her team in Brawley, and she lived in an RV on site. When she was not working, she swam at the Zorro pool, an imaginary cenote. Fund raising took the rest of her time, which is why she spent any with me, expecting a prosperous looking, Anglo to be connected to some cash, somewhere.

This devotion to something that seemingly had no obvious external value, for the unbounded bliss of it, seemed as foreign to me as Izzy finding a stone over 1500 tons to throw down here, as though nature intended it. A notation suggesting no rule of order, nature, or purpose. That might offer only what her Temple of the Dolls proclaims, "we were here".

Frankie was about to leave for Malibu. The desert air, and the quiet nights, even if pierced by the unbridled yelps of Tina, and the bursts of AK fire, did not satisfy his yearning to host the cognoscenti of gossip and gore. I joined them at Maqroll's, where a small, secret reception was underway.

Maqroll had invited a few of us, and some of his subjects, including the gigantic, Madrid to his gallery in the back of the store. On a table there was Dos Equus, and White Castle sliders, a favorite of Frankie and some high end finger food for the rest of us. Under two white sheets, two paintings of wall size 12x 6. Maqroll called Madrid next to him, she seemed twice his size, and she stood stiffly at full attention. He unveiled the work, that showed her from neck to high thigh, in the tradition of all the rest. But, his style was of Goya. Soft colors, rich background, and a skin, off white, to frame a untouched triangle of a dark, black patch. She grabbed him in a masterful bear hug and screamed at him, as though she had been given some gilded award. The anonymity preserved as he called the work only, "Reclining Woman". Mujer Reclinada

Tina seemed focused upon the picture and came close enough to it to observe every brush stroke. Maqroll gently grabbed her by her pony tail and yanked her over to the other painting. In a flourish he pulled off the sheet, and revealed a slimmer figure, with perfect breasts, and under an impressionistic use of light, a body divine in it's modernity. Lean, muscled, exercised and dieted. It was, of course, Tina. He had taken a picture of her, talked her into it, with little coaxing. Now, she was one of the immortals. Unique, modern day, fresh, and fetching.

Frankie was amused and begged Maqroll to sell him the painting. But, it was a bargain, for which he had no interest. He did not want the world to know of this passion, that he saw the world through this unusual prism. A beauty, headless, but enduring. Whatever, it meant to him, for whatever reason seemed to be compromised or lost to him if he sold one, especially Tina, a modern departure for him.

In the front of the store someone was crying for some help to pay for some supplies. I told Maqroll, I would get it, and ran to the front, putting on his apron. In his twenties, unshaven, and frightened, with a rumpled white dress shirt, he came at me. He grabbed my arm and pleaded for an ambulance to take his brother's wife to the hospital. He pulled me into a refashioned school bus that was half camper and half moving van.

In the midst of the clutter, another man, his twin, and a very young woman, obviously in labor. She was far along in her delivery. I picked up her dress and could see the crown of the baby's head. This required nothing more than some firm direction, which I supplied to the expectant mother. A few breaths, a push or two, and the baby came with a slight twist of the shoulders into my hands and onto the apron. I took a few towels and opened the breathing passages and exalted with the trio on this birth of their first boy inside this Ken Keasey bus.

Two EMT's came and transported the couple and the baby. His brother, Seth grabbed me and after an extended hug, unraveled the story that brought them to Maqroll's. They had spent the day driving to the desert for a few days to observe the spring wild flowers, they had no idea of how close Rachel was to a delivery date. So the brothers just went on this excursion. Trusting, he said, that what was meant to be, would be. And that God would watch over them. I was about to inquire which God he referenced, but his skull cap gave him away, when I told him my name, he sat very still, gazed at me, put both hands on my shoulders, and shook me hard.

Lamedvavnik. Lamedvavnik.

You are one of the 36. You are, I know it.

Not understanding him, I calmed him down. And simply asked for some explanation. Which he provided in only short sentences. There are wise men, concealed ones. They do good, righteous things. They balance this world from evil. Always 36 of them. They do not know who they are, but, they are revealed, only at certain times.

Sweat overcame Seth. He was awash and trembling, and placed his hands on either side of my head and shook it from side to side. And he chanted the word Tzaddich, Tzaddich.

The spell subsided as quickly as it had arisen. And, as though, none of the last minutes had happened, he simply said he would send me a gift for helping birth his brother's first born, who they were to name after me, Jacob.

I told him where I was, at the Zorro, room 36. He waved broadly from the seat of the bus, and promised that a gift was on it's way. And the bus, departed creating an opaque cloud of red dust that covered my face.

Tina and Frankie offered to host one last night of drinks to celebrate Dr. Cohen's "unimmaculate conception", before they headed back to the city. She wiped the dust away with a red bandana that came off of her neck and kissed me like I was Frankie, bringing on that glee that comes when you actually believe you have done something worthwhile.

And I actually had an elevated world view, until I got into the back seat of the Bentley and began to wonder what the hell Seth's exuberance and mutterings were all about.

I was in the hot tub soaking away the blood, the sand and red dust, when Joey came in unannounced. He had a sack in his hands that when opened revealed a single book, which he left by the bedside. I emerged nude to Joey's wolf whistle, and threw him out of the room.

The cover was in Hebrew and English. Sefer HaGanuz, the Hidden Book. The prose was in a rudimentary English, most likely a translation of the Hebrew text. I did not find it difficult to read, but it seemed like a handbook of how to live a righteous life, and had many references to Torah that I could not grasp, since I had no clue to what it referenced.

It was, however, obviously a treatise of some kind offered at the end of the 18th century by this famous Rebbe of the sects of Jews from the Ukraine. Nachman, it claimed was a descendant of the founder of this side of the faithful, the Baal Shem Tov. And was, I could tell Nachman's take on the elements of being a Jew and some connection to God through good works.

So, I found a section on Tzaddicks, and read that good deeds, and righteousness was within us all. And that Nachman felt that at all times there were 36 special righteous ones upon the earth, but they did not know who they were. Only events might reveal them, and not even then, unless God willed it.

The book seemed to have some code in it, linked by one Torah passage to another. I could not discern it. It had demands about circumcision, and Abraham being cut at 99 to seal the covenant with God and his people. And the demand to be a good person, who followed the commandments. A seemingly honest, and straightforward litany of wishes.

I could connect to the text, as it explored stories of messiah and lost chances for generations of Jews. It seemed at times narrow minded and insular and then celestial and universal. It had no prosaic flow and brought an anger up in me, since I could not command the text.

I put the book away and dressed for a night with Frankie and Joey and his friends. I did not expect to see Frankie again for weeks, and was more uncertain about what I might do next. That return to Ruth and work still rumbled through my consciousness, and I did just about anything I could to force it deeper in my mind, so I could not conjur the thoughts of it anymore.

A mist covered the Zorro's main pool, as the heated water threw up vapor into the cool night sky. Torches surrounded the pool and the perimeter of the hotel. Young men in short white coats and linen gloves served champagne, and offered caviar and deviled eggs. It was a going away party for Frankie that Joey was throwing, just to gather the guests for an elegant night of gossip and soft jazz. Joey gave me a white dinner jacket, and I managed a conversation about the congestion of Los Angeles and the quality of high school education with a gaggle of couples.

Young Kittle cornered me for his Borrego Springs paper. He rarely had a story that happened on the spot. Most of his stories were about land use management, the changing seasons at Anzo Borrrego park, or the annual cowboy poetry round- up. But here I was with the episode of delivering a baby in a bus. He seemed excited about having a front page of some tabloid merit. He wanted to know, if I knew the trio was a group from a Los Angeles Chabad. I told him I did not notice anything until the couple were escorted onto the ambulance, and I caught the father's skull cap. I encouraged him to make the story about them, and leave me out of it, as a delivery boy, and some heroic figure.

I found Frankie quickly to retreat from Kittle who wanted more details that I really did not remember and had no inclination to invent to fill in his narrative.

I was not surprised when Frankie managed to force out his feelings. He thought it was time to return.

I had no argument, except I felt uneasy about the old life. I remained hollow, not searching, as much as just adrift, expecting to alight somewhere.

For Frankie it was just avoidance, and a middle aged man's inability to be at peace with who he was, at the moment. Frankie said he had stopped evolving, and once he did he became at ease with himself, and even experienced happiness, on his terms.

But, I was not him. And I told him so. He then pointed to my right eye.

"What the hell is that under your eye, man"

I told him it was a rash that I had developed out here. And he encouraged that I get it checked it by Dr. Bob in the city.

He knew, it might just scare me into seeing Ruth, the DA, and might pull me out of this desert reverie. I put the thought into a pocket of neurons, and proceeded to walk my way through a few other vapid discourses with interesting people, before I collapsed in the room.

By 3 am, the hotel dog Highball, was barking by my patio at what he thought was a coyote or mountain lion. The damn dog was a full size German shepherd, with large pointed ears, with the bark of a Great Dane. Joey got it from his mechanic Ernie May, who gave him up before he passed. Highball was the name of May's grandfather's dog who lived after the St.Valentine's day Massacre, Johnny got plugged. And every dog, after that was named for Highball. This one barked until, I got out of bed and held him, until he stopped shivering. He shut up once he jumped on the bed. I opened the book and attempted to see what else it had to offer.

MOSHIACH

ON THE MESSIAH

There are no messiahs now. They are all false. Sabbatei Zevi. Joseph Frank.

The warrior Bar Kochba. All not worthy, none offered by 'ein sof", the Endless One.

They cannot be Messiah, they do not know the true name of him. Only the Hakohen Hagodol will know his name and call it unto him in the room of rooms, where the Holies of the Holies pray to him.

No Messiah will be revealed until he enters the Temple of the Lord and says his name

Unto him, and knowing it is the Ein Sof, will touch him

There will be a Temple, an unblemished bull, and the right time for righteous men to prosper.... then Messiah, only then......

35

Highball looks at me awaiting a warm body next to him. I put the book into the sack, and pack to drive to Beverly Hills, wanting to understand the text, but deciding to make this trip and see Dr. Bob.

Highball grunts and moans as we both fall asleep.

WEST SIDE LOS ANGELES

Ruth was in the kitchen deep into her coffee and phone. I did not seem to be much of a surprise. I thought we might enter the debate over my absence slowly, without fanfare or fireworks. I had dispatched myself from her and my former pursuits, with no notice or explanation, other than the shop worn despair of a man who had done something long and, arguably well enough to support a family, and pursue a career. The celerity of it caught me unguarded.

She was adamant that this was an aberrant phase that needed to terminate. Everyone, she claimed had lost their sense of place because I had removed myself from their game of life. Ruth thought I was overwhelmed by the attractiveness of unusual people, of weirdo types with their own purpose that had no value to anyone but themselves. Purely self- centered bohemians and sociopaths who were in the desert for a reason: they could not survive nor fit in anywhere else. I was drawn to them as a man in a zoo, curious to see the cheetahs and jaguars, pretending, he could run with them, only to be consumed by them if he did.

She did not shout, or cry.

For my part, I admitted to my search for solace, and this certain comfort of having no agenda, no calendar and being about nothing. I did not tell her of the delivery of the child, nor the book, the Black Ethiopian, nor about some mystery about me that was collecting in my forebrain. I sounded unmoored enough, as I continued to express my need to not return to this house, and my lot. Not out of disgust or lack of ardor for her or that life, but instead a desire for what is next, not knowing what that might turn into or around.

Ruth did not bring up a divorce or some other plan. She wanted me to seek help, get some other opinion, renew that therapy, I began after my brother's murder, and this time stay with it. I said I would consider it, but I knew then I would not. The wave of retribution seemed past, when arose a tsunami of grief from within her. Standing at full height, she turned off the phone, and coming close to my face, slapped me with her left hand.

"This is what I get after these years. This. You self centered, bastard. It is always about you, isn't it? What about my future, my dreams. Do you give a damn? Follow your fucking bliss, right? Your damn bliss while what happens here?. You don't know from happiness, you are the most sullen, darkest man on the planet. And now you want to follow another path, a new road…really"

"The road you want is not spiritual or deep. It is the shallow rut of a lazy man, who is too afraid of the future to work, and yield something of any value. You are not some deep thinker, just an old man who wants to roll over and dry out in the desert sun, like some old lizard, with as much value or meaning." A total effort to simply escape from reality.

I retreat to my office overlooking the backyard, with it's small pool, a large Jacaranda about to burst into a purple flowering, and the lilacs offering up their aroma. I should be in tears, or composing a letter of regret and offer some détente. Nothing comes. I gaze outside, change into my work clothes and head off to see the D.A.

And the great manipulator is ready for me, and is not about stepping lightly upon the issue ahead. It is time to end it all. At my advanced age, there is enough of a pension to provide for a remarkably comfortable life, and the case load for the high profile cases is better put into younger hands. While she does not doubt my stamina, she does my desire. She passes a final check and pension form my way, and reaches for a jigger of Maker's whisky, and pours two glasses. She wonders if we cross paths again. I am reluctant to offer any future intercessions, but, I tell her I will be in Borrego Springs, and she can reach me through Ruth.

After decades together, less than 58 minutes ends it.

She is less interested in my next chapter, than her own. I sign the pages, and exit, a made man with enough income to follow what I will follow, if I can find the way to it at all.

My face tells a short story in the morning, as I look into the mirror. There is a darker skin tone, a few days of white beard, lines from nose to lip, the creases from a lifetime of scowls. Eyes still sky blue, and afloat on sea of pure white. Hair white, now, all traces of grey gone, and my father's eyebrows at fully grown and unkempt, all 19th century in style, suggestive of Darrow or Bryant.

Then under the right eye, this triangle patch of rough, discolored skin, mostly reddish, with some purple in it. It is worth seeing Dr. Bob about it, and whether it is a benign spot or something more frightening. He is Dr. Robert Yissa, a highly regarded plastic surgeon, a friend of Robert Shapiro, another expert in the above the neck arts, who announced Copley's death years ago. Bob and Bob were frequent visitors to the Copley estate back in the day. Shapiro straight and a philanthropist, Dr. Bob a sexual athlete, who enjoyed all the delights of the Copley excesses.

In his office, there were patients in various stages of healing or repair. A tall blonde with a pink plastic cover over her nose, and her eyes hidden behind two holes cut out of more pink gauze. A short brunette with enormous breasts, sporting a neck brace, holding up whatever he cut off her neck. A few older women with untouched bags under eyes, and one with a fresh scar stitched across her forehead. The attendants all had flawless skin, no wrinkles, and no bags, even the chief receptionist, named Clara, who was probably 60.

And in a corner away from the enormous television, where Wendy Williams was talking in High Definition, sat a tall older woman. Very proper, regal actually, with a visage like Jane Fonda, much older, 70 or 80, but with an uncommonly youthful face, but a smile like my grandmother. She nodded to me, and her perfume, Chanel filled the room.

I small talked the blonde in a pink mask. I told her I had this patch and was worried about what it might be, even, melanoma. To which, she explained in some clinical detail the symptoms, look and feel of many melanomas, and she did doubt this was more than a piece of eczema, easily treated with a topical application. I was actually relieved, even though, I had no idea who this woman was or what she might actually know.

Clara, took me by the hand, and firmly, with the determined hand of a wrestler got me into an examination room. Dr. Bob surveyed the spot. Put a laser on it. Asked me more about my birthing experience which he had seen in his email, posted by the Borrego Sun, than the clinical history of this spot.

I wanted to trust Dr. Bob. Yet, I knew of his penchant for publicity and pulchritude. On some reality television program, he was a genuine star, as starlets took to his manner and Lebanese good looks. Yet, the producers found they could not contain his bedside manner, as he nailed starlets and production crew alike. They finally ended the series when he bedded a transgender woman, she taking virally spread pictures of their many positions and poses. The network just could not quite stand the embarrassment, Dr. Bob's business soared.

Still, he was one the most respected surgeons of his type. He told me it was likely some form of eczema, and that it would fade with treatment. He wrote me a prescription for a suave and for a cover up, and I was returned to Clara, who by now was giving me a flirtatious come on, which I denied, afraid she was a transgender woman with a functional penis, that I, unlike the good doctor, did not want any part of at all.

When I came out the Grandmother Fonda called me to sit next to her. She asked what it was, and I told her his take on it. She put her hand on my next, pulled me close to her mouth and softly said he was wrong. I politely asked what she thought it might be, and she replied with, a line I did not expect.

"Come join me for Sabbath dinner tonight and you will leave knowing"

She typed her phone number and address into my phone, and I agreed, not exactly knowing why I would say yes, but I did.

Shabbat Shalom

I have been in these elevators, going to some fund raiser, for some candidate the D.A. was backing for some elected post. High rises out of place across a Los Angeles landscape, creating a corridor of high concrete, housing the rich, the influential, and the aging intelligentsia. At least they all thought they were. My thoughts were of legal briefs, jury selection, and bill paying. I had not been to a gathering for a Friday night candle- lighting service, since I prosecuted an Israeli Rebbe who molested a few teenagers in his youth program one summer in the recesses of the Santa Monica mountains.

My mother recited the prayer once or twice a year, usually when my father's mother was visiting. Fanny made it a solemn ceremony, holding on each word of the prayer, and reminding anyone who would listen that is was the Fourth

Commandment to observe the Sabbath. And more, to remember that it was part of our emancipation from Egypt. So, the two candles were to observe and remember. God rested after creation, even though, for him it was not much of an effort, he willed it. The rest of us worked for a living, but as much as I knew of it, I never observed it.

My host was Esther. She opened the door to what seemed to be an entire floor of an apartment. Within was a collective of couples. An architect, a reform Rabbi, a woman Cantor, a few lawyers of various disciplines, a forensic psychologist, a folk singer with his guitar and hippie looking wife. Beards, skull caps, and shawls.

Esther rose from the idle chatter and moved towards the candles. Her dress was dark blue and a white shawl covered her bare shoulders. The cantor explained that the prayer did not originate at Sinai, but came a thousand years later, and was an addition by Rabbi's to serve as a bond to the Jews scattered throughout the world. And when it was offered it brought the world together, all the world, Jew and not.

Esther recited it, with the shawl over her head and her hands shielding her eyes. The cantor sang it.

They all sat at a long table, and drank wine and sang songs, I heard, but did not know. I was uncomfortable with them, as they spoke of temple activities, rifts between local congregations, and the need for a two state solution with Israel and Palestine. I participated carefully, offering only the most tentative thoughts. Esther held my hand beneath the table through the discussions, and rubbed her leg against me.

The folk singer handed out sing along sheets, and offered everyone his latest CD.

I forced my baritone tones into the melody, hoping to pass the time as pleasantly as I might.

By nine we were alone.

She sat close to me on an enormous sofa, pulled me on top of her. And said I had a special gift, but she could not reveal it. She put one hand inside my pants and the other behind my neck, and pulled my face to her face. She knew what was under my eye, but she would not offer the answer, until I was inside her.

This Esther who I had known since this afternoon had a key to unlock some mystery about me that I did not seek or understand. Here I was about to be with a woman who was born in 1929, had the face of a well preserved 70 year old, and, as I found, a body with round hips and thighs, and breasts implanted by some Svengali of silicon.

Her vaginal grip was vestal virgin.

She held me tightly with both hands at the back of my neck. I thrust slowly, until she slapped me for more rpm's. With the heavy bed coverings over me, I broke into a sweat, as did she. I paused to gain a breath, and rose up at the full length of my arms, where I saw what appeared to be a healed scar, that went from under her left breast across her chest and ended down by her ribs on the other side of her torso.

I was startled by it. It was a scar I had seen as a boy of 11 or 12. It was narrower, older, and faded, but it was the same. I was at a nephew's Bar Mitzvah, in west Philadelphia, at an old hall, Uhr's. It smelled like brisket, and fried onions. The walls were painted yellow, the table cloth ivory, and the waiters had brown gloves, so whatever they spilled or thumbed would not show. The older boys would smoke in the alley with the waiters, and attempt to catch "a feel" with the most flirtatious girl from the Five Towns.

That night my aunt, Tanta, Tanta Rose came to our table with her brother Usher. And both were drunk on plum whisky, Schlibovitz. To scare us, Usher retold a tale, I had heard of how he and Tanta escaped the Cossacks who came through their shtetl with swords drawn on horseback. It never frightened me before, it was the stuff of diaspora lore, usually not true, but meant to encourage small boys to remember we were always targets as Jews, in Russia, the Pale or here.

So I was not afraid. Then Tanta Rose pulled down her dress that night and revealed the scar from the saber of one of the Cossacks. She threw her head back and laughed with Usher. It was enough to see her flash her ample breasts at a table of boys, but to see the scar, brought out a scream from me, the other boys ran away.

I ran my fingers over the scar, and Esther stopped her movement. Looked at me and rolled on top of me. She vigorously rocked me towards an orgasm, leaned to my ear and offered another cryptic message.

"...that spot is a mark, Jacob. A mark of your lineage. You are Kohen."

I wanted to learn more from Esther. So, I continued to penetrate her from other angles and exhausted my limited repertoire of reliable positions. But I could not coax more insight from her. Afterward, I told her I had an old book the Sefer HaGanuz. She laughed and taunted me, as though I was a child.

"That Hidden Book does not exist, nor does the Sefer HaNisraf, the Burned Book!"

I insisted, but she told me both were written by Rebbe Nachman, but he had them burned on his death bed, worried that God might be angered by his guidance and insights expressed in them.

She told me, my copy was likely just a hoax. And she wanted to see it, and burn it.

I felt oddly threatened by Esther, who now seemed to be what she was, a old, superstitious woman, who had used me, offered me a single sentence insight and was done with me. Her face had aged, her shoulders hunched over, and she appeared smaller.

The elevator came, and I next remember being headed towards the beach, with nothing in my mind. I awakened in the car, facing the surf. Young men in wetsuits were happily running to the waves. The sun was hidden by the marine layer, I took out an abandoned wet suit from my trunk and waded into the sea, that had an emerald hue. I stroked 300 times out, further than I had in twenty years, and 300 back.

In my best handwriting, I composed a letter to Ruth on my ubiquitous yellow, legal pad.

>Ruth

>I am not angry, nor mad. I just believe, I am, for now better away.

>You can find me in Borrego Springs, and can write or call Maqroll at the store. He will bring me any message. And you can come anytime.

There is something there, I think. Something, I must do or find.

I will be there, after it. The checks will come to you, use them as you will, leave some there each month so I can take care of essentials here.

Love

Jacob

I put it into a purple envelope from a birthday card and dropped it into the post office at 5th and Colorado.

Headed south and then east, until I got to Julian, and ate a piece of apple pie.

CHAPTER IV

FROM JACOB TO MOSES

SUMMER
BORREGO CONSTRUCTION SITE

Izzy does not see me, as I walk towards her, she is naked from the waist to her purple hard hat. She gazes out at the crane and yells to her crew to line up the next boulder, number 20 of the planned 73, monolith trail. This is about 300 tons, and serves the progression of rocks until she finds her 1500 ton monolith that caps the line of stones. Izzy believes this earth art will attract millions to this lazy desert town. She turns slowly to greet me, her pendulous breasts sway, collide and settle on her powerful, if small, sturdy frame.

She dazzles me with her broad smile and "Ola, Jacob". I walk with her as she dons a white T- shirt with the declaration, "The Path of Stones", on the back. She asks if I want to sign on full time, as laborer, and maybe be her flak with the media. I agree only to show up at times and prepare the ground to receive her stones. This morning, I dig with a team of energetic Mexican women, who manage to barely stay dressed, as we etch out a home for the big stone. It is good work, unencumbered by anything, but moving some sand out of one place and putting into another. The essence of Sisyphus, except I never imagined him happy, and, here we all were, having a grand time, shoveling sand in 102 degrees of California sun.

It is a fine way to pass time, as that night with the 80 year old Jewess, mingles between thoughts, as I swim with Highball in Joey's pool at the Zorro. Could I have had intercourse with the aged woman who said goodbye to me at the door, or was I with a preserved Barbarella? And, that whisper as I thrusted, that I was a Kohen, and the mark below my eye proved it. It certainly had not faded, and turned a deeper purple, in the form of a triangle, it was pronounced enough that I had taken to covering it with L'Oreal, crayon concealor. Coming out of the pool, I saw it in the reflection in the sliding door, and stopped to ponder, if I should explore any of it, or just move along in my desert escapism.

In the 36, a note left on my pillow, under it a test tube. The note from the young Chabadnik, Seth. "spit into this, mail to them. You will see what kind of Jew you are"

It was upon examination, the pop DNA business, that for a 100 bucks will turn your spit into your family tree and ancestry. I knew enough, I thought. But, Seth and this mark certainly spiked some interest. After a gargle of peroxide, a good piss, I managed enough saliva to fill the tube and road the off road to a mailbox. But, thinking the better of it, I also sent a sample to Ollie Landecker at the forensic lab in Los Angeles, to check for any specific DNA clusters, he might find.

The pattern of the next many weeks, had an easy pulsation to it. Run before the sun on the desert trails, dig holes for Izzy, sweat with the women, learn to drive a backhoe, nap before a small dinner, swim with the dog, and read the Nachman book, a mystical pile of instructions and constructs of biblical events. On the weekends, I would spend time at the trailer, shooting traps, and firing rounds into old wall boards. I also never missed a Sunday, after church with Maqroll, who always seemed to have found another woman who he conned into stripping for a photo or live model for his collection of the Courbet, The Origin of the World, through the hand of this, one crazy hombre.

He introduced me to, a striking woman, over six feet tall, with a long neck, once labeled, pseudo-goitre', after the swan necked women of Modigliani, the Modigliani syndrome it was dubbed. This one named, Sarah, had the grey-green eyes of Anna Akhmatova, Dedo's muse and, lover, of course. To Maqroll her neck and face did not matter as they were obscured in his renderings. Still, she had a haunting look, as though she could have lived in Le Bateau- Lavoir with the starving Bohemians in Montmartre. She had no connection that was genetic or lineal, as far as she knew. But, Maqroll conceded, she was at least a blazing drunk and cocaine user, like her Bohemian look alikes.

Dedo, Modigliani as he was called, abruptly changed his worldview, even through his bouts with illness of all types, including the tuberculosis that would kill him. He destroyed his early works, ripped apart his "bourgeoisie "apartment, and launched himself into his most heralded works in sculpture and canvas. But, it took hashish and alcohol, perhaps, to soothe and mask his illness, and to release the fury inside of him.

He was an artist released to find his destiny. Bold in his commitment to his image of art, beauty and how to live a renewed life. He took enormous risks, suffered greatly, and had but one show, sold paintings for food, and died with nothing. Would I be capable of such an epiphany and its consequences?

FROM THE GROCERY TO THE TRAILER

It is a short jog at sunrise, the clouds turned salmon as the sun begins to warm the sand, from the grocery to the trailer. I rarely see the postman so early, but he makes his rounds as quickly as he can, sometimes, parks his truck by the trailer and sits on the back porch, knocking back a brew or two before he ends his rounds. This day, he is there, as I return, gazing at the salmon colored clouds, as they fade into a perfect blue, cloudless canopy. He picks up the Maverick 88, and asks for me to pull off a few discs. For a tiny, bow legged guy, Alvaro, can shoot, and hits six in a row. Only Highball is unimpressed and watches with his jaw firmly planted on the ground, only his eyes rolling up at each pull.

Alvaro gives me a small packet, with no markings. He rouses Highball and they go off and play fetch with a favorite rawhide chew toy. I open the packet that contains a scroll of papers, the results of the spit DNA test.

DNA RESULTS

Mr. Jacob Cohen

85 % Ashkenazic Jewish

10 % Middle Eastern

5 % African Neanderthal

I found this totally unremarkable. It followed the maternal and paternal line of the line of Jews I knew. And, the line from Levi tribe of Aaron and Moses to me, was impossible to trace, back past the original 300-600 Jews, who came to Europe out of the Mid East, 32 generations or 20,000 years before. But, there was a belief, around our Passover table, that we were there, when Moses left Egypt, traveled the desert and watched over the Temple, until it was nuked in 586 BCE and the tribes dispersed. If, I was a Kohen, as I was told by Esther, between ins and outs, this DNA would not offer much, but more imaging of the past. It was worth 100 bucks, to confirm I was all Jew, mostly and my thick bro's brow from Neanderthal ancestors, perhaps.

I had a spot below my eye, a word from an old Jew, and a book supposedly from Rebbe Nachman of Breslov, that was esoteric and obtuse. And that black, Ethiopian, Abdullah had not reappeared. My dream life was of nothing, I could remember, and my gnarly feeling that some change was upon me, had not materialized. If there was a sign, I could not find it. Whatever path was to appear, was still unrevealed.

I walked into the outdoor shower, dressed for work with Izzy Kim, and decided to keep it all to myself.

THE WORKSITE

Perez, Rodriquez and Vargas, were all with me, casually talking about their men and laughing about a fellow, nicknamed, El Hombre Bravo, who wanted in the worst way to be dating Cecilia Vargas. He had a reputation as a tough guy, who had successfully, fought off Sinaloa cartel thugs, from taking his brother into crime and his sister into their gang life. He was a gemstone of a man, but, Cecilia was playing the demur, hard to get woman, and her co-workers were supportive. They spoke of his valor and his sizable dick. It seemed a good way to pass through the afternoon heat.

A crane was constantly over our heads this day. Pulling supporting rail ties into place, to form the perimeter of a path. We were so engaged with our bonhomie that the gals did not see the crane operator lose, his focus, and swing the ties towards us. For, an instant, that cannot be explained, I saw it come at us, in my peripheral vision, I jumped at the three of them, and tackled them

47

all, bringing them down to the ground as the railroad tie swung past and over us, and dropped a few feet beyond us, unbound and off the lifting chain.

There was a commotion. Yelling, and screams. Izzy rushed over and slid into the pit, and embraced Perez who had hit her head on the way down, some blood around her scalp. The others seemed unhurt, if shaken. But, an ambulance seemed to appear in a moment, and EMT's ministered to the gals. It seemed a small near miss, to me. But not to them.

In the superstitions that come with the world of hard work, and callouses, my actions were directed by God. I appeared there, because I was needed there, as an agent somehow of the "forces" or, at least, the fates. Izzy shut down the site, so we could gather for prayer, and be thankful, we were not all dead. For everyone, Izzy was a pastor, not a boss, and actually, seemed in contact with some celestial spirit, as ancient as her Mayan forbearers.

And she intoned, finally, to no one in particular:

"And thank you for bringing Jacob to us, so he could act for you, and save these lives today. In Jesus' name. Amen"

Hugs all around, and I finished my workday. Seemingly not phased by the incident, nor connected to some spirit sense. I was just glad the gals were unhurt, alive, and would live another day to contemplate the plight of El Hombre Bravo.

AT ROOM 36

The weeks of summer were blown away by the late fall Santa Ana winds that blew cold across the desert plain. I had spent time with Seth and the baby Jacob, listening to lore of his branch of Judaism, and the impeding hope for a well lived life, by Talmudic rules, and possessed with his optimism about the future for everyone, Jews included. I was not ever so inclined to fervent anything, let alone, religious rapture and zealotry. Still, he seemed imbued with a sense that I had a deep historic past and that I had something to expose, that I was hiding. I told him I was concealing nothing, including my general inability to find the energy most days to search for the next thing, or expect a word or sign about anything.

There was enough wind this one night, to drive me into the room and actually check emails from the last week. My efforts at imposing an electronic Sabbath on communications had kept me sane and detached from the woop and warp of regular folks. I found I could stay away for weeks, and when I would engage, the requests, updates, and emergencies seemed tepid. Yet, this night there was one communique from Dr. Landekker at the lab.

He had taken the DNA sample, and looked for unique indicators. Since he already surmised what I came from essentially. And he found something, again, of more mythical interest than actionable. After all, what DNA might show, was of little interest to most Jews or anyone else. There was no priesthood, no Temple to mind, no Ark to display, no body of wise men to convene. Judaism was not the Catholic Church, there was no hierarchy, right from birth, or special covenant, if there ever as one.

Still, the finding was revealing of who I was on the patrilineal side. The descendants of Aaron and the Levi tribe, who tended to the Ark, and the Tabernacle before there was a Temple are determined from the father, not the mother. The Dr. found I had this Cohen Haplotype:

"In your genetic history, and your chromosomal markers, indicate you have the Cohen Haplotype. This is the Y- chromosomal Aaron. Kohanim are more likely to have this Haplogroup J than the non Kohen Jew. Thus, you have the Cohen Modal Haplotype (CMH). This does not men you are a direct ancestor of Aaron, but it is likely you are part of a genotype on J-P58, that directs your lineage from father to father as being present in the time of Moses and Aaron, or a common origin of the CMH in the Near East, before the destruction of Solomon's temple"

"You are clearly an Ashkenazi, Levite Jew. That is as far as current genetics can bring us."

Conclusive in some measure, but a leap to Aaron's progeny. From Eleazor who receives the word from Aaron in the cave to Phineas, and his ancestry to Zadoc, the first priest and keeper of the Temple. And from those, priests of Levi to the 600 Jews that go to Europe in the Diaspora to the Pale of Settlement, and then to this Cohen household, a stretch, a miracle, a burden?

And if so, what then. Holding a genetic marker is only that, in a world uninterested in any of it, including the faith itself. Mormon's more likely to revere an actual descendant of Aaron, than, even, an Orthodox rabbi. Who cares what you came from, it matters not, without a Temple to be minded, an Ark, or artifact. For Jews, there is rubble, and some artifacts, but no piece of Christs' cross, no Shroud of Turin, no bones of Peter. There is but the "book", the Torah and Talmud, and a story of Moses and Aaron, just that a fable, unsubstantiated by archeology or an actual record. So what of a man who is of Levi, so what can it mean, proven or imagined?

And for a man who never remembered his dreams, who would talk in his sleep, but never had a dream to recall. I would walk from room to room, muttering as a child, some lngedcord around my neck, nearly jumped off the bureau in this noose. But, even through the worst moments, when a son died and then my brother, when the marriage to Ruth began to dissolve, or an especially horrendous prosecution, if I dreamed any of it, when I rose, there was no memory of any of it.

Then, after I read the Dr.s report, I began to dream and remember. It did not matter where I slept. I had dreams of walking in the desert, unable to rest, at room 36. At the trailer, I heard sounds of great stones moving, and men being crushed. I would wake up in a sweat, soaked after attempting to scream for some help, to what, I did not know, and no sound coming out of mouth. I began to see myself clean shaven, all in white, surrounded by white sand dunes and being sucked into a sand hole, until sand poured over my lower lip, and down my throat. And then a recurring dream of me, with hands outstretched, addressing an empty stadium, and crying for one person to show up and hear me.

The memory of these dreams left me unsettled and often tired. I found I could sleep in the afternoon and dream nothing. I pointed the day around those long, dream free naps. But, the dreams continued, and I wrote them down. I assumed they were about anxiety of one type or another. If they were from some "other force", they were damn hard to interpret. If God is still speaking to people, still has a prophecy, these dreams show his special touch to be in need of more practice and repair. I longed for an angel, a Michael or Gabriel or a Moroni. None came, no clarity.

I was tired, confused and doubting this desert transformation. I loaded my .38 and had it by the night table. I shot all five rounds into the ceiling at 2:36 one night, when I heard horses galloping towards me, with screaming gauchos riding them, with Buffalo rifles blazing. I went out back and cradled a shotgun, and finally fell asleep without a dream, and greeted the dawn as a though she was a familiar women on the pillow next to you.

THE SUPER MOON

There is a moon that comes full when the Earth and Moon are closest to each other that rises slowly, but fills the evening sky. In the desert, it comes as an enormous yellow disk and rises over the distant mountains. And then it rises, and where the lights are low as they are in Borrego Springs, it is, as though, you are on another planet, in a distant galaxy. It lights the entire landscape, neighbors turn off their lights, click their appliances and televisions off for an hour or so. You feel guided by a cosmic force, your very blood rises like an inner tide, where two hours away the ocean churns and retreats. You can believe you are part of the universe, every atom in sync with the inexorable ebb and flow of particles in motion traveling together, expanding, past the speed of light, through dark space, for no other reason, but it is.

I had beans and rice over a small fire one night. Working at relaxing, as the super moon illuminated everything, and, I hoped my soul. Highball had ventured out to chase some varmint, and I began to sing, some partial aria from Gounouds Faust as loud as I could stretch the baritone. I heard a bark and then a howl from Highball, and saw him being attacked by what looked like two mid sized wolves or coyotes. I grabbed the AK, and put in a clip, and with the light of the moon had no trouble blowing them both away, dead.

I ran out to the dog and saw a few gashes around his neck, but, I thought I could stop the bleeding, until we got him to a vet. I was sitting in the dirt, holding Highball, and I swear that skinny Ethiopian in a ball cap, that had a Charger bolt on it, came over to us, from the desert darkness. He put his hands on the dogs neck, and the bleeding stopped. He looked at me, with a broad smile and asked in a stern tone, "what are you waiting for?"

And as quickly as he appeared, he was gone into the darkness, his running shoes the only reflection I saw as he exited.

For the next few nights, I could not recall a dream. Then, one came of me supervising the moving of stones, with Izzy Kim. Together, we moved large, cut stones, and I could not see for what. As days passed, stones arrived and hundreds of laborers set them in place. Then they stopped again. The dreams ceased.

Highball seemed to like the heated pool at Zorro's and Joey was always pleased to have him around. The three of us were swimming laps, and Joey dived down, and came up to me excited.

'Did you see that Jacob?"

"What, I see water."

"No man, No, I saw an image, a reflection"

"Of what"

"A building, an enormous building"

Try as a might, I could not replicate what Joey saw in the pools bottom. I had him draw me a rendering of it, on the table cloth poolside. It had two large pillars, large box like structure, a tower of some sort, and he said it was all golden. It reminded me of another image. I took him to the room and opened the Nachman book, where a drawing of Solomon's Temple was placed on a single page. Joey saw it and shouted that it was what he saw at the bottom of the pool.

I do not know what drives men forward towards their destiny or paths. Most find their way based upon skills and circumstance, and luck, I suppose. Some believe they are chosen or destined for their contributions, others that they are here to live the best life they can, suffer the vagaries of it all, and get up and do it, until they just can't any longer. I had a reputable place, family and friends. I was not revered, but, respected or putting bad guys away. I was an avatar of justice, honored for it, and good at it. Yet, it did not seem right, to me to continue on with it all. I had this imbalance, a gnawing pain that would not abate that there was something else. Although, I could not know what it was, but it was here in this desert town.

For me there was no epiphany, no direct word. Yet, there was an inclination rising to a certainty that I was here to do something, outrageous, a total and insane step away from any reality of mine. It seemed clear to me, now that I was to take my Kohen roots, my bump ins with Abdullah, and my new friends of masons, stone cutters, and builders, and reconstruct, the Temple of Solomon, right here in Borrego Springs. A later day, descendant of Aaron, with his mark under my eye, to do what Zadoc and the others did, build it, and replicate the house of God, for everyone.

I decided that I would do nothing else. Devote an entire life force to this crazy quest. That it might just illuminate the faiths of Abraham, bring us all together, to have a place to visit that replicates he house of God. To be sure, I am not the Kohen Gadol, I am but a man with a renewed passion to give the world a Third Temple. One that will not be built until the actual Kingdom of Heaven arrives. But, still, of value to millions who want to walk through its halls, see the Holy of Holies, and experience the Temple as did the ancients, not the Temple of Herod, but, of Solomon. Right here in this desert.

It occurred to me that the old name of Jacob Cohen would not suffice in this new life play. I decided to take on a different name, more in keeping with the mission. I went to the Los Angeles Courthouse, petitioned for a change. Judge Marvin Goldstein questioned me about the change, thinking me nuts. But, then, in front of Ruth and the children, and the D.A., I was renamed.

Moses Aaron Cohen

And I asked everyone to simply call me MAC.

We drank wine, and scotch, and hugged and kissed, ate some lox. It was an adult bris', for a man/boy ready to build a Temple for the world, and to calm his soul.

CHAPTER V

※ ❖❖❖ ※

TO JERUSALEM AND BACK

There is no place for ambiguity for an aging man on a mission. Especially, when the goal is building something, not metaphorically, but actually. There is nothing there and then there is something. It is about being committed, and not tentative, seeing it, planning it, and doing it. This building the Temple of Solomon was that now. I could not find space in my mind for anything else.

Maqroll pulled me into his studio, to display his most recent nudes. His muse, the voluptuous, Madrid, began giving me brown bags of food, and included a brownie or two laced with her favorite marijuana additive. And her brother Segismundo, takes to encouraging smoking his own home grown brand, and offering me a blunt. The buzz helps as a distraction, but does not last for long. I am too busy amassing books, drawings, and blue prints. The trailer has become a library of piles of sketches, video renderings, and just about every book, I can get delivered on the Temple. I have sorted the piles into tall stacks of building plans, historical references, current biblical archaeological theories, and the original building instructions in Kings and Chronicles. I cannot draw well, read blueprints, or even know the correct conversion of cubits to feet. There is a debate over this as well, I find. Some ultra-Orthodox sects refuse to even consider building the Temple, because they fear, they do not know what a cubit is, and until the Messiah shows up to tell them, they will pray for his arrival, and not build anything.

I await some divine tap on the shoulder. I read of King David amassing the material to build it. Piles of cedar, stone, talents of gold and silver. And the site at Mt. Moriah, he bought from Ornan, who was a Jebusite, in 1000 BC, as his reign ended. Ornan did not know if the ridges, he owned around this Temple Mount, where the exact location of where Abraham went to sacrifice son Issac, a thousand years before. But, David had a sense that this was the place to finally build the house of Yahweh. Had he not commanded that a house be built, where his presence could dwell, and the Ark of the Covenant rest. The commandment tablets, the staff of Aaron, and other artifacts of the desert journey, were in the Tabernacle for all those years from Exodus to mid -10th century BCE, when Solomon began to construct the Temple. Seven years later, Zadok completes the actual Temple, a replica in largest form of the tabernacle, and another 13 years pass as the palace is constructed. It stands for 470 years, says that turncoat, historian, Josephus. 470, six months and ten days. Then after a siege of over a year, Nebuchadnezzer II, takes the site, and burns it. The inner sanctum, the Kodesh haKodashim, The Holy of Holies, is sacked, 20 metric tons of gold on the walls of this 20 x 20 room are taken. The giant cherubim had wingspans of ten cubits, and their wings covered the Ark, also coated in gold. That day when the Babylonians entered it all disappeared, including the Ark and the commandments themselves, never to be seen again.

I could pretend to dream of the ghost of David, or a casual visit from Zadok, but, no one came. No voices, visions or insights from any Yahweh, emerging through a grey cloud of Siggi's special blend. I was alone with this seething compulsion, to build this damn thing. Not out of a some sense that it would change anything, or alter the world much. But, it might display that there was a Temple, an Ark, a people who actually believed in the presence of an essence, larger than themselves, that roamed through a building for almost 500 years, and had a name, only spoken on Yom Kippur, inside this 20 x 20 golden lined room, uttered by one man, the Kohen Gadol. Tied by a rope he entered, and he had bells attached to him, so others would know, Yahweh had not taken him away.

That was all. No grand religious vision, anymore than that of Ken Ham, the founder of Answers in Genesis, who believes that the writings of that book are actual. The world was created in seven days, there was an Adam and Eve, and the Earth is but 5778 years old. Yet, as unlikely as it may seem, science not considered, he raised 36 million in donations and floated a bond issue in Williamstown, Kentucky for another 62 million, to build Noah's Ark and a theme park around it. This exact replica from scripture is a top attraction in that state. Ham had a commercial vision drive by a deep religious belief that there was an Ark, so he built it. It is the largest timber frame anything in the United States.

Cubit by cubit, his builders decided it was 20.1 inches. This Australian, true believer, refuses to believe anything but Genesis, that there was a Noah, an Ark, and the flood. So he built it. The rest of the world be damned.

Some considered him a lunatic, a backwater hick. But, he raised 36 million, convinced a city to put up a bond, and the State of Kentucky, gave him roads, freeway off ramps, signs, and the embrace that comes when an idea becomes a tax generating attraction.

Not likely, anyone wants this to happen. The debate over rebuilding the Temple colors everything. I am not attempting to rebuild it on the Temple Mount. I am not pretending or expecting it brings about the Messianic era. I do not know if the Rapture only happens after the Temple is rebuilt. I am compelled to build it here, in this God forsaken desert town, for no known reason, other than it seems of some value, to show it, since, the actual Third temple, may never be realized. I'm no Rabbi, but, this mark under my right eye, declares something to me. Blood runs through me, from the tribe of Levi, the same blood as ran through Aaron, Eleazor, Phineas, and Zadok. I have no flock, no brother touched by God, or tablet to protect. I have this urge, to do something here, across, this desert plain, that may be meaningful or not.

But, it will be done.

There are prophets who say there will be another Temple. No one claims to be a prophet today. The Hebrew God was a talker once. From Abraham to Moses, through Gabriel to Ezekiel. Ezekiel said he was placed upon a mountain and saw a city. But, prophesy, may not be destiny in a modern world where Muslims, Jews, and Catholics all claim the same high ground, on the Temple Mount. And even the Rabbi's disagree, which comes as no surprise to me, that they would argue between them. Hell, even Chanukah, was about a civil war between the Greek leaning reform Jews and the traditional Maccabees. Always a battle, internally rarely any unity. Even as the world conspires to kill us all, the men of Torah and books cannot agree.

Take this Temple lore. Amazing as it seems, one group of scholars claim only a direct lineage from King David can build it. Others, await the actual arrival of the Messiah who will then build it. Yet, another faction sees the Temple actually built in space and floating into place. Still others, believe that any Jew can build it, based upon the sage advice of the iconic Rambam, from the 12th century, and that there must be a Temple for the Messiah to arrive. And, this is supported by the Midrash Yalkut Shimoni, another mystic leader from the 10 th century, who tells of the Messiah actually standing atop the Temple and shouting to all, that some level of redemption is coming. So, if the Temple is to be built, can any Jew do it, and where?

This Jew is about to build a replica, in Borrego Springs. Not the Temple Mount. Still, there is not a Jew, not one who has encouraged me. And the few Rabbi's I have encountered have shamed me, to believe that I am of Aaron, or worse that building this Temple is of merit. One, Ronald Berman, a Kabbalist told me, evil would come to me, and any who helped me would be stricken down by a Dybukk, or witch. Only one, Rebka Dayan, a short, thick, sturdy presence, laughed and invited me to her Sabbath service, in the back of a Toyota dealership in El Cajon. At the end of my brief talk, there was applause, a hug from the Rebbe, and she put her large hand behind my neck, and pulled my head to her mouth. She bit my ear and intoned, "build the fucking thing… just build it."

SUNRISE ON A TRAIL

This is the trail of the morning, most mornings, I know it. It requires a slow gait, to avoid falls and stumbles. Like other things, you cannot be somewhere else, when you are on it, no floating mind or Zen trips. It is a place where the birds warble as the sun comes over the dark mountain, the snakes are huddled under rocks and sand, an Indian spirit moves across the plain, and touches your cheek as you amble forward. I am running slow enough to contemplate a prayer, for some guidance of where to find the cash, and the land to build it. I have taken to small presentations at the Zorro, and a few other slide shows that Joey set up. Even Frankie and Tina, detached from any of it, and thinking I am a 5150, have hosted a few gatherings with LA venture types. They were really more about Tina wanting me to get laid than, anything else. She was uniformly unsuccessful in her quest, as I was in my hopes to catch a rich, wild rabbit, to jump start the venture.

This was a one hour out and back. Rarely saw anyone else.

On the turn around, I came shoulder to shoulder with a lanky older man, Jimmy Stewart type, angular, and sunken eyes, with a slow, soft vocal cadence. Said his name was Jeremy Sadler from Sandy, Utah. He knew about me, told me of his home building, up under Olympus Cove, overlooking Salt Lake City, and his blocks of uncharted desert, he and his brother Robbie inherited over the last year. He was in his late 70's, maybe older, but had a steady step, and ran me faster than usual towards the trailhead. Then, he stopped as though he had a heart attack, but, it was not that. He stooped to pick up a pure white stone. It was the size of his palm, translucent.

"You never pass one of these MAC. In a lifetime, maybe you see two or three. You can go out and seek one, and never find it. Or come back to this trail, and think you will see another and you won't. In a way, we all want to be that white stone, unique, a stand out, a rarity. Not everyone can handle that. Are you a white stone, MAC."

I ran silently to the ATV. And Jeremy asked, oddly, what I wanted from him. And without hesitation,

"I need land to build the Temple"

"How much land"

"The Temple Mount is 45 acres, I need 100"

"I have that"

Within a month of signing documents and deeds, I had 100 acres under a far off mountain of just desert, with a single dirt road winding towards it. Jeremy set up a trailer and three large tents, to begin to review the plans and mark off the territory. I set up no sign, and prepared to establish the camp, before I proceeded to present it all to the county and the planning board. Right now, it was a large plot of land with just a few temporary shelters, and nothing on it.

Robbie unloaded a bus sized RV with four boys ages 25 to 15 streaming out to install invisible perimeter markers, and walk off the dimensions of the Temple itself. Maqroll brought Madrid, and Siggi, and Siggi brought his own small army of laborers to move sand, clear shrubs, and hang out at camp fires smoking his weed. The atmosphere was upbeat, more like a gathering for Burning Man than raising a Temple.

Two men were drunk and high. They argued over a woman and one was stabbed in the chest and across his arm, the other pulled out his Glock 17 and shot the attacker twice, killing him. A young vet, runs his Harley at high speed away from the camp, only to hit a block of concrete and breaks his neck. Three men at a distant campfire in the northeast corner of the compound are killed by, what some believe is a cartel encouraged hit, their bodies are not discovered for weeks after the shooting. And, then three pigs are slaughtered and thrown on the entrance to the camp.

Each incident taken alone, would frighten few, or generate a rumor that would rumble through the town of 5,000. But, unified into a single narrative, they suggest a star crossed site that is cursed by someone, or something, even a God of Hebrews. As much as, Kittle, the Editor of the Sun, attempted to report these events as unrelated, residents, on lookers, and detractors began to sum them up, as portents. The prevailing mythology was becoming that the Temple was more a burden than a benefit, even though, not a stone was laid, nothing fully surveyed, and the development had not been approved.

Public hearings were scheduled. Everyone would speak their piece. I hoped for no more incidents or deaths.

THE MAILMAN

The regular guy is not in the truck. The lazy man, who shoots traps with accuracy in the backyard, is not walking towards me and Highball. She is blonde and tan, in shorts with a black stripe, and a tear on her left one. The dog does not move nor bark. I am handed a manila envelope, that I must sign for, old school, registered letter she attests. I offer her a respite on the porch and an iced tea, she declines, and pets the dog, then rubs his belly, as he rolls in the sand, scratching his back. She accounts how the rip came from a terrier across town. Then she drives away, without a puff of dust, as I open the postage.

THIS IS TO NOTIFY YOU, MOSES AARON COHEN OF A DIVORCE PROCEEDING FILED IN LOS ANGELES SUPERIOR COURT. RUTH WEISS JACOB, OF LOS ANGELES HAS REQUESTED A DIVORCE EFFECTIVE IN SIXTY DAYS.

Not unexpected. There had been no engagement or discussion in years. I dutifully kept the same bank account, expected she pulled down on the pension, the annuity, and other small sources of income to pay bills. We had discussed none of it, since, the name change, and I expected she would move on, eventually. This desert life, my relentless yearning to escape reality, had brought me back to it, with the sucker punch delivered by a blonde in a postal truck. My reaction was not benign.

I rushed to the cabinet of arms, and loaded the shotgun, tied the pull cord to my ankle and sent discs into the cloudless sky. I must have squeezed off 50 rounds, before my shoulder hurt, and my right cheek and jaw seemed numb. There was enough self- doubt and insecurity in each round, to sound a message into the heavens that I had screwed up another part of a life, I had crafted, that was about something, or so it seemed. Now, I was MAC, an aging eccentric, after a rather crazy, literal accomplishment. Perhaps, I was unglued, with a brain disease, chemical imbalance, or accelerating dementia. But, it did not seem that way. By all other measures, except this compulsion or revelation, I appeared fit, indeed, normal. And, until this moment, sane.

I drove to Maqroll's, to borrow his phone to call Ruth. When I arrived he was in his painting clothes, with bright yellow on his apron. He escorted me into the studio, where he had a 20x20 foot rendition of a woman in the classic pose, but laying on a yellow sheet. He had etched out the form, and was anxious to get underway from a photograph he took of her, a week ago. He offered me his phone, I dialed, but, then hesitated. I could not face her, this great master builder I imagined myself, I could not bear the essential humiliation of admitting my part in the demise of the long held marriage. I had deserted her for this, and thrown a life away to pile stones across a plain and be the priest, without authority over an ersatz sacred place. I gave him back the phone, took some toilet paper rolls and two loaves of bread and drove back to room 36 at the Zorro, to soak in a hot tub, knock back a Black Russian, and gaze at the stars.

ISRAEL- THE TEMPLE MOUNT

All the anger of the divorce, the need to prove something to myself brought me here. There is a line of tourists from everywhere awaiting a brief walk on this sacred site. It is morning and the only time Jews are allowed here, I stand with a group from the Temple Institute, who engage in an 'aliyot', this "going up" to stand where the Temple are alleged to have been.

The scholars are not certain, exactly where it is that the Temple rested. But, most agree, Solomon's Temple was near the site bought by David. And that the Holy of Holies was under what is today called the El Kas fountain. The foundation of the Temple near the Muslim Dome of the Rock, and that fountain between the Dome and the Al Aqsa mosque. I can feel the tension, as we wait.

I cannot pray, I cannot walk freely. I must gaze only briefly at the surroundings. Everyone is on edge. The few who have attempted to pray have been arrested by Israeli cops, some stoned by Palestinian zealots. That Dome of the Rock shelters the mystical journey of the Prophet to heaven, where he meets the patriarchs, including Aaron and Moses. Orthodox seers forbid their flock stepping foot here, believing it an 'unclean" visit that might defile the Holy of Holies, since they know where it actually may be.

Not so the Dome, where it is very clear where the Prophet stepped, as an oblong imprint appears in the Rock. His last step before mounting, al-Burg, and ascending with Gabriel in tow. Twelve marble pillars support the inner dome, the focal point of the Haram al-Sharif. This vast place, where pigeons fly, as they have for centuries, and where blood has flowed from soldiers that mark the march history across this small battlefield. Romans, Greeks, Persians, then Ottomans, Mongols, the Brits and now this. You must be here to sense the complexity of it all. Even Moshe Dayan, who liberated this place and the Western Wall, did not let the flag of Israel wave over the site, instead he gave it back to the Waqf, the people in charge of the site to manage it. Since, then, it has become a battle ground.

Radical Jews come at times to challenge the rules. Some have fought, Palestinians have died in riots to reject any changes. Even the Israeli Supreme Court ruled that Jews do have the right to pray, but if you do, you will be removed or arrested. Evangelical Christians have a stake in the debate, as the entire prophecy of the Rapture and Tribulations rests upon the Temple being rebuilt, here. Without it, the Anti- Christ has no Temple to reside, the tribulation itself of seven years, is when the Temple is built or delivered by God from heaven. Without it, Armageddon is stymied, the great battles that presage the return of Christ unfought, the Gog and Megog unmatched. And the defenders of Islam want none of it, they simply want this spot to be the center of a holy revival that rids Israel of its Jews, and returns Jerusalem to them.

And it is not lost on me that I would not be here, if Moshe Dayan and the Israeli IDF had not won that war. The entire Western wall and all of Old Jerusalem was in Jordan's hands. No Jew could pray at the Wall. Dayan, it is said, wrote a prayer that he placed in a crevasse, "May Peace descend on the whole house of Israel". Then, he ordered the flag over the Dome be taken down. And ever since, there has been no peace.

I had the feeling of others, I expect. This was a place for Jews. The Ark was here from the Tabernacle to here for hundreds of years, then, lost or stolen, by the Babylonians. The vestments of the Temple; the silver shovel to remove the ashes of the sacrifices; the mizrak, bowls to hold the blood; the gold plated Shofar; the golden Menorah; all gone, taken to Rome by Titus, or buried even, in secret places revealed only in the Copper Scroll from Qumran from Cave 3, in scroll 15. All gone. Not a single real trace of any of it, except for some sonar scans, the catacombs beneath me, the Western Wall. But, enough to fight over, die for, and contest.

I could not stop and pray. I knew no prayer except the Shema, which I said through my mind and did not utter. But I also did ask for guidance, to build the Temple. I asked for some divine direction. In doing so, I found, I was shedding tears. A guide came to me with a purple handkerchief, and frantically motioned me to wipe my face, for fear I would be arrested for praying. I complied and stuffed it into my blazer pocket.

THE TEMPLE INSTITUTE

In the Old City, the streets narrow, enough room, barely for four people to walk abreast. I walk tall, as if, I know it. I do not look so unusual here, in some ways, I have a white beard and longer hair, a dark tan, and blue eyes. But I wear no long coat or hat of some slaughtered animal. I cannot be mistaken as a Haredi, with a book under my arm. I am decidedly Western, and can utter only a few obvious phrases in tourist Hebrew. Still, I feel as though I have been here, and walk the path to the Temple Institute with a certain confidence.

And the purple triangle beneath my right eye is concealed. I have the Mark of Aaron, but choose to show it sparingly.

The Institute itself is part museum and a center for the rebuilding of the Temple. There are re created artifacts, that are replicas designed to strict specifications to resemble what was once used at the Temple of Solomon. There is the breast plate of the Kohen Gadol, with a jewel for each tribe; the garb of the priest, and even his golden crown. You walk into a place where you sense a virtual factory of creators, intent on offering all the ritual objects, so that, when the Temple is rebuilt on the Mount, everything will be exact.

And behind another door, sits Dov Salomon, who is the keeper of the blue prints for the rebuilding. His brother was run over by a tank and crippled in the Golan Heights in 1958, and was an advocate of the immediate bulldozing of the mosque and everything else on the Mount, so the reconstruction could begin. He and Dov where, in their way, radicals whose evangelical yearnings would destroy peace in Jerusalem. And, for Dov, the Temple he wanted was precisely accurate, including the return of animal sacrifices.

But, these Institute people were also committed to the actual hierarchy of the ancient Kingdom of David and Solomon. They wanted to train Kohanim priests, restore the Levite control of the Temple, reform the governing body of 73 men, the Sanhedrin, separate men and women; restore cleansing Mikvah baths; and reformulate the faith in its most odious, hierarchical form. They were modern day Pharisees.

They saw form and spectacle, the word and ceremony, as the be all and end all of the faith. When I raised the question to Dov, if Jews would be better off without the ceremony and the reinstitution of the priesthood, he lost his temper, and called me a "secular" Jew, as though it was tragic curse, and that I was to blame, and others like me, for the loss of generations of faithfulness. Still, I persisted.

If the Jewish world looked like the Christian, with the Pope and the Kohen Gadol, with a Temple and the Vatican, with priests and Aaronite priests, and the ancient texts and rules, would the future be brighter for the world's 15 million Jews? Are the outer trappings of a faith, the faith? And has not the Diaspora sustained Jewish thought, through two thousand years of hardship?

Dov was unconfused by my inquiry. He found me Western, frivolous, if serious, and unlikely to understand why their way of rebuilding was the only way. He welcomed support from the Israeli government, who gave him small funding; Revelation filled Christian supporters, and even an American billionaire, the son of two Holocaust survivors, and an Orthodox Jew. He told me to track down, Henry Swieca, and his Israeli- America, wife Estee Tobaly, to get his take on why he supported them.

Swieca, at 19, lost his mother to ALS, his father in the same year to a heart attack. This orphan had a knack for investing, and forced his way into Merrill Lynch, with his only connection his hunger to succeed. He knew adversity, and was not inclined to forget his past, his parents grit to survive, and his own journey. So investing in the Third Temple seemed a natural philanthropic gesture. Dov thought this take would quiet my Socratic diversions. It did.

He projected the blueprints on a large television screen from his computer. It was not unlike what I had found from various sources. The basics were all there. The pillars of Jachin and Boaz on the porch; a main building; an interior outer alter; the holy of holies at the end, enclosed. And outside the inner court, with lavers or baths for purification and an alter for sacrifice; and the massive Molten Sea baths for priests, which was set atop twelve oxen facing outwardly. Then the outer court, the Great Court, that surrounded the building, where the people came and prayed.

There were no surprises, some nuances of where steps would be placed, and the exact designs on the wall or the opening doors. It was as elaborate, as I expected. The structure and gardens and courts, he estimated at 350 to 500 million, but the gold plating, and re-creation another 300 million. So, it was a billion dollars to construct it, as the true Third Temple. They also wanted a conference center for the Sanhedrin, a museum for visitors, and an auditorium and classrooms.

To this point, he was argumentative, but civil. When I told him that I wanted to build a replica in the California desert, it was more than he could stand, and he began yelling in Hebrew and shaking his fist at me. I attempted to calm him with my limited grasp of the scripture that surrounded the building of the Temple in 1 Kings 8:12-13.

And I quoted between tirades, that the priests carried the Ark into the Temple and the Holy of Holies, and the book accounts: that a cloud filled the courts, signifying to Solomon that the Lord had filled the house of the Lord. Solomon feeling vindicate that Zadok had built God's dwelling and Solomon said,

"The Lord has said that he would dwell in thick darkness.

I have built for you an exalted house, a place for you to dwell in forever"

And Dov calmed. He realized, while I did agree with his approach, I was enough of a serious Jew to be treated with some respect. And he reminded me that Solomon dedicated the Temple that day not only to Jews, but to all who came to Israel, to be open to all from all the lands to experience the presence of the Lord.

He offered to email me his plans, and to find contributors from America to support the Institute. I signed a commitment of a few hundred dollars as a contribution to get the plans. I was surprised that he came to me with open arms and hugged me, and offered in Hebrew a blessing for good fortune. I decided to not reveal the other oddball biblical fact that also on the day of dedication Solomon slaughtered 22,000 bulls and 120,000 sheep to Yahweh.

As I walked away from the Institute a young woman grabbed me by my arm, and pushed me into a doorway.

"I am Rebbeca HaKohen, Rabbi. I see your purple marker. Are you one of us"

She had taken the purple handkerchief as a mark of my support for the Temple Mount Movement. A ragtag group of radicals intent upon the use of violence to rid the Mount of Muslims ad rebuild the Temple.

"I am MAC from America."

"Well, MAC from America. I am Crazy Becca. Will you come with me"

As we walked, she quickly recounted in her Brooklyn accent that she was part of the movement and often stood by the Mount and waved an oversized Israeli flags, and shouted for the Muslims to leave the site. She admitted to being unpopular with most in Israel, but, that the movement as growing. She had not done the "deed" as she called it, but wanted me to spend a night with her, and her cadre, at a kibbutz.

MISGAV AM

It was a long drive through the day to get to this place, this kibbutz. Misgav Am sits atop Israel overlooking Lebanon and the contested Golan Heights, the town of Kiryat Shmona to its near South. It is a small place, that overlooks the valley, sees into Lebanon and its enemy of Hezbollah. It is one of the founding socialist enclaves, created by Palmach freedom fighters after the Balfour Declaration in 1945. It came from blood and sacrifice, this kibbutz of about 500 residents.

It did not seem so incongruous that it would be the place where Crazy Becca and her cadre might hide out and plot the overthrow of the Temple Mount. She was radicalized, this bright, tough, girl from Sheephead's Bay, when Rabbi Yehuda Glick was shot after a speech to foster the Judification of the Temple Mount. It was an assassination attempt by Mutaz Hijazi, a local Palestinian, who the Israeli cops tracked down and killed. He came from Abu Tor, and Crazy and her group protested and demanded sovereignty on the Mount. Police and Hijazi supporters had violent clashes. The streets filled will the scent of tear gas and the rock throwing popularized by the intifada.

The band of radicals was a mix of millennials like Crazy and a dozen friends in bandanas and purple t- shirts. A few older men had KACH emblems on their jackets, which I knew where from the outlawed party once run by American born rabbi and radical, Meir Kahane, of the Jewish Defense League. Glick had ties to Kach and to these kids as well.

The discussion was a teach in. They wanted my support, thinking MAC, the Temple builder would be able to raise funds for their efforts, even if it supported violence. They were, as a group, convinced that the only way to jump start the actual building of the Third Temple, would be by exploding the Mosque. It was guerilla talk, like the conspirators, from the Irgun, who decided to bomb the King David hotel, where the British Mandatory authorities were housed. The attack killed 91 and injured 46 others, and although there were warnings, they were ignored. The Irgun operating independently from the Haganah, that ran the Jewish insurgency, did not know that an attack was nixed.

I wondered if they even knew of the Palmach, Irgun, and Haganah. And if they did know would it matter. They seemed imbued with the same zeal and devotion to getting a result. For those groups it was freedom from the British and independence. For this group of zealots, it was the building of the Temple on sacred ground and the expulsion, not the détente with Islam.

Into the evening hours, they created a warming bonfire. The ardor seemed to ease, as a man of my age rose to tell a story. He spoke with an Eastern, USA accent, that sounded nasal enough to be from Bayonne. On his hip was a 1911 style, 9mm. He looked to me to begin:

"Welcome to you MAC. I know what we propose may sound extreme. But everything in Israel is extreme. Our politics. Our dream of a homeland. A Third Temple. And who denies us this, Palestinians, Jordan, Islam, America, and even some Jews. But, we must fight for it, for the dead, and the living.

You know, here in 1980 a band of terrorists, funded by Iraq, came into the camp. They took over the nursery. They murdered the teacher, then shot an infant dead in a crib. It took two raids by the IDF, the first failed. Two more workers are killed. The second raid, they kill the terrorists, liberate the children.

But, as the years pass, we attempt to conciliate as God commands us. Yet, the real peace never comes. Here at this kibbutz we make bandages and dressings for the sick, wounded, and poor. This is our purpose. And to have a Temple again, will that too be denied, never to be seen in any Jews lifetime, a 1,000 years from now?"

I rose and walked towards him, and hugged him before the assembled. They applauded. I was about to return to my spot by Crazy Becca, when a man shouted out,

"Tell him who you are Yaakov. Tell him"

And I paused, as Yaakov held my wrists tightly and said to my face,

"I am the infants father.

I could not flee, nor cry, I was startled and transfixed. Becca came for me, and took me inside the dining hall, where she introduced me to a woman who had her eyes and coloring, but with grey and white hair, in long pigtails. Obviously her mother, who seemed interested in my tale of prosecutor to MAC. Becca left us.

Perhaps, it was the campfire, the stories, the shared angst over the future for these young folks, or just loneliness. I expect it was that. We merged into a tiny bed in one room, overlooking Lebanon, and had a slow, soft joining of two aging bodies. With few words needed, an offering of solace and companionship only the most alone can know, we held each other until sleep came, without a dream, or commotion until dawn.

BORREGO
ZORRO ROOM 36

Madrid had gathered her family with Siggi to prepare a feast for the hotel staff, to thank Joey and his partner for employing them for the last year. The long table spread across the pool area and a band played Mariachi tunes. Izzy had a few workers from her crew, and Roberto has an entire table of his laborers. It was a fiesta of craftsmen and working women. Everyone danced and sang. I sat with Maqroll who was less joyous than the others. He was concerned that the money needed to fund our venture would never be found, he foresaw darkness, and trouble ahead. I attempted to reassure him that we could begin with modest funds, on the land we were given.

I had convinced myself that immediately building the Temple would take many years and millions, even in replica form. If the real Temple was a billion dollars, we needed a few hundred million, like 350- 400 million to totally complete the project. I was going to give it 7 years, just like Zadok. But, I thought, the first thing to build was the housing of the Ark as it traveled through the desert, the Tabernacle.

I could see the tabernacle in the center of our land, and build everything around it, so that the most expensive part the Temple itself would be build last, as we raised the money to complete it. The Tabernacle requires a few hundred thousand, as a replica, but a few million for actual re-creation. And, people could come and visit the Tabernacle, and help build the surrounding grounds and structures.

I announced the Tabernacle construction to the group, Roberto pledged construction help and Izzy, now at monolith 60, agreed to begin her thinking about the quarry and moving of the foundation stones for the Temple. I had the purple, triangle mark showing, this night, and Madrid, after a rousing dance with Maqroll encouraged the story for the group.

In the most irreverent manner, the story came out of me, from Rebbe Nachman's lost text. Aaron was in charge of the flock, as Moses goes to receive the covenant and Commandments from Yahweh. He comes back and the people have made a Golden Calf. In anger Moses destroys the tablets. Aaron, his older brother, apologizes to Moses, and a single tear leaves his right eye, and it sears his skin. For all time the true, descendants of Aaron have this mark, this only revealed to the most pure and holy, and to those who will guard the Ark, the Temple and Gods people. I have only the mark, I tell them, and only the compulsion to build this replica Temple.

When asked why now. I have no answer, other than I am here, with this marker. I am of Aaron and I am driven, by a force I cannot control, to give up everything to build it, here.

But, it starts I tell them with the Tabernacle that is logical since, after the Golden Calf, Moses instructed Aaron to build a place for God to dwell, a Mishkan, or dwelling place. It was to have an interior tent for the Ark, a gold plated, lamp stand, or menorah, with 22 bowls for oil, shaped like almonds and blossoms, a table for bread, seven more oil lamps, and an altar for incense. Surrounding it layers of curtains, some with polished gold.

Back in 36, Exodus is the source for the Tabernacle construction. I lay out the requirements, awaiting Roberto and his expertise on building materials. There is more curtain than wood, some four pillars, and artifacts to be rendered. I have a thought of Hollywood set designers for the Ark and the Menorah, the table, the oil lamps. It does not seem too costly- less than 300k.

Roberto sees the 48 boards, more to create a tent over the ark, some pillars, an eternal light, called the Ner tamid, an elevated altar for blessings and incense, and the perimeter behind curtains, attached to pillars. It was for him a few weeks of easy labor, as the structure was designed to be moved, across the desert after Moses returned with the second covenant. Roberto seemed relieved. It was not difficult, at all, and for this God, not much to ask.

The Roberto meeting encouraged me. I looked into the sky, knowing the Tabernacle did make the journey to Canaan, and was there as they fought with Joshua at Gilgal. It found its way to Shiloh, and stayed there for 300 years. The Ark, eventually separated from it and found its way into a tent David struck for it. But, it was the first synagogue, the first pre cursor to the Temple of Solomon, and even that Temple was modeled after it, as are most modern synagogues. A wall, a reception area for worshipers, an eternal light, menorahs, a bimah or altar, and then the Torahs or the Holy of Holies. The same walk, as did Aaron and the Levites in the desert.

How crazy was any of this? In one week, astronomers found a black hole 800 million suns of density, and a complete eight planet solar system, some 1200 light years away with a third planet from a sun like ours. Is there a Temple about to be built there, is there an eternal essence there? Or more unknown, is this all from one source, one bang in firmament that brought us all to this? Pondering all of that makes this quest seem smaller and achievable.

NIGHTFALL AT THE SITE

Weeks have passed. I have given some speeches, lined up providers of materials, even convinced a set designer to render the Ark and other ritual items for cost, with durable materials. Yet, there are only a few funds, raised on the various funding sites, on the internet.

It is the darkest of nights. A thick cloud layer has shrouded the sky. Highball and I are alone, in the RV, when the sound of trucks at high speed cross into our perimeter. I hear shots fired, and we roll out with the AK and the .38 holstered on the ATV. There are two trucks, one with three men shot on the ground. I see two others by the side of the other truck holding shotguns.

Highball jumps towards them. One man raises the gun, and I fire a full clip, as a shotgun blast rings out. In seconds, they are dead. Highball is a clump of flesh and hair, also dead. On the ground, are four large duffel bags, they contain packets of 100 dollar bills.

I know what I should do. I know, but I do not hestitate.

I throw three bags into the ATV, throw them into a storage shed.

I drive to the store and have Maqroll call in the shooting.

The Sheriff of San Diego County comes out to the scene. Bill Gore is a Gary Cooper type, a man of few words and possessed of good judgment. He also was the protégé of Bill Kolender, who had reformed the cop shop as its chief, and became the long serving Sheriff. He was proud of his Jewish heritage and we would share family stories, when we met at conferences. Gore had rubbed shoulders with me through the years as well. He was in no mood to do anything but get the crime scene under control and move on. He called the D.A. directly.

I spent the night burying the bags, and locking a hundred thousand in a metal box, I kept in a shed. The D.A. arrived at dawn, alone. She was in no mood for pleasantries, considering me an outlier, who had turned a little crazy. Still, she saw what it as self defense, and would not charge me. When she what I had buried, I told her it was a grave for Highball. She gave me a hug, and stepped away.

The AK was registered under Frankie, and she could have fined me, but, let it go, for old time sake. She coaxed me to call Ruth, and, revealed Ruth was very serious about Arnie Reingold, a Superior Court judge. I nodded and said nothing.

A few months later, I call Roberto, have him buy the material.

By Fall, I call everyone together to dedicate the Tabernacle.

May God forgive me.

CHAPTER VI

❖❖❖

THE TABERNACLE LIFE

There are tours of the site. Buses coming from Los Angeles and Ventura County, to walk the grounds, and see the Tabernacle. There are more Christians, church goers, than Jews. On weekends, cars stream past the tiny Christmas Circle, and follow our signs to THE DESERT TABERNACLE in white letters on a blue background. One hundred a day, a thousand or so each weekend.

Maqroll and Madrid have taken over the parking concession charging for buses and cars. The fee to the Tabernacle is whatever a person can afford. But most folks throw in a ten or twenty. They have set up tables for picnics, established clusters of areas for children to play, and set up canopies for shade. Every sign is in English and Spanish, every exhibit has a docent, who offers an explanation for the elements of the Tabernacle, the Exodus journey, and the role the Tabernacle played in preservation of the covenant and the Ark.

The grounds are still more sand and dust than structure. But through a ranch style gate, there is the beginning of an outer wall, and inner wall to surround the Tabernacle and eventually the Temple itself. On the perimeter there are yurts, that sleep five people, for those who sign releases to stay the night and help construct the walls. And there is an earthen amphitheater, where I hold a late afternoon seminar on what we are doing and why it matters to have a replica of the Temple here in the California desert.

And twice a month, Seth and his Chabad group dress in ancient garb and populate the site as docents. They also gather to sing prayers and chant in Hebrew to enhance the authenticity of the surroundings. It is all upbeat, cheerful and a celebration of the past, than an overly serious rendition of the struggle of the Jewish people. The mood captures my feelings that this is a quest of enormous positive energy flow, and not some darkly rabbinical undertaking.

However, there is a reverence inside the Tabernacle that comes naturally to patrons. It is a replica, they all know this but it is also compelling somehow. The sign explain, how and why is was built, and the role the Levi tribe played in carrying it through the desert, and the 300 years it rested, before the Ark as placed in the Temple. And each day, twice I would stand in front of the golden altar, and burn incense. And the fire before the goat and ram skinned canopy was always burning. When they entered, there was a hush, even though the replica Ark was just that, it inspired awe. And the mocked up tablets, also inspired quiet discussion. For there, they rested with a urn for manna from heaven, and a rod that was to be Aarons.

There was controversy about all of it, especially the rod of Aaron. Some scholars saw it as a rod of a shepherd, plain, yet, blossoming, as though it was eternally alive, and yielding almonds. Others, the version we created, was majestic with the names of the twelve tribes, and a gemstone for each tribe, mirroring the stones on the Kohen Gadol's breast plate. And when they exited there was a path to a large tent that showed them blueprints of the proposed Temple, renditions of it from various sources, including the Temple Institute, and then the entered a smaller tent, where a scale model of the Temple rested behind plexiglass. A docent stands by the model and explains as the groups gather how it will be built and displays the inside with computer video, that he projects on the large screens around the model.

And, incongruously, there are always food trucks, of some sort, that offer the cuisine of the trucks, that has nothing to do with the Temple. There was no special food, the recipes of today that suggest food types are all derivatives from Sephardic or Ashkenazy traditions. Yet, people pause and eat, and picnic, and contemplate returning as the Temple gets built.

I was surprised to see that when we offered, special rates to use the grounds for services of any denomination, we were booked for months in advance. They came in cars, and buses, and conducted their services. There were groups of all sizes, pastors in colorful frocks, holy rollers and Gospel singers, and on the rare occasion a men's club from a synagogue, but never a rabbi to conduct a service or say a single prayer. For a fee, I would show up and give a simple, if inspiring sermon, on David and Solomon and Zadok and the creation of the Temple and its purpose. I found I had tendency to dress in all black or fully in khaki and black, like an evangelical Marlin Perkins or Jack Hanna. I did not want the trappings of a rabbi or priest. Although, I did find myself, rising at dawn laying my tefillin, I would put the shel yad, on my arm, and the shel rosh on my head. Something I had stopped doing after my bar mitzvah. I was in a small chapel, in an airport at Inchon, on a trip to Beijing and a man was praying there, twenty years ago, who gave me his phylacteries, and we prayed together. He said through a Slavic accent that I would return to it. Two decades later, under these circumstances, I had.

It was now a symbol that had meaning again. The process of tying the prayer boxes to my arm and between my eyes. All from Exodus to remember the journey and to bind, literally, man to God, as written in Deuteronomy:

"you shall tie them for a sign upon your arm, and they shall be as a memorial between your eyes"

It brings me back to those days, when I found it a pain, to wrap the forearm, stand with this prayer box at my hair line, and pray quietly, then walk to Beth Emeth and the farmhouse synagogue and have a bagel. Then nothing righteous flowed through me. Now I was tied to this ritual, a Jewish meditation, that recognized my heart and mind were a blessing from God, and that I was finally on a path to be an instrument of some measure, or so I imagined.

But, not to the traditional Jewish power brokers. In Los Angeles, I was a pariah. Since, I was instructed by Joey from the Zorro to get hip to social media, he had his marketing expert, Cynthia set up everything. The Temple in the Desert was everywhere from Facebook to Snapchat. There were pictures of everything, my lectures, people taking selfies by the Tabernacle and the model. And the groups of Mormons who bused in most weekends to stay for a week and move rocks into place on the outer wall had their own followers. And, as expected there were haters, and these people she called trolls. I expected the anti- Semites, the Jew haters, even the threats on my life. But I did not anticipate the ire and disdain of other Jews.

Rabbi Jacob Mendelson had made it his mission to destroy me. He posted constantly to anything we offered. He organized a small protest to picket our compound claiming I was a P.T. Barnum character intent upon defiling the faith. It was a circus, to use his phrase, a vastly preposterous scenario that was about ego and, even, dementia. He could not stand our popularity, and worse, brought in the Israeli orthodox sects to condemn be, and send a note on every platform he could that, while I was a Jew, I was neither Levite, Kohanim, nor a descendant of Aaron.

In his most unkind declaration, he found me a "common Ashkenazy Jew". And, he had convinced his inner circle that no good would come of the Tabernacle or the efforts to build the Temple. He wanted me to fade away, and crumble into a pillar of desert sand. This was of some consequence, since I had hoped for funds from Jewish supporters. This runt of a man, with a hunched over gait, and closed left eye, seemed more upset with his lack of vigor and popularity than he really was upset about my efforts. He could not stand that I was getting attention that even his wealthy congregation could not give him. He saw it outwardly as a challenge to the faith, while, it was instead a personal challenge.

Thinking me a fool or lunatic that he could easily outmatch, he invited me to visit with him to run over Judaic philosophy.

WILSHIRE BOULEVARD TEMPLE CHAPEL

I had been here many times for Bar and Bat mitzvahs, the services of High Holy days. I prayed under this dome and sat in these seats, surrounded by the murals of Jewish history crafted by Hugo Ballin, who painted these massive canvases in the Pacific Palisades and had them glued to these walls. He and Rabbi Magnin, debated over the depictions, and exactly what he would portray. And it was all funded by the Warner brothers, and a young, movie savant, who rarely came to pray, Irving Thalberg. This was a place where the powers of Hollywood, the secular dynamos who built the city, merged with families of lesser status, and standing, but who had a reform minded faith. Yet, a faith that ram deep through their generation from immigration, through the American dream, the depression, the Holocaust, and the era of American dominance.

Rabbi Mendelson sat in the front aisle, a few feet from the massive stage, the bima, and the ark was closed. Above him the full figure of Moses with his hands flayed in the sign of blessing by the Kohen over the congregation. And surrounding, the dome, the Shema, in Hebrew, "Shema Yisreal, Adonai, Elohanu, Adonai, Ehod." He immediately challenged me:

"So you are a Kohen, from Aaron. Who appointed you the Big Mahoff."

I told him my tale of the mark, the visions, the odd happenings. Which he rejected categorically.

"You are a mythologist, not a rabbi. There is no mark, there is no proof of the line from Moses and Aaron to today."

I told him, even if he rejected all of it, I was still compelled to build the Temple. He accused me of creating a Jewish Disneyland, which was an affront to all Jews, and inevitably to God. I asked how he could know what God wished, and how he came to this certainty. And he offered that he was convinced that the only Temple to ever be built must be on the Temple Mount. His agitation grew with each exchange.

He pulled himself to his full height, pointed his finger at the Torahs. And intoned,

"You will be struck down for this. It is not written. There is no text !"

And he reached up to my lapels, and pulled me close to his mouth, and screamed,

"Who are you... you fake ... you impostor of a Jew... stop it... stop it..."

His voice carried in the empty chapel, I could feel the historic figures in the murals watching and judging it all. He unmoored me, and then left listing to his left with a slight limp.

I sat and gazed into Moses' eyes, read the Shema and uttered the full verses to myself, under my breath. I might have felt scared or chastised, but, I did not. A calm came upon me, as a deep melodic tone, like a cantor warming up his voice, filled the place. I imagined my school boy practices, the barely adolescent voice, memorizing the chanting codes, "mah pach, pash tau, zau kaf, ka tone". My eyes closed and fell into a sleep, until a janitor came by, in his yarmulke, and with the same face as Abdullah, gently shook me awake.

I wiped the naps drool off my face, and drove for the next hours without any thoughts back to the Tabernacle.

ON THE RUN

If you had to cast the founder of endurance athletics, go find a six foot four, blonde, hulk, with swimmers' shoulders and deep blue eyes, you would have to find, Dave Horning. He invented with Tommy Warren and a few ex – Navy guys, swimming, biking and running for fun. Dave has swum around Manhattan and swam away from Alcatraz, all the while creating a business that encourages average guys, like me, to compete. I would show up for his events, and once won my age division in a race through Death Valley. So, he was natural to have him and his all women team establish a race to raise funds for us.

This was the second annual, Temple in the Desert, race weekend. Some raised 2500 hundred dollars to run, and other offered up 200 dollars to enter. It was a small race by most standards, but it was respectable at 7000 entries. Some ran the 5 and 10k, but most the half marathon, a flat jaunt on desert roads, with five miles on a trail right through the Anzo- Borrego park preserve. I promised myself, I would run it every year until the Temple was completed. I was a sight in my shorts, white hair and beard, and the shirt saying, in the front, Temple in the Desert, and on my back, "follow MAC".

The race finished at the Tabernacle, and we had bands play. It was like any other race, awards, refreshments, and the docents available for tours. The trophies were all stones, that were being placed round for the walls, with a small bronze plaque. Every finisher got a medal in the shape of the Temple, with a gold color. It helped spread the word, to but another group of would be allies, and translated into modern lifestyles. The goal was solemn, the quest to achieve it was modern, upbeat, and vital.

I finished, worthy of no accolades. Horning promised another effort next year, and proposed a direct use of the funds to buy trees and landscaping for the site, which he thought would entice even more to come, especially if they could actually have their name on a fruit or nut tree. It was as old school as they come, with the twist of a footrace. The Jewish National Fund claims it planted over 240 million trees, since Zvi Hermann Schapira, convinced Herzl, himself to accept the proposal, as Zionism grew in 1900. As did the groves first of olives and other desert hardy trees, proliferate over the years. There was a blue and white tin can in my grandmothers house that seemed to be eternally full to go to JNF. Perhaps, the idea from this athlete turned entrepreneur would help populate the desert, as well.

BUILD THE WALLS

Izzy looked like a Sabra. Her dark skin and cannonball shoulders busting through her white tank top. There was an exotic aura around her, as her team of women commanded our volunteers at Yurt City. They were mostly Mormon boys and some women, who had organized their wards to drive from the Great Salk Lake to labor for a few weeks to move stones, dig post holes, and spend some time working on a spiritual dream. Izzy was a hard boss, she had to be so no one would get injured. Her team ran the dozers and back hoes. She could see the outer wall nearing completion. She split her day between the big stone placement for her project, and this supervision in the afternoon.

It had been years now, since I first met her. And I was not that lost middle aged man. I was in the final third of my life, now. Driven to get this Temple done, in my time. I was free of the old "reality", but tied to this created one, with a vengeance that it had come so late to me. I did not seem to have my energy, or well being. Yet, I was concerned that I would not see the end of it.

Izzy was hardly consoling. She had no sympathy for my muses about my age. In fact, she had no idea how old I was, or cared. She seemed to believe that time was granted for how ever long you needed to start a project or insure that if you expire, it will still get done. Through her eyes, everything imagined was accomplished in stone, and brick and earth. Whether it was the Pyramids, Chichen Itza, Rushmore, Crazy Horse, or Sagrada Familia, which 133 years in the making begun by Antoni Gaudi. All were completed, somehow, including Solomon's Temple. The creators often did not live to see completion of their projects, but many saw most it realized. And to Izzy, this made them saints. Each a timeless force, against a world ordered to the mundane and not the epic. In her small frame was housed an enormous spirit, that seemed unbound by age, and the worries and concerns of men of merely flesh and bone.

Izzy had no age, no facial lines across a soft face, not a fold or deep furrow. She seemed eternal, perhaps, she built all those projects. But, she was an inspiration to me, as I soaked my bones at the Zorro, and prayed for stamina. She shocked me with her candor about my life style.

"If you are so concerned, what do you eat? What are you drinking ?"

"You need to dedicate yourself to a better regimen. No meat, no booze, sleep".

What she demanded seemed suddenly reasonable, if harsh. But she convinced me with the tale of Gaudi's death. He was a master builder, artistic, an inventor of new forms and fused high art and function in his many buildings. He was a strict vegetarian, often fasted, starved himself at times to gain clarity. He was in his later years a true ascetic. It gave him power and energy.

But, on a walk to prayer, he is hit by a tram. He is dressed, as was his way then, like a bum. He was left in the street, until some citizens, out of kindness, put him into a cab. By the time, he was recognized and treated he was dead, at 73. Izzy drew the lesson firmly, as she massaged my neck.

"You must take care of yourself to do the work. But, no matter, when the tram comes for you, all that is left, is what you put in place. We cannot wait, MAC, to get the stones, the big stones in place."

I told her I would find the money to bring the foundation stones which would signal the seriousness of this compulsion, and tell the world that a Temple will be built here. But, I could not tell her, that I had no more cash, and not a prospect to raise funds for the next phase and years before us.

Inside the Holy of Holies

I know this is a created place. Not holy or in anyway divine. Still, I feel something under these ram and goat skins, in front of this fabricated Ark. I am alone, the nearest person in a yurt, and there is not a sound. There is no wind. I came here to seek guidance, while it as likely, I could have sought it anywhere. But, I came here to speak to God. It all seems so infantile, or at least childish. I have so come believe my own narrative, that I come here expecting a divine conversation.

I am not Kohen Gadol. I am not Aaron. I am the only one besides a few unusual desert spirits or old women who think I actually have the mark. I am, however, utterly certain that this is the right quest, the perfect journey to build this Temple of Solomon. It is inside the Holy of Holies where the name of God was spoken. Dare, I attempt to utter it.

It was spoken before the Temple, then restricted. Only the priests knew it, and now it is lost. Some say it is Yahweh, that's Wilhelm Gesenius, who sees the letters YHWH, called the tetragrammaton, and sounds them out this way. Others forbad the use of the name of God, and substituted this array of names, Hashem; Adonai (very popular); Hakodesh baruch hu (the holy one, blessed be he); and non Jews, sounded out YHWH as Jehovah, which most scholars think is dead wrong.

After the first temple destruction, there is a sense that the name of God became, "ineffable", except to the high priests. And some zealots believed that the mere utterance by the common Jew was a capital offense.

I do not know the name, raised to call the essence or presence of the Lord, Adonai. But, it does not seem right to me, here. As I studied the original form from Abraham's time and through the Aramaic that is spoken for centuries, until block Hebrew emerges, it looks like Yod He Waw (Va) He. Which sounds more like a native American chant, but, why should it not sound that primal. Yod He Waw He! Vowel less.

I say the Shema, think all the other names, and feel compelled to utter

"Yod he waw he !"

Then I talk to the Lord, like others do. In the reverence that comes from a deeply held belief that there is a receiver, a listener. I ask for no money, only guidance, admit to frailty, and offer gratitude. I sink instinctively to my knees, place my face on the ground and pray for forgiveness and then, strength.

I stand, a wind blows across my face, cold over the tears.

At the Zorro, Joey looks at me, and claims I have a sunburn, on top of the dark tan.

I look in the mirror of the room, and it is as though I had been under a sun lamp.

THE GROCERY

Carl Gustave Jung thought we all had the same instincts and archetypes within us that went back to our ancient beginnings. He had little clue of genetics, DNA sequences or the genome. Yet, he posited this "collective unconscious" that bound us all. A counterpoint to the personal unconscious driven by upbringing, sexual dysfunction, and an imbalance of ego and id. He rejected his rival Freud. There was something there more primordial, deeper. And, then tie that to the unexplainable, interconnection of one action to another, unchartered by a time span. A Monarch butterfly flutters in Mexico, hundreds of thousands fly North, a baby is born in South Central, a young cop becomes an expert marksman. Somehow, over time they all collide, in death, defense, or a simple outstretched hand saving a life. Is it from an unconscious source, or merely coincidence.

Then at a random moment, as I am buying soup, yogurt, and napkins, someone yells FIRE at the Rams Head gated community for seniors.

A 92 year old man, named Sergei is overcome by smoke in his home by the 16th hole.

His niece, 24, Anna Akhmatova sleeps soundly in her rear bedroom.

Her namesake once the mistress of Dedo, the miraculous bohemian from Livorno.

He dressed in a brown corduroy suit, yellow shirt and red bandana, sat with his sculptured limestone heads in 1911, in Paris. One with Anna's face. He lit candles and held a séance with them. And lost interest after creating only 25, gave some away.

The smoke alarm has no batteries.

I arrive with Maqroll and jump from his pick up. He turns the garden hose on the house. I rush into the living room, engulfed in smoke, and carry a frail and very light old man out of the house and place him on the lawn. He is alive and speaking loudly, I cannot hear him, as the first fire engine arrives. When the siren stops,

"Anna, Anna is inside"

I run back into the house, and towards the back. There is a long haired, tall girl, motionless on the bed. I throw a chair into the sliding door that faces the golf course, and carry her outside. The EMT puts an oxygen mask on her face, and she begins to take a breath.

A firefighter points a hose at me, and douses me. He tells me my hair and beard were on fire, I am a charred mess.

Maqroll knows the girl. And he drives me back to his studio, for a change of clothes.

THE STUDIO OF MAQROLL

Maqroll has a collection of women painted in a myriad of styles from traditional to modern, even, in abstractions as a homage to Gustave Courbet and his origin of man nude. Maqroll has managed over these many years to take pictures of women, and have some sit live for him. There are almost a hundred of all sizes and hues. His success mostly due to his overwhelming charm, and the fact that the face is never painted or shown. Thus, they can be anonymous, enjoy his rendition of their torso to their ankles and reveal their pudendum.

One such subject of his last year, was of an Akhmtova, a slim and taut body, with well formed, but smallish breasts, and beautiful long thighs. She now hung in his behind the store gallery. He painted her in a Warhol manner, with reds, yellow, and blacks behind her pure white skin. It was a striking, larger rendering of 10 feet x 10 feet.

It was the girl I pulled from the fire.

BORREGO CLINIC

As a courtesy I went to visit the old man at the clinic. He had a breathing tube, was ashen and suffered with a saline IV drip. He motioned with a single finger to come nearer. And then he surprised me.

"There is an object, in the garage, inside a trunk, wrapped in towels. Take it, it is yours."

I objected to anything, since he seemed not long for the world. But he insisted,

"You saved her, Anna lives. Take this, it is yours."

I agreed, reluctantly, figuring it was some artifact of the old man's life.

The doctor told me, there was no one to decide, when they stop the artificial apparatus, so they expected he would be gone in days.

THE GARAGE AT RAMS HEAD

I returned the next afternoon with Anna and Maqroll. I found the trunk, and a large object, wrapped in towels. I took it to the lawn, and unwrapped it, to reveal a chunk of limestone, as I turned it was a sculptured face that was the image of Anna, sitting in front of me. Maqroll gasped, and shouted,

"It is a Modigliani head, MAC. Amedeo Modigliani !"

Anna hugged me, claiming it was worth a fortune.

Somewhere, a man hits a mallet, a stone falls from a quarry, a man falls in love with a married woman. The unconscious connections collide, or not. Jung and Freud forgot the great unknown essence, the eternal movement of spirits and results from the power beyond us, the ineffable.

Then,

> From: Ricardo Guliani, art investigator and authenticator

> "Your Modigliani head is not authentic. It is most likely one of three crafted in 1984 in Livorno, as a hoax. This piece was created with an electric drill and has traces of river residue that we believe comes from the Fosse Reale canal.

The actual head depicted is still missing, and may have been swapped for this copy.

While the piece has some historic value, it has no value as part of any Modigliani collection"

Ricardo Guliani

I give the head to Joey to place in the lobby of the Zorro, even as, he begins construction on The Inn at the Desert Temple. He saw enough tourists and buses coming to the Tabernacle to build a hotel to accommodate them all. Now, we are a not for profit corporation this Temple of the Desert LLC, where we build a hotel, collect tourist dollars, run road races, have concerts, and conduct tours. There is cash flow, to be sure, but not enough still to build the Temple as a contiguous project. It took Zadoc and Solomon seven years, it may take us a lifetime. Still, it is happening with these funds, and, a sea of volunteers, who build the outer and inner walls. And Izzy continues to bring large quarry stones to create an authentic foundation for the project. Izzy brings her trucks and cranes and unloads a stone, even as she, continues her project now at 73 stones across the desert floor. The stones matter, but, it is more her presence, her Cheshire cat sized smile, sturdy, tanned frame, and her almost mystical assurance that this Temple will be built.

I had taken to giving a sermon most Sundays for the buses from church groups. It was about the history of the actual Temple, the fight over the Temple Mount, and why this place, this Temple was worthy of their support and cash. At first, it lacked eloquence, and even passion. I was so worn by the process and tentative. But, over the years, my commitment matured, as did, my belief that my destiny in this quest. It was not just a trip to oblivion, it had some rationality. God had not spoken to me, directly. There was no burning bush. I had this mark under my eye, a night in bed with an old woman, and the encouragement of this enterprise with the Tabernacle, the tours, the volunteers all working towards some result, in this patch of the desert. So, the mission speech had gravitas, now. There was always applause, no one seemed to brand me as a religious zealot or, just, a lunatic. So, the speech brought more folks, buses, and revenue.

The Inn prospered, Joey brought in another staff, for year around business. And the stones on the outer wall began to form a perimeter, the inner wall had a corner done, but, the actual Temple was still a blueprint, the Tabernacle stood as the promise of a Temple.

Izzy pulled me aside after one sermon, put her calloused hand across my face, and grabbed me by the old man's white beard. And in Spanish, whispered, You must get off your ass and tell the world of this. It is time you are ready. "She then kissed me on the broken skin of my lips, and in English exhorted, "you have a strong message, you cannot get what you need here alone, you have not moved from this desert in five years, it is time MAC. I know. I will watch over this for you. GO."

I was at first furious, my expansive ego, unprepared for any critique. Then awakened to the fear of scrutiny that held me back, and the prospect of ridicule. But, I was no longer a former District Attorney, a husband or father. I was now totally transformed into MAC, the Temple builder. Perhaps, I could venture forward, raise funds, face the forces that stood in my way, and find more allies. But, I could not organize a day, usually, let alone a world tour. I sat in the trailer, attempting to mind out a calendar, and found it paralyzing.

Then there was Fran. Izzy asked her to come in from Don's Trailer Park in Ventura. She arrived in an old RV, with two dogs, Spike, and Lobo. Lobo, was a Shepard mix, Spike a rescued Greyhound. She let them out and they ran towards the horizon. Fran settled into the canvas chair by the shotguns. She was a master booker for Hollywood types, actors and music groups. From the Grateful Dead to Betty Davis to a handful of current rap artists with names like Chrissy X and Del Mar, and George Ah. It took a few days of her in the trailer, the dogs, running, cold beer, and a sneak peek at Maqroll's private gallery that got her interested. I thought I had convinced her to do the scheduling and bookings, but, it wasn't me.

In her visits to the store, Maqroll still had enough bullshit and charm to con this 65 year old roadie into his studio, where he photographed and painted her, in the style of the master himself, Courbet. Then, as the days passed, and the acrylic dried, they started screwing in the late afternoon. They were both entwined in a brief interlude, that filled for them both, that long stretch of loneliness, and being untouched that can come over people devoted to their work, and detached from their own need for intimate contact. And who have left their youth, the passion for the pursuit of another, and have been hobbled by a few blows to the heart along the way.

She decided to stay around. Fran said it was because I got along with the dogs. But, it was Maqroll for the moment, and the chance to park the RV, live in a yurt and hang out with Izzy. Maybe, building the Temple mattered, but, it was a small thing. She began to create this MAC persona, set up a better You Tube channel, jump into Twitter, and began Instagram for the Temple MAC, with a constant stream of pictures from the compound. In a few weeks, she had a schedule, starting in rural America, and building to New York and larger media markets, over a years time. It was gradual schedule that allowed for speeches and interviews, and some side trips.

I was reluctant. But, I had no doubt that I just might rub shoulders with someone, or group that could offer a substantial pile of cash that we could finally plan the long term construction of the Temple and build out the surrounding accoutrements. I had a five year horizon, maybe even ten. We agreed I would wear mostly black, appear in a business suit, and trim the beard and hair for neatness. The mark of Aaron would be uncovered, although, it would often bring controversy, Fran did not feel it would harm the tour, and might create a stir in some quarters.

The face in this mirror, that I had seen change from puffy assistant DA, to MAC had not aged so much, as the years might suggest. I was leaner by 30 pounds, my skin tone was darker, almost dark caramel, the blue eyes clear, and my head of hair and beard a lush, full cinematic prop. I could not detect any real sign of aging, over these last seven years.

And I felt ready for the road.

CHAPTER VII

THE TENTH COW

OGALLALA, NEBRASKA

There are 1.92 million people in the state. Five million cattle finished and marketed. Texas has more of everything, but Nebraska has the highest percentage of cattle to people. In Sand Hills country there are ranches of enormous size, some of 45 square miles, others divided between the North Platte and South Platte rivers, mostly run by families who have raised beef for generations.

I'm sitting with Roy Robbins, rancher/ cowboy, who is over six feet two, in a pressed and laundered fancy western shirt, and blue jeans that are stiff, clean, and pressed. He wears a simple black cowboy hat, pulled with a right handed tilt towards his right ear. He owns a smaller ranch with 900 head of Angus, all red. He raises them until they are 900 pounds for males and 850 for females, then, off they go for finishing, then to market.

I came to this café overlooking, Lake McConaughy, that is the visible outcropping of the massive aquifer that underlies the region. I am here to talk about red cows, female heifers to be precise, who, by definition have not had a calf. And to learn from this Red Heifer Association of America founder, if a calf could be birthed that was without a blemish.

No one knew more about applying science to agriculture and in his world, Red Angus. He knows how to artificially inseminate his cattle, how to breed them, and has enough prize bulls to put him into some sort of AI Hall of Fame. He has personally run his arm, deep into a cow vagina, and maneuver past the cervical rings to plant a vial of 20 million sperm cells inside her. He had yet, to breed the best Red Angus bull, like the legendary, Cherokee Canyon or the most revered, Make My Day, but he is working on it.

Robbins is a Catholic, goes to church. He knows about Revelations, but does not make it, any big part of his life. He is just pleased that God has given him, good health, a strong family and the cattle, and the great state of Nebraska. Not so some other cattlemen from Texas and Mississippi, who want him to spend more time on breeding the unblemished red heifer.

During my speaking tours, in city 19, in Tupelo, I came across a bent over, preacher, Eli Buell. Who proceeded to tell me the story of Clyde Lott, who like Eli was a minister in the National Pentecostal Assemblies of Jesus Christ. Lott was a rancher, who was a student of the end of times, and the coming of the true Messianic age. He told Eli of a passage in Numbers 19 that intrigued him:

"Speak unto the children of Israel that they bring thee a red heifer without a spot, wherein, there is no blemish, and upon which never came a yoke. The cow will be an offering to me. You will slaughter it, and burn it on a pyre of cedar, hyssop, and with a strand of scarlet thread. Then mix the ashes with water and purify all those who have been exposed to death. Anyone who fails to be purified, shall be cut off from the congregation, because he has defiled the sanctuary of the Lord."

Lott knew that it was unlikely that a red heifer existed on the desert trek to the Holy Land. Yet, he was a believer in scripture, and mostly believed that he could assist the Jews by providing such an animal, so that when the Temple was rebuilt, prior to the coming of Christ to earth, they would be able to have a line of Red Heifers, to tend to the Temple needs and those of the Lord.

Old Eli played out for me the End of Times rag. There are seven years of tribulation. A battle ensues, Christ wins. Some true Christians are part of the Rapture and are sucked into heaven; most others convert or die. Eventually the final battle, Armageddon is joined and Prince Gog, from Magog, is destroyed by God. The dead rise, forgiveness reigns and the Kingdom of God prevails.

But rancher Lott knew that none of this happened, not any of it, unless the Temple was rebuilt. The other criteria seemed underway. Israel was back in the hands of the Jews, and Jerusalem was the capital of Israel. But that Temple, on the actual Temple Mount had to be rebuilt, either by man or by God in heaven. Either way, Lott believed that it would not be sanctified without this unblemished Red Heifer. He was so committed, he actually convinced the Mississippi director of Agriculture to send a note that made its way to Israel, remarkable in its simplicity:

"Clyde Lott is prepared to offer Red Angus suitable for old testament sacrifices, will have no blemish or off color hair, genetically red will produce red eye, nose pigmentation will be dark, heifers at a year old will weigh approximately,700 pounds."

It never made it into the hands of serious diplomats, who were too occupied with keeping the peace on the Temple Mount than building a Temple. Yet, it did make its way, as did Lott, to American born rabbi, and keeper of the Temple Institute, Chaim Richman. To me, Richman would have seemed an extremist, who wanted animal sacrifices, the Temple built and ruled over by his very own Levites and Kohanim. He was man of tradition and rules, of his interpretation. For this Rabbi Richman, all Jews were impure because there is no Temple and, they are not sprinkled with the ashes and potion as commanded by God in Numbers 19. They visited in Israel, Lott seemed devoted to raising the cattle, including from ranchers in Nebraska. But he was more visionary than that, he also wanted to preserve the DNA so, should he be caught in the Rapture, the specimens could be used for the new Temple.

As I traveled, I had Joey, send me the Nachman book, that started me on this journey. And as I remembered, he outlined a portion of the Mishnah, the written version, of the sketchy oral tradition, that did deal with this ritual. Nachman was not a believer, and thought Numbers 19, a glitch in God's conversation with Aaron and Moses in the desert, most likely a misunderstanding, that came after the golden calf debacle. In any case, he said there were nine calfs, and when the tenth came, so would the Jewish Messiah. The timetable made no sense, of course. How could only nine provide enough ashes and potion from Solomon to Herod?

And through the years, there were red heifers. Most from the United States. When they came, a holy man, of some sort sojourned from Israel to declare it unblemished. In 1996, they came upon such a heifer, dubbed, Melody. The extremist Rabbi's caused such a stir, because they proclaimed her the Tenth Cow. This excited their base of zealots, who wanted to use her presence to push for funds to actually occupy the Temple Mount and build the Temple.

89

Such, an approach brought attention, but, not the kind they preferred. The unresolved Temple Mount issue was not to be changed by the identification by these Rabbi's of Melody the Red Angus. Melody eventually grew a white tail, and ended the dispute.

It is after all, a place of myth, that has become substance. Of story turned into immutable beliefs. And of unresolved conflicts. As a Jew, I believe there was Solomon's Temple, Herod's, and it was destroyed by the Romans. I do not believe Mohammed ascended to Allah on his horse/man Barak; that Cain killed his brother there; where Isaac or Ishmael were offered to Yahweh by Abraham.

I do know that the Golden Dome of the Rock, and Al-Aqsa mosques stand today on holy ground claimed by three faiths. What it will take to build the Temple here, may take the battle of the revelation, or the act of Yahweh returning to his house to dwell. I doubt all the claims of the extremists like Rabbi Richman or Rabbi Yosef Elboim, who wants to start an institution that raises cohanim, the boys who will be the next priesthood. He wants people to "donate" their children, so they will not be in touch with the dead, until the ashes of the tenth cow can be created through sacrifice.

It is such ramblings of the zealots that remind me of my mission, I tell Robbins, over coffee, and eggs. I am not here to build that real Temple, in Jerusalem. I am uncertain it would be good for Jews, or the world to upset the forces that keep the Temple Mount a site of such controversy. I tell him, I am certain that building a replica here for all people too see, will serve a purpose to inform, entertain, and engage people of all persuasions who can experience the edifice as described in the bible. It did not surprise me that most of my support and funding was coming from Christians who believed in the preservation and power of the holy word and spirit. Whether evangelical or not, they warmed to my personal story and the vision of walking their families through a replica of the Temple of Solomon.

Robbins knew all I wanted was a few head of Red Angus to begin a small ranch near the Borrego Springs site. And, I wanted to see, if we could create an alliance, to attempt through good science to raise at his ranch, an unblemished heifer. He could not see, anymore than could Lott how a Red Heifer made into the Middle East, thousands of years ago. The cattle in Egypt were spotted, and brown. You only needed to go to the King James version to learn that they were more likely Holstein. In fact, the Aberdeen Angus was a Viking cow, transported to Scotland and England. The Red Angus was less preferred than the Black Angus, even though, when you reviewed the animal, they were mostly identical save for their color. But, from the 1860's onward, they became a popular breed. They were docile, could be breed for large beef yields, and a much preferred, well marbled beef steak. Robbins told me he could provide some cattle, and sit with a rancher who wants to raise the heifers. But, he thought it could take a few generations to get a pure one that would pass some test. To him, it was more an experiment in genetics and selection that ranching. But, he thought my efforts to build a replica in the desert had some value, and he would not discourage me. He wondered, if we hit on the true Tenth Cow, whether that would erupt another volcano of hope and fear, as did Melody. I thought it was likely, but, still worth the effort. That cow would be at my place not Israel, and it was for a purpose of enlightenment, rather than the disruption of the Temple Mount.

We rode in an ATV across the grasslands. Nebraska has the perfect topography for cattle ranching. Cornfields in the east, grasslands, a bountiful aquafer. A short distance from raising and breeding, to finishing and the market. The red hulks against the grey sky, the aroma of cows, and cowboys doing their work, seemed idyllic. It was a long way from Borrego, and a universe away from the Los Angeles courtrooms. Our conversation, started with Red Angus and floated into faith and family. Here was Robbins, as disconnected to Solomon as any man could be, never saw his Temple, nor thought about it. But, it seemed to matter to him, mostly, I expect because he respected a man with a dream, any dream.

His was to raise a family, be right with God, help those who needed help, and raise the bets damn angus in the world. Here he was working on all his goals, at once. An unwavering, fearless man, who was the rock upon which this nation was built. Perhaps, if I was raised here, I would not need a Temple dream, I would have a built in purpose, instead of this mission that is inside me, my mind full of it. He has no strain or compulsion, his life unfolds as suns rise and set. God leaves him alone to his own devices, but not me, not now. I wonder, if I could put on his big, black hat, and walk the stalls, put my arm up a vagina, find the right spot for the 20 million sperm?

Would, I be driven by a presence I can feel, a force I talk to at night that never answers, or would I be like Robbins, at peace with who I am, what I have done, and who I love and protect.

I would have ten cows, when I could provide the right essentials to raise them. And he would agree to a project with the Temple of the Desert to attempt to raise an unblemished Tenth Cow. If it happened in his lifetime, he agreed to have the celebration in Nebraska. Robbins took off his hat, and waved at me, "don't give up MAC".

EPPLEY AIRPORT

I made my last speech in Omaha to about 200 civic leaders of mixed faiths, from a Lion's Club. They were enthusiastic and had many questions that centered around the value of my replica or "tourist temple" and the one that might actually appear in Jerusalem. I found, I was most effective, when I spent more time on the project and not the contorted history of the current politics of the Temple Mount. It was largely a conversation, I could not conclude, as I sailed through the labyrinth of the three faiths and the conflict for the holy ground. The audiences seemed much more at ease, when I appeared more as a later day, bearded, Walt Disney of religion, than a man on a mission of faith. Still, church groups had no issues with the history lesson, the discussion of revelation, or the Kingdom of God.

I had honed my pitches into these two approaches, now. The Disney version, and the more pious, descendant of Aaron. The religious speech was my power, and came from a well of belief and passion that felt more like Billy Graham, than the more modern, patter of the Joel Osteen. I existed on that continuum, with some comfort, and found the best response from people with strong beliefs. Fran booked me through a few Reform synagogue groups, and they mostly thought the project frivolous, and saw me as a somewhat demented prophet. I doubt the prophets of the old testament where any better received, carrying the obtuse words of God to the people of Israel. At least, they had God talking to them, all I had was a mark on my eye and a compulsion.

23 cities, 23 talks, 10 radio shows, 2 major articles in newspapers, the Red Angus, and now a return to the Tabernacle. I was not weary, nor depressed. But, I feel alone here, in this old place, where Hollywood put George Clooney for a movie, and Christopher Walken in another. It looks like what it is. A place between places. Where souls are in transit from where they are to where they want to be.

CHAPTER VIII

∞∞ ❖❖❖ ∞∞

RABBIS GONE MAD

TRAILER BACK PORCH

The shotgun blasts signaled a return to some normalcy. Izzy and Fran busting clays, as they arced out over the desert scruff. Fran was learning, but had a steady stance, and determination. And Izzy sat in the Adirondack chair and pulled the rope, shouting out instructions. The blast had purity, the clays a linearity, and the hits on target, a finality that mocked the rest of my stochastic existence. Only the barking of Lobo and the whines of Reds, the Irish setter disturbed the moment.

I hit 18 of 25 with the 16 gauge Mossberg, finding myself pleased to not be MAC, the builder but that ex DA, escaping from Los Angeles. This life of purpose, and construction seemed more intended for Job than Aaron or Moses. We walked in some imposed silence, until we got to the pieces of the clays, and began raking up the debris. Izzy felt the stones walls were beginning to take shape, but the main walls, needed more stones than they could quarry, at least, in the short term. But, the project now had form and shape. She wondered, when I would finally seize on a real architect to build the Temple itself. The Yurt People could not further the development of the actual construction, they could treat the walls, and the park, and Tabernacle, but not much else.

Fran seemed almost serene, in her telling of the impact of the promotion tour. Money was coming into the Go Fund Me site. Contributions from Pay Pal were now growing. We seemed on our way to enough new cash to acquire an architect and general contractor who could begin the process, finally, of crafting the Temple replica. It was still, at minimum a 300 million dollar project, the cost of a modest high rise or auditorium, maybe twice that figure. No happenstance would yield that, it would take more interviews and intervention from some source, that was not, yet, identified. I expected no divine intervention, nothing I read or dreamed gave me a clue to our economic salvation. And Fran was not waiting for a word from God, either.

Rather than fly me to the hinterlands, she opted instead for a new strategy, where she would lure a major news organization to visit our compound, and reach, in one airing, millions of donors and supporters. Izzy was unimpressed by Fran's name dropping and television knowledge, she rarely watched any of it, and found it mostly drivel. She playfully grabbed Fran's wrists in her powerful hands, and proclaimed Fran's soft hands to be no match for her at the hard work of getting the Temple built. When released Fran took out her cellphone and proclaimed, she needed only this, not a crane, or pick axe, to accomplish her tasks. She went over to Izzy, and grabbed her butt.

"I'll get Sixty Minutes out here Izzy, Sixty Fucking Minutes, and then we'll get this damn Temple to rise."

ROOM 36 THE ZORRO

Some nights, I leave the compound, after tending to the eternal flame, a small bonfire, like those that dot Will Rogers beach most summer nights, before the Tabernacle. The trailer often occupied by dogs, Fran, or Tina and Frank pumping their way to togetherness. I settle in here, like an old Tzaddik. Pretend, I am one of the Lamed Vav Tzadikim, the "hidden righteous ones". One of 36 holy men, or at least one of the 36 outside of Israel. There are 36 more in Israel so says the Talmud, according to Nachman of Breslav. He quotes the Talmud, Succah 45 (b). To that text, there are always at least 36 righteous ones to receive the Divine Presence. So here in Zorro 36, I look at a desert mountain, hear the slosh of the hot tubs, and the occasional orgiastic sound from a nearby hut. I do not feel like a Lamed Vovnik, no wiser than others, for taking on this mission, this calling to build the Temple here. Aaron was 71, Moses 72, among the other 70 wise men who preserved the world from God's annihilation by being righteous, kind, and toiling to redeem man and the world. Building this replica, seems hardly worthy of such distinction. I am not David, nor Ruth. Certainly not Esther who saved all Jews or Deborah, who took us out of chains from overseers.

Into the Lamed Vav, all flows and is redeemed. Because God knows that the unknown 36 can save mankind, through their good will, faith, and deeds. Nachman says, "they lead. They comfort. They teach. They protect. They are filled with compassion. I wonder do they, or one of them also Build? Then again, I have never pretended to be, but what I am.

A secular Jew, who is a descendant of Aaron from the tribe of Levi. Beyond that I no holy man, seer or Messiah. I simply am driven to build the replica Temple of Solomon in this California desert. I do not pretend this will bring on the Revelation and The Rapture, nor that is a substitute for the real thing, on the Temple Mount. Who knows what is to be? Who can say if this is built what cosmic forces it may unleash or none.

God has not been much help. He has not spoken. No prophets have arrived. Hell, the grand founder of Hasidism, the Baal Shem Tov, who we always wrote as Besht, the acronym for the bet ayin shin tet, The Master of the Good Name, got a visit from Elijah, himself, when he was but 16. I get nothing, bupkis. Yes, now I pray, lay Tefillin in the morning, sing and chant prayers, and talk to God, in my own continuing conversation.

But to Aaron and Moses, he was heard by them along the desert journey. Or perhaps, he did not speak, but, his voice came to them. It filled them without a sound. But, they could summon the "ineffable" by knowing the true name of God, in the Tetragrammaton. I had no way of knowing how to call God. I just sat down, like this night, and asked for some guidance, some cash, and an angel to keep us safe.

Then, a sip of Glenlivet, or two, and sleeps comes. Often dreamless. And at times not, transported to a vivid other world, as part of Walter Cronkite's, You Are There program, I watched transfixed on my father's RCA.

A DREAM

I am at a large table in Cairo. Men are dressed in pants, covered by tunics. All have head coverings, some in turbans. They are at a dinner, as am I. The master is a Jew called Halabi, a man of great wealth, and some power. He handles money, and taxes for the Ottoman rulers. The talk is of how to live a righteous life under the eyes of God. There is concern over deprivation as the way to show

95

piety. They fast, jump in vats of cold water, and beat themselves with knotted ropes. Some read the Talmud, others the Zohar. Halabi hands out some gold Sultani's coins, I grab a few, dated they are, at 1663.

A man enters, and the room turns silent. He is introduced as AMIRAH, Our Lord and King, His majesty be exalted, they say. It is, none other than, Sabbatai Zevi, the fake Messiah. This charlatan pretended, nee believed he was the Mosiach. It is Zevi who claimed in 1648, the very year the Zohar said it would happen, that he began chanting the Tetragrammaton, or so he claimed. He was a mystic, like many of his time. Jews were ready for some redemption, being slaughtered across Europe and the Ukraine, by peasants and later Cossack hordes. He either came to believe he was the messiah because he was a lunatic or was a lunatic and true believer both.

But, here he was. I tried, in this dream to tell them all. That he was a pretender. But, as in dreams, nothing came out of my mouth. I screamed in my head, but there was no sound. Instead he told the tale of who he would marry. It was to Sarah, a whore from Livorno. This girl, was a refuge from the Khmelnytsky Uprising in Poland, where Bohdan Khmelnytsky, successfully fought his Polish overseers throughout Poland and the Ukraine. The Cossacks destroyed villages, and murdered, dismembered, and crushed thousands, upon thousands of Jews, and some Catholic clergy. It was Malthusian solution to Jews existing in Europe. A soaking in blood, that burned into the souls of those left, and of the superstitious Rabbi's who stood by and watched them all die. It was no wonder, that a from a cleansed Europe Zevi would come, so desperate they were for deliverance. But to this fat, little man?

Sarah escaped the Cossacks, fled to a convent. Then found her way to Livorno. And along the way became convinced she would marry the Messiah. Zevi was nothing if not an opportunist and sent for her, to be married in this room at Halabi's home.

Then, I yelled out. "He is not the Messiah. He will become a Muslim to save his neck."

I am beaten, stripped naked and hung upside down by my ankles. And they throw food at me, until I am beaten with a knotted rope, until I collapse. Convinced they are that God will deliver them to Israel through Zevi and his whore wife, Sarah.

Then, I awake, my T-shirt soaked. The sheets wet. I strip and throw myself into the hot tub, and gaze at the stars, still shaken. In the time of false Messiahs, they believed him, for no reason. He managed to surround himself with rabbi's who agreed with his claims, he was declared a Messiah by many Jews in the late 17th century, But he was a delusional, worthless pig. And, eventually, he was given three choices by the Turks.

He could survive a volley of arrows, if they miss he lives. He could be impaled, no hope there. Or, as he chose, he could convert to Islam. So, by 1666, he was an Effendi, of the Sultan, and he practices Islam, although, he still played around with mystical Judaism.

Zevi gave it all up to live, consort with Sarah, and take another wife to please the Sultan. Jews buying into a promise of redemption, offered by a pretender. No further ahead than behind, and the rabbi's who supported him returned to their internal battles over righteousness from the Talmud to the mystical Zohar. And some small joy returned to some places, as Jews worshiped, and were, at least not being murdered in their beds.

A chicken dealers son born, 1626, on the 9th of Av, the day the Temples were destroyed had risen to be a false Messiah. And died of old age.

SIXTY MINUTES ARRIVES

There was a time when the executive producer, of Sixty Minutes, Don Hewitt would proclaim, "the last person you want in your living room is Mike Wallace". Now, both of them long gone, the most watched news program was still able to move public opinion, even, if its sharp teeth have worn down, under the crush of an expanding media landscape. I had been interviewed enough, now, to know what I was doing was not received with universal acclaim. Too many, I was a nut, or more generously, an obsessive religionist.

The producer was a mean spirited, agnostic. She had no interest in the compound, and was vocal about her desire to be in Afghanistan, rather than tracking an aging, self appointed Temple builder. Whether I took her through the exhibits, or walked her through our scale model of the Temple, now a new feature in 1/3 size, she was unimpressed. Only the tabernacle seemed to engage her. The replica of the Ark and my explanation of the contents, seemed to touch her curiosity.

She pushed me in our pre- interview process. The approach was obvious, to make me say I heard from God, was a later day prophet. Every question returned to the unanswerable, of why me, and why here. I offered my most honest reply that it came to me, internally, not from a voice or sign, other than this mark under my eye. I read her the passage from the Rebbe Nachman book, which she dismissed as some fraud. No matter, my passion or my resolve to be at ease, she did her best to rile me, and even, used her physicality to unbalance me. She wiped her chest with a towel, opened her khaki shirt, and leaned forward to whisper in my ear, that it would all be over shortly, as though she was a dental assistant, coaxing me through a root canal.

No matter, I did not yield to her view that I was a goof. I attempted to be thoughtful, quiet, and devoted to my mission, but, little more. She seemed to have softened somewhat, and, offered a hug, when she left, awaiting the correspondent, the next day.

I greeted Leslie Stahl by the main gate, in my ATV. The expanse of the compound behind me. I had decided to take a somewhat different tact with her. This was a woman of great experience, who pioneered for women at the network level. She had been to the toughest battlefields, interviewed warriors, kings, and presidents. I elected to be, what I was, an eccentric, but not deranged secular Jew on a mission to complete the destiny of my line of descendants from Aaron to Zadoc to MAC. I thought a ride through the compound, like the classic ride of LBJ through his ranch across from the Pedernales River. She seemed up for the ride, dressed as though on a combat mission, but pleasant and seemingly open to my self- imposed obsession.

The desert wind lifted her hair, and she smiled as though this assignment was a relief, and not a burden like it was for her producer. She wondered how, we could ever find the money to complete the Temple, and why unlike the ARK built by Christian fundamentalists, who did not acknowledge evolution, we were struggling. Was it because I was Jew, or that the Jewish philanthropic community refused to embrace the project. How could it be, she asked, why it was not an obvious win for everyone.

She asked, but knew the answer. I asked if her father would have approved. Would his Swampscott shul embrace this effort? I became the inquisitor, and she the respondent. I pulled over by the far Northeast corner of the compound, where Julio Rodriquez and his security patrol had their yurt. He explained the dangers of night raiders, and vandals, and how they patrolled the perimeter 24/7. She pulled out the pistol on the ATV and asked me to use it, on the cans and jugs Julio had for target practice. I fired five rounds, and hit the big jugs, not much of a feat. She laughed, then she probed more on who supported me and who was opposed to all of this.

Stahl

When you line up supporters, they are ?

MAC

By faith, Catholics, Mormons, and those uncertain, agnostics and atheists, who just like the idea of the Temple.

Stahl

What of the Jewish faith? I would think they would be enthusiastic.

MAC

There is a complexity here. I am building a replica. I am not building the actual Third Temple, which by biblical injunction, would be constructed or delivered by God to the Temple Mount. But, some Jews off all types, are wary of this project. They do not want it as an attraction, nor as an ordained Temple. Individual Jews seem to think it is of value, regardless of the view of their Rabbi's.

Stahl

You say that you 're a descendent of Aaron, Moses older brother. And therefore, are destined to do this? That sounds like a tall tale.

MAC

It is an article of faith. I came here to rest many years ago, from a hard year as a prosecutor. I had grown weary of putting away the bad guys for terrible things. Over time, I came to believe that I was from Aaron and the tribe of Levi. And I saw this mark below my eye emerge, that every descendent of

Aaron is reported to have, by legend. I do not know, if any of it is scientific, but I do know, this must happen, here.

Stahl

Has God told you to do this?

MAC

I wish I had a voice, a sign. The "ineffable" presence has not exhibited his presence or desire. But, it may not happen that way, or ever happened like that, you know. I feel a presence, a driving force, that compels me. I have retained that inner knowing for all these years, and it moves me, everyday, every moment to complete this, as long as I have the time.

Stahl

Will it ever be done?

MAC

It took Zadoc and Solomon seven years. It has been eight, so far. I cannot know, I have no timetable. But, God will give me the time, and it will get done.

I took her into the Tabernacle, and said a prayer, out loud. I chanted the Shema. I embraced her as one Jew to another, not television, journalist star to desert madman. I hoped for a fair treatment.

And, when it aired that next month, it was more than fair. It offered the project some credibility. Even though, she explored my connection to Aaron and the connection to the faith and the Temple; she also explored the value of the project as a demonstration of faith, and pure history. She also interviewed a few New York based rabbi's, and other detractors, who thought the project unneeded, and worse unwanted. She showed me firing the pistol, and downing clays with the shotgun.

Still, on balance it was a fair appraisal and more captured what I had become. I felt that she had captured the essence of MAC. I knew that man on the screen, I was thoroughly this transformed, hardened person. Whatever, I was, now long gone. I seemed devoted, but not maniacal. Yet, there was a vulnerability, as well, that there were forces, that could end this all, unless, we moved to protect what we had built. A force of ignorance and fear more powerful than, even, the Babylonians and the Romans.

When, we looked at the incoming revenue, there was certainly a rush of dollars that related to our Sixty Minutes exposure. The 501 © 3 continues to grow in revenue, and more than sustains our daily needs of security, the docents, and our basic construction. We have a hotel, seminars, tours, and lectures on the compound. We can take a visitor through a 1/3 replica of the inside of the Temple, and show them the replica Ark and have them stop for a moment of reflection at the Tabernacle. But, there are no walls for the building itself, the grounds empty, awaiting a benefactor of some size, or enough waves of small contributors to begin the actual process.

Yet, each day Izzy sends crews to move what stones we have on the perimeter. The Yurts are usually filled, the visitors willing to groom the grounds and offer special skills, and artisan crafts. Food trucks appear on weekends, and buses come on a strict schedule for tours, and lectures. Some groups continue trek here, to conduct their own services And, on occasion there are concerts, some impromptu. This desert spot has become a gathering place for spiritual thoughts, and a blending of faiths.

It is, as God commanded, a place for all to dwell, not just Jews. Even without the Temple, they come to experience the vibrations of a place constructed, not for profit or glory, but simply to remember that there once was place, that the mythology claims was God's house. It does not seem to matter to anyone, if it is true, as much as it is a belief. And that belief empowers their own concepts of a force beyond us all. No one walks the paths, in silence, people are engaged, mostly upbeat and happy to be in this place, created from an idea, that seems when discussed, just, nuts.

TISHA B'AV, AUGUST 9TH

Fran was right. The impact of the speeches and the CBS exposure brought both praise and opprobrium. Money came from many sources, international as well. But the main censure came from the traditional Jewish hierarchy. Not officially, the Jewish Federation and Congress of Reform Rabbi's and a multitude of others, sent me letters of condemnation, and individually made certain that I knew the building of the Temple, even this replica was improper, somehow, in the eyes of the Lord, and their interpretation of the value of rebuilding in the first place.

I decided to conduct my lecture or sermon at the Tabernacle on this holy day of Tisha B'av. I had long ago fasted, on it, as was the tradition in my conservative family. My grandfather, Thomas, always said prayers, for the destruction of both Temples, on the coincidental 9th of Av, each August. It was always a day of fasting until sundown, and the story told of the destruction by the Babylonians, then the return under Cyrus the Persian, and the final blow by Titus and Nero to level the Temple and disperse all the Jews. And then Thomas, would intone that we were better off as mobile religion, than if the Temple's survived. Better to be at large and nomads, moored to no brick and mortar, than the Pope and the Vatican. Rigidity of a faith, frozen by its edifices.

I often wondered in these last years, if we had not survived because the Temple were gone. By 135 AD the Jews who were left, dispersed, the Ten Tribes long gone after the 586 destruction, the diaspora was the only reality. The Jewish people could not overcome, the weight of the Romans, nor the rise of a new faith that was part Jew part Christ. The persecution of the Jews, never ended. Eventually, Christianity found its way into the halls and palaces of power. Judaism died, not only because it had no center, but, it battled internally. The priests soured and turned to narrow texts and the ways of the Temple, now gone. Then, the Ashkenazic influences splintered through pogroms and travails, while the Sephardic suffered with exile, the Inquisition and conversion. Judaism was a grand mess, as Christianity rose. If there was a Temple, the priesthood, the Sanhedrin, would Jews be any better off, spared the horrors of the Cossacks, the Pogroms of the Tzars, or the Holocaust?

And now, we had the Talmud, the mystics and the Zohar, Orthodox, Reform, and Conservative. All with viewpoints, that eventually converged, around a God, the Book, and some rituals. But, few of their leaders, thought my Temple project was of value, and most just avoided it. I was fine with their silence, some Jews came, mostly those who were free of affiliation, without a synagogue or rabbi. And to them and others, I addressed this day, as a commemoration.

I saw a few hundred in our outdoor theater. It was over 100 degrees, as is the way of August, in Borrego Springs. I stood in white, no vestments, just white trousers and open collared dress shirt. A small ensemble played some Jazz and traditional music, and played under a few prayers. The audience sat with their plastic water bottles, and waved hand fans, we provided to everyone. About twenty bikers pulled in at the back, and seemed content to kick back and hear me out. I waited until the wind calmed, the band stopped, and I began my lesson about the Temples, and did it with an honesty, that just poured out of me, a holistic purging of truth.

I told them :

There is no archeological evidence that the Temple stood where we think, on the Temple Mount. Some think that Solomon, was but a two – bit warrior king, and that the Temple was built later. There is a dispute over how long it stood, most think it was 410 years, 6 months, and 10 days, before it was sacked. When it was dedicated the priests slaughtered 22,000 bulls and 120,000 sheep. The myths are that God filled the Temple, but his spirit occupied, the Holy of Holies, a room that held the Ark and the ten commandments, along with the staff of Aaron, and manna from the trek across the desert.

And if you believe the accounts of the Tanakh, and Kings it was a magnificent building, filled with gold and silver, cedars, elaborate carvings, and was a place for all people, or so it was meant, and therein dwelled, the presence of the force, in a cloud, that was the, "ineffable". Today, if it could be replicated, it would be billions in gold and silver, and as grandiose as the Vatican.

Yet, it was unlikely it would be rebuilt. This, Beit HaMikdash, given politics, the clash between states and the realization that it might only happen, if you are a believer, tied to a larger landscape of redemption and revelation. Still, this one, old Jew thought it would be of value to millions to build a replica of it here, where you are sitting. For historical value, education, and some element of faith.

There is a spirit here, I recounted, that was not of one faith or another, but the essential bond between us, that we should treat each other as we wished to be treated, have faith that something out there is bigger than our lives, and universal in us all. We are all part of it, the stars and elements of the vast unknown, and it exists right here, in this heat, on this compound, and inside of you. I asked them to be still, and be silent with me as I uttered a simple wish:

"May the spirit of the people here, create a feeling that we are all one. Let each one know we are here for each other, no one here today is ever alone. This ground is not hallowed, but the people who come here are... blessed. We are united, in the belief that every dream, every path that has heart can be realized. Even this one."

I roamed the crowd taking pictures and becoming an Instagram regular. Fran pulled me to some autographs from some friendly Hollywood types, who had sources of cash. She eventually wanted me to get to her yurt, to escape the heat. I felt the need to walk out the energy of the sermon and the handshakes. We were alone, as we approached the yurt village, except for Reds and Lobo.

Two black Fords pulled in front of us. They emptied quickly. And we were surrounded by eight large men, all with yarmulkes and beards. And one slim, pale white man, in a white shirt and a daily talis hanging out of his pants. He shouted at me, as his men surrounded us.

Lobo barked and attacked one of the large ones, grabbing his trouser leg. Reds took to the perimeter and barked. Fran calmly took out her phone and signaled security. I engaged the slim one in a dialogue. It seemed he was a Kahane follower, from the outlawed Kach party in Israel. He said he was sent from the Temple Institute, which I knew was bull, to stop our project.

His name was Dov, and he threatened to destroy the compound, and bring this outrage, he called it to an end. He claimed he had allies, like Crazy Jake, and other former Jewish Defense League adherents who would make our lives misery, unless we stopped. I doubt he had ever thrown a punch.

He screamed that I was a Frankian. A totally obtuse and 18th century reference to, one, Jacob Frank. Who claimed, with many adherents, to be the Messiah. This Frank was a Pole, who said God spoke to him, and he was the heir to the mystical crown of the charlatan Messiah Sabbati Zevi. Smart rabbi's excommunicated him, but, a local bishop embraced him, because he adhered to the Zohar, and not the Talmud. So, nuts they were then to find a Messiah, to overcome their horrendous tribulations, from ghetto to slaughters. The bishop ordered all the copies of the Talmud in Poland burned, all of them.

Frank made up his own religion, called "das", Then he took his followers to be baptized and converted to Christianity, and thousands did by the French Revolution. Eventually, Frank, in his obvious madness cloaked in a mystical charm, found his way to Offenbach, lived a nobleman's life, with armed guards and visited by converted Jews, and, even, czar Paul, before he was Tzar.

A grand, mad, fraud, who spoke to God. I was not any of that. But, this shrill, punk was screaming this bull history at me, as though, I was a later day Messiah, and intent on destroying his view of the faith.

It was all crap.

So, out of some fatigue and just street smart bravado, I walked up to him and gave him a short palm hit to his nose. By the time he started bleeding, our security crew drove up with Rodriquez and two cohorts, with guns drawn. Rather than hold them, I let them go with a soft voiced warning to not create trouble again, or they would be cited.

Dov turned to me, with his nose still bleeding into his white, handkerchief. And proclaimed,

"The rabbi's will not allow this! This is not allowed! God will not permit it!"

I looked at Fran, put my arm around her, gathered the dogs, and walked towards her yurt and the prospect of a cold lemonade.

Chapter IX

The Prince and the Indian

Across the Desert Plain

The sky is streaked with salmon colored clouds. The sun about to rise in the crook between the mountains. Izzy stands alone, she faces towards a serpent of stones, she has placed across this plain, she has decided to stop at 73. The last monolith over 40 tons. The crane, nearby, will reposition this last stone and face its flat face towards the East. I walk towards her, then offer a hug and a kiss on her cheek as a salutation.

Izzy has completed her project. A long path connects each stone. A small placard explains where the stone came from, some as far away at her native Central American roots. There is nothing else to read, only to contemplate what one will as, the trek from one stone to another, a Neolithic experience. Some walk it in silence, others with their electronics sharing the adventure. Children and mothers with backpacks, and, even, some runners, like me, who strip down and conquer it as a Tarahumara might, with ease and grace and no timeline.

This strong, block of muscle has accomplished what she had designed in her imagination. I had spent as many years, and still had no Temple. I had much to be sure, but, not the place I had envisioned that consumed me. Izzy vibrated her destiny, and exhibited it in a stunning smile erupting across the features of an ancient face. Always offering insights that come from hard labor and calloused hand philosophers, more Hoffer than Socrates.

She has a passion for Sarah Manguso, who overcame, that malady, only Izzy could remember, Chronic idiopathic demyelinating polyradiculoneuropathy. It was a rare auto immune disorder where the immune system attempts to destroy the nervous system. Surviving it, requires the most arduous regimen of plasma transfusions and the insertion of device in the chest, called a Hickman, where the tubes for transfusion are inserted to save the veins on the arms and legs. Manguso was a heroic figure to Izzy, and as much for her struggle, as her poetry. Izzy often uttered from Manguso's pages:

"You can't learn from remembering. You can't learn from guessing. You can learn only from moving forward at the rate you are moved, as brightness, into brightness."

The sun rose as she expounded. Izzy emphasizing the light, placing her hand on the last massive rock. Manguso lives, overcame the tubes, attributed her recovery to gamma globulin, and intercourse with a friend, Victor, what a combination, Izzy mused. Still, there was something to be said, for moving forward, regardless of circumstances, and obstacles. Her stones across the desert, were not obstacles, but milestones, each marking a journey taken. They exists on this desert floor, as though, they were dropped from huge hand, like a crumb trail. And, Izzy saw it that way. Some "ineffable spirit" scattering huge stones, like pebbles to mortals. She never cared what anyone thought, stayed bright and seemed to possess an internal guiding light. She claimed my impediment to completing the Temple was not money, nor desire, but my link to the behaviors of my upbringing. I was still trapped by approval, and, at times, paralyzed by either fear or too much introspection.

I stayed through the morning and helped the team reposition the stone, by turning it 180 degrees east. I felt strong, with the sun tattooing my bareback, and watching Izzy use her hand signals to direct the crane operator. I imagined a symphony before her, and a baton in her right hand. As usual, when they took a break, she had them haul Dos Equus from her truck and, we all collapsed, by the shade of the rock, and she sang with the others, whatever tune came into their heads, usually in Spanish.

I climbed to the rocks top with some others, and sat silent, listening to her strong voice, and gazed back miles across the plain, now marked by a rock path. It seemed meaningless, to a cynic, or even useless to some, but I knew it was created with heart, and it would attract thousands each year. The notion of a devoted artist has its own energy and power, it attracts because it exists, and is brought into the world through a creative process that gives its meaning. If no more meaning than, it is done.

I slid down the rock face, and she caught me. Suddenly, I felt an actual spark of electrostatic energy, easily explained. But there was also, two other surges. The first the obvious sexual charge of being near this nexus of all energies, including sexual attraction; and, something else. The feeling of needing to move on, with more vigor.

Izzy grabbed my neck with her thick hands and shook me.

"Damn it MAC. Now is not the time for reflection"

"You must Escape from Reality"

"ESCAPAR"

MAQROLL'S STUDIO

Madrid was moving the nudes and rearranging their place on the walls. The collection had grown through the years, and there were many that had no place to hang. Madrid had her rendition prominently shown at the center of the western wall, and her enormous loins and lower torso was exquisite, and sensual. She had managed Maqroll's store more now, so he could paint, when a subject became available, and he was spending time on constructing a larger place for all his renderings. Even though, it was a hidden pleasure, by word of mouth, women came to have their picture taken, and some returned to see the painting hang. Often now, they merely asked Maqroll to send them a photo of the work, with snapped picture or email. At times, a clique of gals would come by, and ask for a sitting nude for one of their group, like a birthday gift or a tattoo. Maqroll, now charged a fee for such a service, and he needed room outback for them to sit and chat and snack. So, he was devoted to building a larger studio and place to display his artistry.

Unfortunately for him, the original painting of Gustave Courbet was still banned on Facebook and other social media sites. They could show murders, hangings, and even the beheadings of radical Islam, when their monitors missed it. But, you had a fight on your hands if you dared launch the image of his famous nude, L'Origine du Monde, anywhere. Imagine an 1866 nude, still considering risqué and pornographic.

Madrid and Maqroll were debating with Akhmatova, whether to open the gallery for visitors, and make it a new desert attraction. Double A, as I called her, remembering Anna Akhmatova, Modigliani's first serious lover, stayed in the town, even after the house fire and the death of her grandfather. She was stunned by the Modigliani head being a fake, but channeled her energy between the Zorro, the grocery, and raising funds, for a fee for the Temple. That I had saved her life, by her judgment, gave us a unique bond, more like father and daughter, than any other pairing.

I sided with her. The artistry and pure cleverness of Maqroll made this gallery a natural attraction. Certainly years before, this small desert place might have been offended by the nudes of all sizes, shapes, and hues. But now, as women have come into ownership of their bodies and psyche, these depictions are empowering. And, that no one is revealed, the genius of Courbet, is translated here, and does attract adventurous types to be models, buy the pictures, and celebrate their corpulence.

Double A had another motive as well. She believed the attraction would bring high profile and wealthy visitors to Borrego Springs to see the works, and experience the Tabernacle compound, walk the Boulder Trail, and stay at the Temple of the Desert Inn. She was a schemer and entrepreneur. Her sense of the value to people of wealth, to these attractions, was intense. Double A had lists, within lists, of contacts globally, and she used her connections from her high art associations to spread the word. But, she needed Maqroll to come across.

He was not a man without foresight or passion. Maqroll had many adventurers in his life from Mexico to become a citizen of the United States. He was proud of his legal status, his service in the Marines, and his ability, found late in life to paint. And he had a twinkle, in his coal black eyes, that his love of the woman's body was realized through his hobby. But, he was also humble, reticent to share his secret passion with others. And afraid, the sheriff would bust him, or worse, he would be thrown out of town on a rail, by the conservative town council.

The land was his, as was the zoning as commercial. Double A enlisted Frankie, who was a hellava lawyer, and just a guy out of central casting to go before the planning board. But, it was through his long time and, at times, suffering red head, Tina that Double A made the deal happen. Through the years, Tina had honed her body into a toughness, and sinew, few could match. Now, she wanted an updated oil painting to hang in her Malibu home, the one that was steps from the ocean. Her bedroom looked out onto the beach, and she had a wall over her bed that was destined for her origin of the world rendition.

Maqroll saw her in bright colors, with a California tanned torso, tan lines at the bikini imprints, and a well etched Brazilian shaping of the hair of her mons pubis. They settled on the colors, as Frankie convinced the panel to allow him to finish the expansion and open the obviously named, "THE ORIGIN OF THE WORLD GALLERY ".

By the end of summer, it was completed, a spacious large barn with high white walls and the paintings, a few collages, and the replica of the original work on a kiosk at the entrance. The studio was now just that and Maqroll accelerated his work and collection of pictures. And what a collection it became. The allure of anonymity brought would be cowgirls in pick ups, the Beverly Hills women in their Jags, and the occasional Bentley. It was all very proper, and above board. Some took pictures, and had the image sen t to them electronically, others had the finished product sent as an oil, another fee for the actual painting; and, some were cleared to be exhibited, and that had more appeal than anyone thought. This was certainly not Ars Gratia Artis, what had been a satisfying, if sensual hobby, was now a modest business. For Madrid it was a just result for years of putting up the "mistresses" of his paintings. Once muse, now curator. And for Maqroll, he found he could afford to paint and hire others to run the store.

It was not a surprise, exactly, when a Rolls pulled into the lot, and a modestly sized, slim man emerged in a business suit, cloaked in a brown Bisht with a white keffiyeh on his head. For an Arab man to enter such a gallery would seem, outwardly a violation of the ethical code of some branches of Islam. Madrid greeted him, just as Double A intercepted him before he entered. She knew who he was, and why he was there.

She had connected with a girlfriend from Geneva, who now was curating the vastly expanding Louvre' in Abu Dhabi. This Celeste Greenblatt was monitoring the movement of a painting of Jesus, garbed in Renaissance clothing, that the hoped to acquire through Saudi contacts. The intrigue that surrounded this, Salvator Mundi, was due to its creator, DaVinci. It was a major acquisition that was worth, at auction, 350 to 500 million dollars. For Greenblatt, there were a few bidders with that kind of discretionary cash on hand. She had tracked down a few sheiks from the line of Al- Saud. As a Jew she could not easily travel to Riyadh, but did manage a clandestine meeting in Abu Dhabi, with three sisters of a crown prince, who was buying what he could of high value for the Louvre', but had a secret penchant for erotica, or what his culture claimed it would be in their eyes.

He was in the hunt for the DaVinci, but Celeste could not be certain, he would bid. But, she did have the photos of the Maqroll paintings, that intrigued the young prince. He vowed to head to Borrego Springs on his next visit to the Beverly Wilshire near Rodeo Drive. So, Crown Prince Mohammed bin Salman was now at the doorstep of this oddball place, looking as though, he belonged there, from a long line of al-Saud monarchs. Double A with her braided, blond hair and cut – out jeans, and Madrid in a flowing purple, cotton Mu, Mu.

The Prince would not be the first of his faith to be enthralled by the Coubert painting. After all, it was Khalil Bey, the Ottoman diplomat who commissioned it from the artist. He owned it, even as he collected other "erotic" works of the 1860's. Yet, he was a gambler, and a diplomat on the run. In his Paris flat, he gave up large sums at the gaming tables, avoided his work, and eventually returned to Vienna, just before the Franco- Prussian War. The painting went on a journey that, at times, kept it hidden.

The Prince was here for a jaunt, and pure fun. He had no designs that these paintings were of any actual value to a collector. Still, he enjoyed the prospect, and bought three large renditions, and wanted Madrid. Double A refused him, and Madrid did as well. Instead, he chose a slim, redhead, a hard bodied, blonde, and a Sofia Loren sized, brunette, perhaps the most voluptuous of all.

Maqroll suggested the Prince visit the Tabernacle, and walk the grounds. It was an opportunity to watch me, address the Sunday crowds.

THE COMPOUND

The Prince watched the speech, I gave most Sundays. The history of the actual Temple, the current impossibility of building on the actual Temple Mount, and the dream here, of building a replica to be a place of reflection, worship, and gathering of all faiths from across the world. It was always led to a crescendo of passions and usually touched the crowd of a few hundred. That day, I was more energetic, and focused than others. And I walked towards the Tabernacle to say a private prayer for direction, stamina, and deliverance to complete the project.

As I prayed inside the Tabernacle, the Prince also prayed. He was a Saudi prince, descended from Muhammad ibn Saud, reaching back to Najd, in 1774, when this forefather joined his tiny mid Saudi town with the growling spiritual force of Muhammad Ibn Abd al- Wahhab. It is, of course, Wahhab that brings his brand of radical Islam to the house of al- Saud. Together, they form an alliance that lasts from then to now. The most righteous sense of Islamic purity, and its enforcement through the imposition of medieval sharia law.

But, that backdrop is fading, finally. This prince lives with 28 million Sunni's, and five million Wahhabi's, intent on destroying everyone, including other Muslims, who do not believe in their strict, extreme interpretation of the law. They are people of wrath and want the end of modernity. Not this prince, nor his Crown Prince Muhammad bin Salman, who his driver refers to as Mbs. His approach is to retain religious Orthodoxy, while opening up society to modernity, for women, recreational pursuits, and the freer flow of ideas and information from outside the kingdom. The hammer of Islam, radical Wahhabism that rules by fear, Mbs wants to crush. The modern battles over dominance from the Iranian revolution, the incursion of Americans on their soil, and the horror of 9/11, are in keeping with a long, bloody historic line of conflict for hegemony, where hundreds of thousands were beheaded and thousands more stoned to death.

The desire to find a faith that honored Allah and the Prophet, but did not retard progress and destroy a people and a region, is foremost in the minds of this current generation of leadership. They have traditional battles, religious obstacles between Sunni and Shia that will not subside, but, they want to be able to walk this earth in reverence to Allah, without defiance, but with peace and dignity within themselves.

Knowing this, I find the young prince relaxed, and at ease with me, in this place that symbolizes a Jewish past. I do not bring up the paintings, as, I fear, I may embarrass him. Instead I invite him into a well outfitted yurt for VIPS. I ask for everyone to leave us alone, and only bring food, as we sit and talk of life and our dreams.

I begin, where I always begin with men of power. I ask simply what do you believe? I ask not to argue, but to discover whether they have faith and in what. He expresses his view of God, his adherence to the Q'uran, the pillars of his faith or his practice, and the daily living of it all. In this we have more commonalities than rifts. I hear him, then expound, as gracefully, as I can. I dearly want a single malt, but settle for tea for obvious reasons.

The Quran comes to Mohammed from Gabriel, who carries the word of Allah. Moses goes to Yahweh, who delivers the code, twice. The Torah comes from God, as does the Quran. There are 114 suras, 613 mitzvahs, other books, like Talmud and Tanakh, all from the original word of God, interpreted by subsequent scholars. There are temples and holy things. Wars are fought, the Prophet overcomes division and challenges. Moses Aaron and others through the texts are also men who hold the word of God, and his prophecy.

I tell the prince of the Mark of Aaron, show him the triangle. He asks if God has spoken to me, I tell him, no. But, I admit to dreams, and deep feelings, and constant questioning of what I am doing. He turns into a inquisitor, and bores into my belief system, and mostly, why I chose to leave everything to come here to this desert to build the temple of Solomon. I have no rational response, really.

I have this destiny, revealed by this mark. I have found solace in this. I am driven by a "knowing" that this must be done. And so, far it is happening. He seems bemused, and content with the answer. He wonders, if having built, it might encourage a view of the actual Temple Mount, to change towards a reconciliation. He is much more interested in future outcomes than am I.

Time passes quickly. Two men of different worlds and generations exploring the larger questions of faith and conflict. For these hours, it seems that the rifts are not chasms, and can be bridged by one person reaching another persons heart. We walk the compound as the buses depart, the food trucks are being cleaned. A lone security man drives his ATV around the perimeter. Lobo and Reds are roaming, around the yurts, and charge up to me, the prince lights up, as he plays with them. Their bark, penetrates, an otherwise quiet night. The crescent of a new moon, emerges to light a dark blue sky.

Having no reticence, I attempt to escape reality, and tell the prince, I need funds to start and finish the actual temple. He seems concerned that the "usual" Jewish benefactors would not fund this project. And I tell him, some have offered funds through the years, but, no major contributor has come forward. He asks if the funds can be anonymously offered. He would not want his family or the monarch to know, he gave to build a Jewish temple.

I do not press him. I escort him to his Rolls, and actually bow, for some unknown reason, out of deference, I suppose. He nods and smiles. And offers, "Allah will provide"

The Trailer – A Year Later

It is an oatmeal and toast morning. The winter winds are sharp, and there will be a cold front upon us, slowing construction of the Court of the Gentiles and slowing down the Inner Court preparations. We are moving towards having the grounds prepared. But, I have not approached an architect, or taken bids, without enough cash on hand to begin with confidence we can conclude the process. I do not want to start this movie and not be able to finish it.

I have plastered the walls of the trailer with blue prints, pictures of the Temple, inside and out. This old trailer is construction central, all it needs is a general contractor and a budget. All our businesses are turning small profits, the compound is still vital, but the numbers have slowed, over these many years. The dream needs more evidence for the public to share in it. It is becoming a MAC thing, one old mans', adventure with no obvious happy ending.

Fran drives up with Izzy and the dogs. They enter the house with a bravado, as they often do, all fast pace, bumping into things and shouting. Yo MAC.

Fran pushed me onto the sofa, and opens her laptop. She pulls up our bank statement.

And there, as they laugh. I cry.

50 million dollars is in the account. 50 million wired from somewhere.

Who could have sent this, they ask. I cannot know, I tell them.

I walk out back with the 16 gauge, Mossberg, load a few shells and fire them into the sky, and I scream to God. Then, I fall to my knees, and hold my head in my hands, and cry some more, whispering.

Allah will Provide... Allah will provide...

CRAZY HORSE, SOUTH DAKOTA

Somehow, it is hard to imagine what makes for events across a historic timeline, a century, era or a millennium. The 18th century ran through my thoughts, as 100 years of tumult and contrasting change. Did the people in it know it? What is discernable as the zeitgeist changes, as new thoughts and ideas evolve, or as mores and ideals change. Some drift away, others are slaughtered by new ones, and, what of the people, are they but, travelers surfing a wave of change, or without any chance to alter the course of history?

In the same time frame, a man claims he is the Jewish Messiah, only to convert thousands to Christ; another in a tiny central Arabian village, Muhammad Abd al- Wahhab, decides to reclaim Islam; Polish Bishops burn all the Talmuds they can find; even as, Rousseau, and John Locke write of a social contract that illuminates the rights of man. There is revolution in America; revolt in France, followed by the terrorism of Robespierre, and a struggle in Europe, between the ancien' regime and divine right monarchs, and the unalienable rights of men. All in one period. Freedom fighters, fundamentalists, sheiks, and emergent nations and empires.

And now, it moves at hyper- speed. New technologies and advances, but, what of our fundamental beliefs? Have we evolved at all?

Certainly, from my closed corner of the room, it looks grim. An actual Temple on the Temple Mount seems remote. Palestinians continue to protest their rights to Jerusalem, as the would be capital of a Palestinian state; even as Jews are restrained from just praying near the Al-Asqua mosque. The Dome of the Rock, a tribute to blind belief and superstition that Mohammed stepped her on his way to Allah, one miraculous night. And, I still battle with the traditional Jewish groups, that my replica Temple is, if not a sin, is certainly not a mitzvah. Now, with funds, in hand, perhaps, the realization will calm all troubled waters, on this thing I know, I must do.

Have I lost my mind? Am I so detached from reality, that I cannot see the folly of this quest? As Izzy drives from Mt. Rushmore to Crazy Horse, I keep the questions to myself, afraid I am to reveal my ennui. It is all smooth black top, surrounded by rock faces of granite. Rushmore was really a government job, it took 14 years, and cost about a million of 1930 dollars. It was carefully planned by monumental sculptor, Gutzon Borglum, who with son Lincoln wrangled enough federal funds with the help of Senator Peter Norbeck, and even, Coolidge himself, who famously wore a Indian headdress, and ten gallon hat on his visit to the mountain.

It was not one man's obsession or dream. It was a project, that Borglum designed, selected the Presidents, and attacked like any other dangerous, construction job. 400 artisans worked the scaffolds, and they had a carver of immense talent, who gave the faces their expressions. He was, of course, Luigi del Bianco, who even on 60 foot heads could apply his finesse. They dedicated the heads as they were completed. They even fought off a bill, passed by the House of Representatives to include, Susan B. Anthony on the rock face. The bill failed, claiming appropriations were frozen for the project.

The monument at Crazy Horse was a passion project. A unique obsession of an entire family for many decades since 1939. Korczak Ziolkowski was an accomplished sculptor in his own right, when he was fired from the Borglum team site. He was headstrong, and his day work of blasting, clearing and then "honey- combing "the rock in small segments did not suit his need to build epic things. And epic came along in a letter to him from a tribal leader, a Lakota chief, Henry Standing Bear.

He has a piece of granite that was Indian, and he and others were outraged by Mt. Rushmore on land that was in dispute since the Indian wars. Somehow, KZ saw a model of it in his minds eye. He knocked out a model and stood it on a log pedestal, in front of the site. It was of Crazy Horse, to revealed out of the mountain and it would dwarf, Rushmore. 563 feet tall, 641 feet long, a warrior on horseback with an outstretched arm. His head would be 87 feet, versus that of the Presidents at 60 feet.

For over 65 years, the entire family was raised by that mountain face. He gathered, dynamite and later plastic explosives, like C-4. Paid for bulldozers and back hoes, and all along taught his children to blast and clear. They lived in cabins, and he cultivated second wife Ruth, to handle the finances, a gift shop, and the food concessions. She dutifully handled it all until he died, and the sons took over. Korczak went from Connecticut artisan to master builder, his strong body and handsome cowboy face, turned through the years to a long, white haired mountain man, with a rugged, wind scarred face, protected only by a white beard that grew to mid chest.

As we approached the mountain, Izzy stopped the car. She got out and just gazed at the enormous Crazy Horse head. It was spectacular, and the nose alone, she estimated was over 20 feet. She went from excited to solemn, overtaken by the decades it took to get just to this. How could I be so short sighted and of such weak will, to complain that I was not making progress. Here was a family with a grit of cosmic proportion who went from nothing to this, formed a foundation, taught kids about Crazy Horse, and refused to give up. Even Lincoln Borglum left the mountain, when funding ceased, the full figures of the Presidents left undone, as funding dried up, and the war began.

Izzy walked with Monique, one of the ten Ziolkowski children, who is the Luigi del Bianco of this project. They shared a love of the conversion of rock to something, of monoliths, and the almost cellular connection they both had to epic projects, that are out of reach and imagination for mere mortals. I went up to the site with sons, Casimir and Mark, and they reinforced my sense that they were there to the end. They did not care that it was slow work, but acknowledged, it was Ruth who saved the project. She redirected the carving from the horse head to the face of Crazy Horse, a simple change in direction. But, her foresight made the project real, gave it form and suggested the end result. Without that change, they would have lost without funds or interest.

Now with the founders both gone, it fell to the seven of the ten still there to carry on the effort. And they had more than the adversity of the construction. They never had support from the Native Americans around them. They were often seen as building a monument to their father, not Crazy Horse. There were demonstrations, some vandalism, and most it they just ignored, and continued to blast and carve.

Yet, some philanthropists only saw the positive opportunity, not to enhance tourism, as much as to make a point about the story of the Indian past, in these Black Hills. T. Denny Sanford, took over Dakota bank, made a fortune, and gave them ten million, not caring a hoot, how long it takes to get it finished. He has invested in medical research, funded centers for children's health, created new disciplines to improve education, and they all may pay off sooner than this he told the boys. But, he said, "I don't care if it takes another 100 years."

117

Izzy took me to a room behind the gift shop. There grandchildren, some grown, where working on turning fragments of rock into everything from bookends to candlesticks. The commitment they had inspired me. It was a much needed tonic. I put a few candlesticks into a bag and vowed to light a candle each night at the compound to remind me of their certainty that Crazy Horse will be finished someday.

I sat on the back porch, with a coffee mug chiseled from the rock, filled with Starbucks, as heavy mist descended in the late afternoon. I turned to chat up an old Indian, with features that were familiar to me. I had never seen him, then, I thought I knew him well. As if he knew me, he asked,

"Do you have a big rock with a spirit inside of it?"

I admitted, I did in a way, a building, yet to emerge. And he said,

"If you are not patient, it will die, as will you"

He huddled closer, and gripped my left wrist firmly. Telling me every dream has its own spirit life, and I can not bring it before its time.

"It will not come, until, it is time. This dream has its own spirit and its own time"

He released my wrist, gazed into my eyes, with his grey eyes, and for a moment I was frightened of him. My cup dropped, and when I had retrieved it, I turned and he was gone.

CHAPTER X

CRASH AND BURN

THE COMPOUND AT DAWN

There was smoke, and that distinctive smell after a major fire. A dampness in the early morning, everywhere, and it had not rained for months. I drove past the outer gate that now had two white swastikas painted upon them, poorly executed and backwards. But, the meaning was obvious and evil. Then, I turned into what was a crime scene and it was filled with firefighters, black and white sheriff cruisers, and plain clothes cops dotted the compound, their gold badges on their belts, shining in the emerging sunlight.

The tallest man was the Sheriff. I knew these scenes, I prosecuted from evidence gathered at them. He came to me and offered a hand, then a hug. And, delicately, but, with clarity told me what he knew. Gently, he sat me inside his white, unmarked cruiser, and handed me a shell from a spent AR-15.

From what they found, when they arrived at the compound, a band of three truckloads of White Nationalist, Skinheads attacked the area. They deployed across the compound and destroyed the Tabernacle, and burned it. They tore down the history center and the scale model of the Temple. Simultaneously, they burned the surrounding exhibits, and spray painted any wall they could find with a swastika. Every book, sign, and replica exhibit was riddled with bullets. The replica Ark was defiled by human feces, and they urinated on any Star of David or sacrament, they could find.

In sum, it was a sacking of the Tabernacle compound. Three security guards responded and fired on the intruders, all were killed. Maqroll, who was alerted by the guards, came to assist and shot and wounded two of them, and they are in custody. By the time, the deputies arrived, the bad guys had fled, the damage done. Only the yurt village was untouched, the residents unharmed. Everyone was evacuated to the high school gymnasium, until crime scene was secure.

Maqroll appeared with some abrasions to his forehead and a wrapped hand. Considering the fire fight, he seemed, his usual calm self. He asked the Sheriff for armed guards to protect the yurts, and he nodded. He thought, it was clear, this band of anti-Semites would return, unless force was obvious. And, he was confident, they would break the men he wounded, now in custody, to collect the others.

I was far from my years as a prosecutor, but, wanted to be updated on the progress of the investigation, while my limbic system wanted immediate vengeance and retribution, my heart and spirit wanted to rebuild. I had not a single thought of walking away, not one. As I walked through the rubble, I knew my tiny compound was not an analog to Tisha b'Av and the end of the real Temples. And then, Jews were enslaved, dispersed, and forced to hide their faith and begin again, without a Temple for God to dwell. I have it better, much better. The 50 million is there, I have not lost my passion, and I am imbued with this damn thing, it will not leave me. Still, I am unconvinced these rag tag Jew haters plotted this on their own, this mass destruction.

We had constant protests. All non violent, but loud, and, at times, disruptive. Dov and his band of Jewish Defense League followers, came by most Sundays to picket and scream at the buses. He threatened me regularly with emails, nasty Facebook posts, and even am actual letter. I could have pressed charges, but, found him, largely benign.

Others, were the standard assortments across a broad spectrum of protesters. We attracted pro life supporters; Black Lives Matter advocates; many evangelical street preachers; and the most bizarre, group of anti – viva section folks dressed as cows. The crowds, we generated brought them all out, and they were not really a burden. In time, we engaged some of them, with food, water, and the occasional tour of the place.

In the end, our good will, and the upbeat spirit of the place, warded off real evil.

But, I knew that there was a group of usually poorly organized Hammerskins in the far desert regions by Blythe. They are the best organized of the classic Neo- Nazi, Jew hating, kill the "mud" people genre. They also have bands, and a musical style that appeals to their amped up followers. The suspects shot by Maqroll, one had the distinctive claw cross hammers logo tattooed on his left upper arm. Another had their slogan,

"H.F.F.H", Hammerskins forever, forever, hammerskins, as a tattoo on his butt.

This group had murder in their blood, if only rarely. Wade Michael Page, was a band member, played some tunes with his chums. Until, on a summer day in Oak Creek, Wisconsin, he slaughtered six people. Why? Because they were worshipping in a Sikh temple. No one knows, if he just mistook them for Muslims, because the sick bastard blew out his brains, rather than face prosecution. He is revered by the Blythe chapter, that calls themselves, WMP's. Clever as they are, their trucks all have 838 in their license plates- H.C.H translates to $8^{th}, 3^{rd}$, and 8th, letters of the alphabet.

We have Pink Floyd to thank for the identification of such an odious group in their film that became the contorted symbol of these thugs.

It would take many months, before they flipped enough of them to get to their leader, Jackson "Bad" Weathers. By profession, he was a skilled carpenter, and often found work on subcontracting jobs in Imperial and Riverside County. He was well mannered and, by, all accounts a skilled carpenter and mild mannered co- worker. But, there were times, when he could not find work, as housing starts diminished under the eight years of Barak Obama. His three children went to schools that were not well staffed, they ate a meal at school, his wife tried to spread the EBT card as far as she could. And he, read whatever he could mostly about World War II, and, then, more on line form home grown Neo- Nazi's.

He was imposing at 6'6", and clean shaven, from head to chin. He had the body of an NFL lineman, and a strong, deep penetrating voice. As, his good times, seemed harder to come by, he attended a few Hammerskin meetings, and found, the group often in turmoil. And eventually, there was a split, between those with more violent tendencies, and those just happy to have their music, and a club of friends who thought the way you did about the problem of the world, namely, Jews and blacks, the Mud people. Jackson eventually became

121

the leader of the 838 WMP's chapter, and was more a Nazi club type than a murder.

Still, as he sat in an interrogation room, it was clear he led his group to the compound, but, not only because of his hate of all things Jewish. While, he admitted, he despised my Temple project, he was not there to kill anyone, and he certainly did not fire the shots that killed the guards. He knew his entire crew would be indicted for mayhem, destruction of property, and a few of his members for murder. To keep the D.A. from charging him with murder, he surprised them with a fact sequence, they could not have known.

They were paid for their assault on the compound. For fifty thousand dollars, they were hired to destroy the Tabernacle, and wage enough havoc to convince me to leave Borrego Springs, forever. The man behind the raid, had no criminal record, was not a member of 838 WMP, and had never stepped onto the compound. He was a scion of the community and his family had lived there for generations. He was a mean spirited, universal hater, but he had a special distaste for Jews, and had his own interpretation of scripture.

Jackson gave up his name to avoid a murder charge or conspiracy to commit murder indictment.

"James Stepler. Stepler Citrus Farms. He paid me, the 50k."

THE TRAILER AGAIN

Philip Rivers was an under appreciated, but, skilled Quarterback for the San Diego Chargers. He was on a team that was always rebuilding. He was ranked 9th best as a passer, and 4th in all time consecutive starts, he completed 94% of his passes. For this he makes 21 million a year. Still, he has sense of humility, and the grace to honor a higher power in his life and considers his talent, wife, and his eight children a blessing from God.

With all the rebuilding and the losses, he often appeared at practice with a T-shirt emblazoned with a Latin phrase, attributed to the Opus Dei, and Saint Josemaria,

Nunc Coepi. It means, "with God's help I get up and Now I begin again".

Fran brings the wooden sign, with blue letters, rimmed in white. I hang it over the front door. I began in this trailer with nothing, and I have returned to it. There is only room or me inside, the blueprints and compound plans clutter every flat space. I vow to use this place as our center of reclamation, as we begin quickly to rebuild the compound. There is agreement, we should not rebuild the Tabernacle, but spend all our efforts on the grounds, the walls and the actual construction of the Temple.

We will have to now find the architects for the Temple, artisans to craft the Ark, the oil burning candelabras, the tables, doors, and the elaborate interior carvings. Then, there are the outside baths, the massive, Molten Sea on the backs of twelve metal oxen, and the other inside artifacts. All requiring housing, on site feeding, and recreation after a long day of work.

I could not know who these people where, but, I trusted we could identify them. But I was adamant that all the Sunday services would continue. Fran moved her trailer back into our backyard, so she could co-ordinate incoming media that was now worldwide, due to the raid and the murder trails ahead. We had become a center of national attention as well, as rumors developed along a few story lines, including who were the killers, what was 838 WMP, and who was this man Jonas Stepler, now charged and arraigned for murder.

STEPLER CITRUS FARM
BORREGO SPRINGS

It seems like what it is out here in Northern Borrego Springs, citrus. Acres of lemons, tangerines, tangelos, and grapefruit. And there are palm trees farmed here as well. Every acre needs water, and plenty of it. These farmers like Stepler take 70 % of the water pumped from underground wells, the rest goes to golf courses, and then what is left to residents.

Now, that was not problem for Stepler's grandfather, and his father before him. There were no golfers and very few people. But there were farmers and farm workers, and people who got it all to market. But, now the water table, and that is all the water they have, has dropped 119 feet, with a 26 foot decline in the last ten years. And, so far it has been a 16 year dry spell.

For Fran and I this was all an education in how Borrego Springs got its water, from NASA hydrologist, who claims this area is in, "critical overdraft" to hear Armand Vigolo tell it. 128 private pumps, that feed these farms, and they are all pulling from the same aquifer. The state has mandated that a plan is in place by the Borrego Water District soon, or they will impose a cut in all consumption, to 70 % reductions by 2040. To do that on the present use rate and aquifer, will mean farmers must find another way to water, reduce crop output, or grow less water needy crops.

And even though, from the satellite, Armand can show any farmer here, the reality. Water is getting harder to find, the basins that accumulate water in wet seasons are depleted, and the regeneration of the underground water supply cannot catch up with the use.

And the farmers, like Stepler are not all believers that they have not done enough. When the look at their pump gauges and their reductions, they believe the state and county should be protecting them, not forcing land to be fallow, or outright pay them from state funds to stop farming.

Stepler is 82 with a Jimmy Stewart frame and manner. He speaks slowly and rarely. He can shout in anger, but usually not. His wife Jean had Alzheimer's and after being in a nearby home, died four years ago, and Stepler is even more quiet and troubled. But, then Armand tells us of his last visit to a water board meeting. There he screamed a warning about the valley dying, if they cut his water, and others. He was so upset, they called an EMT to check his vitals.

He still travels to a small evangelical church, where services are at the back of the Borrego Springs museum, by Christmas Circle. He drives his new truck, with his name and logo on the door. They preach the Second Coming, the Rapture, and the end of the Jew, the non believer, and the sinners. For Mr. Stepler there is no dispensation, Papal decree that frees the Jews for their killing of Christ.

The prosecutor in me, induces that an aging man, loses his wife, is threatened with the loss of his farming due to water restriction, and his lifelong dislike of all things Jewish, might add up to a conspiracy to create mayhem, but not murder. The murder is on 838 WMP, the havoc on Stepler, but both charges being sustained seemed unlikely.

Could my project alone have prompted the raid, probably not. But, the button, I had hit was water rights. I was becoming a concern, as I sapped vital water from a place that never had enough. He saw me as an interloper, a water guzzler, and, a Jew who thought he was priest.

If, things move as they often do in the system, it will take a year or so, before any of them go to trial. I would travel to the San Diego, Superior Court to witness that trial, if the Temple is back in business.

I am more concerned about the cleanup than I am about incarcerating the lot of them. The compound must be made ready for rebuilding, and I need to find the builder, and the artisans, I am feeling pushed, a weight descends on me, that lightness is gone. I can feel it between my shoulders, and I am stooping. I struggle, now, each day, to stand taller, eat less, and adopt a stringent ascetic style, that is more monastic. I want to appear lighter, at ease, so I fake it. Inside, I am darker, as though a great river runs through me, carrying a cargo in barges, to a distant port. The sooner, it gets there, the better for everyone, and my aching soul.

The Compound
A Sunday

The families buried the guards weeks ago. But, they wanted a memorial here, on the ground they protected and died for. Carlos Rodriquez, 27; Emilio Perez 47; David Rosen 56. Each a family man, who was moonlighting from his day job. They were on an overnight shift, armed with a sidearm, and a shotgun. They were outgunned, and outmanned. They could keep vandals away, and did that effectively, but not a quasi- military group of Neo- Nazi raiders.

An ensemble of musicians who knew them played their favorite songs, as family members offered the eulogies that over time have the same cadence. Everyone cries, the wives can hardly speak, the oldest children offer a strong appearance, and there is often a friend or buddy, who attempts to remember the full person, with a story and some humor. In the end, the loss is too much to process. The guitar riffs all seem incongruous, the virtuoso playing, as if rising into the sky, with their spirits.

Then all goes silent.

I look into a thousand eyes, to offer something, perhaps, solace.

Carlos, Emilio, and David were all here to protect my dream. It was not theirs. I know they cared about the concept of building the Temple of Solomon here in Borrego Springs, but, it not something that was their mission. It was a job, that was part time, to fill in the financial gaps, they faced between what they hoped to achieve in life, and what it would take to realize the goal. We all have these gaps, don't we; between who we are and who we want to be. Between what we can afford and what we really want for ourselves and our children.

These three men knew all of this. That is why they road this property in the middle of night, in search of vandals and banditos. Always hoping, they would not find anyone so foolish, and could return home safely, rest and attack that other job, that might help them find their destiny. Carlos was in law school, and sought to be a prosecutor. He could be eloquent, and, at other times, direct. But he from the earliest age, believed in justice. Emilio drove a produce truck, took what work he could, because he hoped to finally rollout his own food truck, with his wife, Lena. They were working on names, now that they had the truck. And, David was a teacher at Borrego Springs High, but, he was more than that to his students. He coached baseball, and track, and served as every ones unofficial college counselor.

The raiders are the personification of evil incarnate. They were wild dogs unleashed to bring havoc to this quiet, serene place. There is no reason for it, but hate. It is not God's plan that hate will endure. It is instead the hope that, we will endure, and find our way to heal, by helping each other. This was not a hallowed place, it was but an effort to provide a replica of something unique that we could enjoy, and use to reflect upon God's presence, but,

It is hallowed ground now. "Carlos, Emilio, and David are in the soil and live in our souls. We will go forward and build this Temple, and bring thousands here to see it, as a memorial to what they sacrificed. I do not know how to reach them, but, I hope I can touch you today. Hold onto their memory, burn it deep inside of you, and count your blessings that they passed through your life."

The band played some fitting overture. I relit the eternal light, where the Tabernacle stood, and everyone rose, locked arms, and swayed in a gentle desert breeze.

CHAPTER XI

❖❖❖

WHO WILL BUILD IT

THE ORCHARDS

Tree planting is a symbol of renewal and recognition that some things will exist after us. In the aftermath of our destruction, I took to spending money on buying fruit trees, planting palms, cypress, and a small cedar grove. As a boy, we would collect for trees to be planted in Israel, a sign that the state of Israel would survive and always be a place for Jews to return. Every year my father would plant a tree for someone in the family, every Tu Bishvat, the holiday for it, he would say, in Genesis God planted fruit trees before any animal or insect came to propagate on earth, for two decades. He always promised, we would go visit the trees, but, like most of his generation, he never saw Israel, let alone the trees. But, I was intent on this, lemon trees, orange, and some dates, scattered in small groves throughout the compound.

There was no grass, only native desert plants. The grounds were beginning to rebound from the scars of the fire. The damp smell of ash yielding to the flowers and the aromas of plant life. Izzy's team trucked in palms to plant, and clusters of birds of paradise and plumeria, throwing off odors of jasmine, ginger, and even coconut.

The pathways to the replica tent, and the walk of history, explaining the history of the Temple and Solomon and David, was now filled in with grey gravel, and a black rock, that is gabbro, lining the paths. Each sign had a precis of a part of the history, and a rendition of the scene. We began issuing museum quality, I pods to give each visitor an audio explanation of what they were experiencing.

And we created, a Virtual Reality room, where for a fee, a visitor could rent an Oculus viewer and see exactly what it would be like to walk through the Temple of Solomon, replete with priests, prayers, a narration, and even simulated animal sacrifices. Perhaps, the majesty of it all drew visitors, or the animal sacrifices, but it quickly became the most popular part of the experience. Of course, I had to listen to Double A, who convinced me to have a VR for children and another, bloodier, version for adults.

I found, I would take to raking the gravel path, after hours, with the Ortega brothers, Jesus and Raoul. They were quiet men, with a serenity about them. Both had a Ruger .357 on his back hip, required by Izzy, just to be certain, if the animals returned, they could protect us. But after, the niceties of a brief conversation, they would settle into the task of raking the gravel. For them it was just work, for me, it was a large Zen garden, where I could let my mind drift, and attempt to not hold onto any thought.

But one night, I could hear the distinctive engine of a Harley 1800cc, and saw it kicking up dust coming towards us. Then, Jesus and Raoul, protectively pulled their pistols. Until, they saw a undersized man, pull up, take off his helmet, only to reveal a white haired, old man, who looked barely heavy enough to stay on the bike. I waved them off. I knew the frame and the face.

Captain Sammy "Starman" Rubin. He was dubbed the nickname, for his two bronze stars and oak clusters, earned in Vietnam. He led a squad into the fight for Hue, when Tet broke out, January 31st, 1968. That date tattooed on his right forearm. In the house to house battle, he took the point, killed the enemy, while suffering wounds to his leg and torso. He also managed to drag two of his men into a safe spot, even as he continued fighting. A fight outside of the city, required he call in an air strike, which saved his squad, but shrapnel penetrated his back and a cart on fire rolled over him, catching his back on fire. Severely burned, he continued to fight and lead his men, until they were out of danger.

Now here he was, after hearing of my trouble, and had left everything, which was not much anymore, in Hemet, to join up with me. His wife was long gone, his night sweats and chaotic personality, now diagnosed as PTSD, too much to take, and his three kids scattered from Seattle to Boston. Even, his exploits in Washington, as a few term, Congressman, provided some pension relief, veteran health benefits, but a sizeable distaste for government, politics, and blowhards. Of which, he thought most were these days.

He had spent the last year, running a palm tree farm in the Palm desert, for no other reason, except it was easy to do, required minimal hours, and trees did not talk back. He required little, he had enough money to live comfortably. But, here he was after some adventure, and to help me out. It was over 40 years ago, I helped him out, this runt of a man. In our school yard, before everything was politically correct, you could get beaten up for being small, looking different, or some combination of any of that. Starman was all of it, small, a Jew, and had a big mouth. The toughs took to grabbing him and hoisting him by his belt onto an iron fence that surrounded the playground. Then, sometimes they would strip off his shirt, and whip him, to the delight of the girls, and, one particularly odious gentile would hit his stomach, eventually loosening his belt, so Starman would fall to the ground.

I was bigger, had some combat Judo skills, my father taught me. And after a few weeks of this, I took on the mob, and beat the crap out of three of them. I even encouraged Starman to help me beat the leader, until he bleed onto his Ban-Lon shirt, Starman, smashed his head into the ground, breaking his nose. From then on, I was his defender, and, it is, most likely, that experience that probably set me on a course to defend and prosecute the bad actors. It is also what galvanized Sammy to never be a victim again. His squad owed their lives to that schoolyard.

And I was blessed, with this guy now taking over our grounds and landscaping. He brought along, as well, some other vets and lost souls, who he housed in a special yurt village, he set up just outside the eastern perimeter. They worked dayside, helped each other with their brain surges, and held AA meetings, when they could. When, I engaged them in the project, they seemed bemused, and most admitted, to some belief in some higher power, but, did not certify as part of any religion. Yet, they all agreed their very presence was a miracle of some sort.

On occasion, Starman would have a plus one on his Road King. She was of our age, with pure white hair, and no makeup. Ruthie sized me up with grey, wolf eyes, and would hug me at the waist, lift me off my feet with a grunt, as her greeting. She did not vibrate like Starman, she was a searcher, almost mystical, and at once serious about everything, and then, on a tear to escape from reality. It was not a bi-polar syndrome, it was something very unusual. She seemed to know exactly what supplies, were needed, or where to plant things. And then, she would ask me about the project, or jump into my inner thoughts.

"Did the Molten Sea have twelve oxen?"

"Will you kill the Red Heifer"

"Can I come to the Temple, if I don't take a mikveh bath"

"Are you really a holy man, and not just a builder?"

And, I would answer, then she would walk away or grab my left ear, with her thumb and forefinger, pull it hard, and mutter, some inane, axiom.

"tune in MAC, tune in MAC, don't drop out"

Then at daybreak one day, Sammy found her naked, cross legged in front of the eternal flame. And, in unmistakable Hebrew, she was chanting a morning prayer,

Modeh Ani.

At night, I gave my weary soul into God's hands, and, he returns it to me in the morning. My soul is within me. How great is your faithfulness.

He lifted her up, and she was in a trance from this morning acceptance of a renewed life, granted for another day. Her soul intact, by the prayers words. She said nothing, until he returned to his place, but, then she would not sleep, and tied him to the bed, and exhausted him with her ardor. He was certain, he was not dreaming, that he was with her due the events he recounted to me. But, Starman was not fully certain, since his mind often imagined scenarios, with such vividness, he, at times, could not distinguish between reality and some altered state.

It mattered not to him. Either way, he experienced something that was inexplicable, but, full of a simple life pleasure. Questioning Ruthie would serve no purpose, if he was insane, or was she, made little difference to him.

WESTWOOD, UCLA, THE W HOTEL

The Hillel at UCLA was not as robust, as it was during the years the Baby Boomers matriculated. It still provided a gathering place for Jewish students, an opportunity to meet young women, and to observe holidays. Then, it was also a place where people of varying political viewpoints could gather and debate, argue, and agree to disagree. The current climate, seemed more puritanical and restrictive. There seemed to be an acceptance of speakers of some views, and the prohibition of other viewpoints. It was less about religious stands than political. The dialogue was narrower, and the attendance at seminars or lectures less.

Hillel might find it all foreign, of course. There is no Torah here being studied, no famously austere patriarch, Hillel, teaching Torah. But, he would understand dialogue, and thoughtfulness. Hillel dedicated the last 40 years of his, Moses length life of 120 years, to being the embodiment of the Jewish spirituality. And in his time, he espoused the most obvious, and succinct learnings of his time, as exhibited in a relief sculpture on the Knesset Menorah today, that shows Hillel teaching a Gentile, standing on one foot, the meaning of the Torah,

"What is hateful to you, do not do to your fellow; this is the whole Torah; the rest is explanation; go and learn"

So to these two hundred or so students and teachers. I am not here to tell them of Temple Mount, the Messianic Age, or that I am Hillel HaKohen. I am but a Jew who has found a mission, and turned his once secular view into one that is more Rabbinic, not unlike Hillel, the Pharisee, who gave his teachings well before the Rabbinic hierarchy took control of the faith, after the destruction of the Second Temple.

I offered the visuals, the dream, and the why of it all. They applauded, if still uncertain of what value it would be, other than, as one student claimed, "its just a mini – Disneyland, MAC, no more or less." And that offered me the opportunity to quote Hillel,

"If, I am not for myself, who is for me. And when I am for myself, what am I?

And if not now when"

They stood and applauded. A young man, in the apparel of a Hasidic, came to me and claimed that those words were not Hillel's, but actually older, and attributable to Aaron, who stood by his belief that the covenant with God, was encased in the Ark, but only two mattered. There is one God, who brought his people out of bondage, and, do unto others as you would have them do unto you. This fellow thought that was the message of Torah, God and Aaron, and that Hillel stole it. I assured him, no one needed ownership of the Big Two, and that Hillel was a hero and icon to me. Such, debate seemed counterproductive to me. Yet, to this young man, it seemed as vital as who would win the Super Bowl, to his classmates.

I took a three minute walk to the W, to just sit, have a single malt whiskey, and enjoy the world I once populated. Women in high heels and black dresses, shoulders bare, the smell of some high priced perfume, wafted by as they sauntered to gather. Laughter, carefree socializing,, lost to me mostly in my desert existence. I could still laugh, but, I was never much of a smiler and found most things, others found of humor, I did not. Still, there was an unmistakable gaiety here, and it was warming.

At some nooks, a language was spoken, I could not discern. I asked a man, sitting alone in a green beret, with a conventioneers tag around his next, that had ROBERTO in bold letters on it, what it was. Roberto said it was, "el vasco, la lengua vasca", the language of the Basques. He was here for a gathering of his comrades, in the Basque National Liberation convention. They were not fighting, any longer, but demonstrations continued in the region. His English was impeccable, since his family emigrated to Nevada in the 1900's, his father a successful sheep herder and shepherd, until the depression drove him into potato farming, some gold mining near Winnemucca, Nevada, and eventually into building hotels, casinos, and restaurants.

All I knew of Winnemucca came from my prosecutor days. They had a notorious brothel, red light zone, called, 'The Line', that often was the subject at our conclaves of the value of regulated prostitution in Nevada, versus what we had in Los Angeles, which was damn dangerous, unregulated and drug infested. This was Roberto Zagarzazu who lived in Las Vegas and was an architect and builder, of things, including one of my old haunts while on convention, in Henderson, the Green Valley Resort. Sometimes, even over a drink, in a familiar place, the world feels five or six people wide.

My story was always easy to tell, if I started it already in Borrego Springs, and left the mysticism of my Mark of Aaron, and the dreams, and unusual happenings out of it. When, I was linear, people got it, and often found it dramatic, and just a good tale. I did not appear that unusual or foreign, and Roberto listened, and then asked the obvious:

"Who will build it, for you?"

I said, I was about to begin the search, but, was unclear of the proper path to find the right contractor, and had no one on our team with the expertise to direct our efforts. When I asked him, who could build a Temple of Solomon, his response was exhaustive, but meandered towards a conclusion that was obvious to him, and startled me due to my self imposed failure to understand the magnitude of the process from plan to completion.

Roberto acknowledged that through the ages, and today there are builders of holy places. Whether Egyptian, Babylonian, the massive mosques of Islam, the edifices of the East for Hindu and Buddhist. All have their own challenges from material to unique symbolism. The Catholic Church alone has a vast variety of places to worship, of varying designs from the Sistine Chapel to the works of the magnificent artisan, Antoni Gaudi, one of Roberto's heroes. Most took years to complete. Some are never done, others have had their opulence fade or were destroyed in war. Still, each place was built with a special purpose. And Roberto, felt that although, this was to be a replica, its essence would still be what one would actually build on the Temple Mount.

And more, no matter what I pretended, he leaned towards me, to emphasize;

"MAC, you are building a dwelling place for God, whether you think so or not"

He admitted there were people who built synagogues. But most synagogues, were designs like the Tabernacle, and later the Temple of Solomon. A large, impressive doorway, a walkway and seating, the eternal flame, the ark that holds the Torah. Then the architecture that surrounds those basics is diverse, unique and stunning. And anyone of those could be a model. But the most prolific builders of Temples, with over 150, across the globe is the Church of the Later Day Saints, the Mormons.

To this Basque, who has watched Mormon money build, and rebuild Las Vegas, and see their Temples rise with majesty, they were the ones to contact to build my Temple. He did not know, if they would entertain it, but, they built buildings with the best standards, the best material and workmanship. The built them to last, and most critical, they built them as holy place.

"Go talk to the Elders, MAC" and let me know what they tell you.

We exchanged phone numbers, and he gave me his card that had the oak tree of Gernika on it as his company logo. I drove past the massive, Mormon Temple on Santa Monica Boulevard, with the highlight lights all on, and gazed up at the angel, Moroni, pointing towards the Great Salt Lake and Temple Square, and wondered if Roberto had opened a door for me.

Now how ready was I to walk through it ?

SALT LAKE CITY

The Salt Lake Temple captures your attention, as it stands with majesty in the center of the city at Temple Square. It has six master spires, that immediately declare the religious significance of the architecture. Three for the higher priesthood, that is higher than the rest, of the Melchizedek, and three for the Aaronic priesthood, or those in preparation to become higher priests, in the faith. There is a natural affinity between the faith of the Later Day Saints and Jews like me, who have come from Aaron and the Levites.

Joseph Smith and Oliver Cowdery were in the woods, near their new homestead in Pennsylvania, right by the New York State border, where he fled from persecution, even though his transformation to his faith was just years old. Yet, that forest, he and Oliver went off to pray, he says, about baptism. And then, in a classic theophany, John the Baptist comes to them, and by laying his hands upon them, restores the Aaronic Priesthood. It is a moment of such power to the LDS believers and establishes, Smith as the legitimate founder of the Church. Thus, it places, me as a Levite, and a purported descendant of Aaron, as, in some way, connected to their beliefs.

To be sure, we differ. I from Zadok, the first priest of the first temple, and Zadok from Eleazor and Aaron. Jesus from another high priest of the Hebrews, who appears in Genesis, Melchizedek, or to me Malki Tzedek. This was the King of Salem (nee Jerusalem), who gave bread and wine to Abram (later Abraham), after he saved Lot from Yahweh's wrath over Sodom and Gomorrah. He was not a descendant of Aaron, nor was Jesus, and to the Mormon faith, his priesthood had higher merit than that of Aaron. They could evolve and study the faith and progress to be a high priest, not of Aaron, but of Malki Tzedek, or Melchizedek, which means literally, My King is the God, Sedek.

I pondered as I walked the 15 foot high outer wall of granite, that surrounded the Temple on its ten acres, if the Elders I would meet with consider me, if not one of them, at least worthy of consideration and assistance in how to build my Temple. Inside, the edifice were marks of the Temple of Solomon, a large baptismal bath, water that mirrors the symbolism of the Molten Sea ; and, there is a Holy of Holies as well. The structure is larger than the Temple by a few feet in height. From the ground to the base of the angel, Moroni, it is 210 feet or 120 cubits; for Solomon's Temple, base to ceiling is only 200 feet or 100 cubits. Still, this was built as the other Mormon Temples to be the "house of God", it was not merely a building.

When Brigham Young came to the Great Salt Lake, he walked the area by this creek, and in his first four days, picked this exact spot as the location for Gods House. He broke ground in 1853, and forty years later it was dedicated. And it happened, even with, battles with the United States, including the Utah War, where the elders had the foundation stones buried, so the marauding army would not notice the outline of the temple perimeter. The faith grew, even under persecution, and the Temple was done.

As I was escorted to the Executive Director of the church's Temple Department, I was uncommonly nervous and apprehensive. Elder William Leavitt, was from central casting, he was slim with closely cropped grey hair, a square jaw, and perfect teeth, white like the dried salt of the great lake. He could have been a Marine colonel, but he commanded the site selection, subcontracting and completion of every Temple built. He was neither abrupt nor warm, but his approach was all business. Yet, it was obvious he knew everything about my journey to build a temple, and seemed reflective about it all.

He started with scripture.

"We build for a purpose that comes from our scripture. We are instructed to build in 2 Nephi 5:16. This not unlike your command by God in 2 Chronicle 5:1-14 or most obviously in 1 Kings 7. And we construct our temples with strict standards, and the highest quality materials. It can take us two to four years to plan one, and another four years to complete it, although we often go from groundbreaking to dedication in four years."

He was concerned that I referred to the Temple as a replica, and not a true house of God. As others have offered, if you build it, it must be properly done to satisfy the biblical commandments, but, I doubted, I could ever raise enough funds to really gold inlay the walls, create the menorahs of gold, buid with cedar logs, and find enough sandstone and granite to install that would be carted to the desert by train and carried overland by trucks. He was adamant about this point, that building a replica was foolish.

"MAC you may think what you are building is not the actual Temple, and that is true. But, you cannot build what is in Kings or Chronicles, without abiding by the will of the author. You either are doing this for him, or you are not. If you are the man of God, you contend, if that mark below your eye, is a symbol of the priesthood, you must get in touch with what is happening."

He was willing to assist me, in finding contractors, and took me in to meet the Chief Church Architect, Jack Williams. Williams had the carriage and shape of an NFL interior lineman. But, his voice was soft and inviting. He had a large blueprint of the renderings of the Temple of Solomon in front of him, and seemed conversant on every aspect of the building. His greatest concern was sending me to a subcontractor who could manage the intricacies of the construction. It was all right angles and fairly simple construction, but, he expected that steel would substitute for the cedar superstructure, and that not all the walls would be pure stone. He thought it would make sense to have a half face stone façade, covering concrete and wood underpinnings. The design was as stipulated by Kings, and was something, he thought any contractor of his could handle.

Fundamentally, the Temple itself, not Solomon's adjacent palace had a few steps up to the doors, two large columns, Boas and Jachin, made of copper, brass, or bronze. They were black, and stood in front but separated from the walls. They alone were six feet around and 27 feet tall, and the top ornament was another eight feet. Or in the Torah, 18 cubits high and 12 cubits around. The cap pieces had rows of pomegranates, and lilies.

The doors were of olivewood, and had upon them intricate carvings, as did the doors to the Holy of Holies where the ark was placed, under the gaze of two enormous Cheribum. The Temple itself a long building with varying levels. The ceiling at 100 cubits, and an Altar for sacrifice, and steps to the Holy of Holies. Outside the Temple was an inner court for priests, a massive bowl of water, for priests to bathe, mounted upon the statues of twelve oxen, called the Molten Sea. More altars for sacrifices, housing for priests, and stewards surrounding the actual sanctuary.

Williams went through each drawing, quoted Kings, Chronicles and Ezekiel. As he turned the pages and placed them on his designing table, I was overwhelmed by the details. I saw in my minds eye the Temple, the columns, the walls in gold color, the central altar, the holy place and then, the Holy of Holies. But he saw it all, a direct interpretation of scripture, and that it could be built.

"MAC its four to seven years, like the original. But, they cut all the stones at the quarry and then only had to put them in place. And, David had collected material for the inside, and they crafted the rest under Zadok's supervision. So, there were two major groupings, the masons and exterior builders and the artisans. But, the columns, the large Cheribum, and the Menorahs were done by separate craftsmen. We can build that structure in four, but what goes inside especially if it is to be authentic, will take more time. So call it seven years, like Solomon waited from shovel in the ground to the dedication ceremony."

Here I was now, a healthy, and seemingly ageless 75, facing seven years, or more to see the Temple realized. Williams knew it was not what I had wanted to face. They built the modern Temples in four year, two for planning, and two building. This project had its own complexities, and the choice of just how authentic to make it. I was already struggling with the comments of Elder Leavitt, that I could not avoid the reality that this not the actual Third Temple, it still had to be built with the purpose and heart of the actual edifice. All this time, I had held out that I was some secular Jew, with an obsession, when I instead was a transformed, secular Jew, who was becoming, the true descendant of Aaron, and charged with a broader destiny, than I was afraid to admit or imagine.

Williams offered me list of his contractors and another list of artisans with skills to create the designs for the interior. He suggested, that I build it using modern techniques and tools, to speed completion. That Ark, in Tennessee was built with the techniques and tools of the time. They had something to prove, about could the Ark as depicted in scripture be realized, he whispered, you don't. He handed me a floor plan of offices and pointed to a door, number 1893, of someone the Church would allow me to employ as a consultant on my project.

The door had a nametag on it. Polly Angell. Architect.

It was right at the corner of the hallway, that was brightly filled with LED lights.

A tall woman with long brunette hair, braided into a single pigtail, and a wind –worn face, extended a long fingered hand, and crushed my knuckles together in a shake. She had a powerful, almost person on a stage volume, voice, that suggested an optimistic outlook. As the others, she knew my tale and required no background, and launched immediately into what she could offer. Which was oversight, occasionally at the compound, but, she would be in constant touch with our chief of the project. I hid my embarrassment, as not having a chief or anyone else to assist.

She also had her biblical history to offer context. King David had wanted to build the Temple, but he was a warrior and shed too much blood, but he also was a man of desire who consorted with Bathsheba, she surmised. A more modern Lord might have forgiven him Bathsheba, but not the God of wrath. So David went to King Hiram the Phoenician, who ruled Tyre, and began to assemble the raw materials, and later it came to Zadok to find more than cedars, but gold, and woods to create the Temple, as God required it. To Polly, this Temple must built like those of Brigham Young according to a celestial vision as expressed through men.

Polly knew something of this. Her most storied namesake and great grandfather, Truman Osborn Angell was the church's first and most acclaimed architect. He oversaw the creation of the Salt Lake Temple, and watched over it through many other projects for, 35 years. In so doing, he buried three of his children, a wife, and sacrificed his life to his brother –in – law Brigham Young. Such devotion and competence served the church well in those early years, even going to Europe, to study techniques and bold new styles. He was the consummate man committed to his work and its realization.

Yet, he did not live to see the great Temple dedicated. His greatest achievement he gave with his life to posterity. Polly would have none of my morose babblings. She noted my youthful face and clear blue eyes, and thought that between us we would have Solomon's Temple in the desert and we all would be there for its dedication.

She asked for a final blueprint to be drawn, and assignments given to my team to divide the labor of masons, stone cutters, electricians, interior designers and steel men. She also wanted a budget. The San Diego, "big Temple" cost 25 million, 30 years ago, what was our estimate on this project 100 million, or what? I nodded, pretending that I had a clue on any of it.

I drove to the Salt Lake, stripped down, and floated, like I was in the Dead Sea, right next to a family from Elko, Nevada, with three screaming kids. Their mother's appellation, "Get your damn ass out of the water, right now, I have lunch" pushed reality into my face.

I was finally near the actual starting point of it all. Did I have the courage to move forward, or would I just continue to float, in an imagined sea in my mind?

CHAPTER XII

❖❖❖

PEYOTE MIND

At a bus stop by a settlement in Israel, the normal sounds of morning stir with the hum of vehicles and the loud voices of people in motion, instructing each other to move or meet. There is no more sense of doom, or impending calamity than on any other street, in the country. Three IDF soldiers, with the faces of very young men, carry their rifles casually on a strap over their shoulders as they walk away with the nonchalance of carefree youth.

A man as young as they, Itamar Ben- Gal, a scholar and Rabbi, waits content to be away from his four children and pregnant wife. It is a moment of some serenity.

Another young man, at 19, an Israeli citizen, raised by a Palestinian father, Ais Abed- El- Hakim, is not serene. He awoke with a mission in his mind, that he could not avoid. His life of struggle, only to be balanced by a deed of vindication. So, he comes behind the Rabbi, pulls a knife and stabs him, until blood covers his hands; and then, as quickly as the deed is done, he flees.

The sirens overtake all the other sounds. The screams of grief are drowned out by the Mogen David teams, far too experienced in saving victims of terrorism, in this part of town. But, there is no saving, Itamar Ben- Gal. By the time, an EMT declares him dead, Hamas has already issued a note of praise for the bravery and resolve of Ais Abed- El- Hakim.

I see blood, hear the sirens. And awake with my UCLA T- shirt soaked.

These vivid dreams are more frequent, often, linked to nothing, but seem, prophetic.

No matter, how I want to be just a man out to build the Temple of Solomon, I know that I am not. Each year the transformation seems more biblical, inspired by something within, but, attached to something not of me, that I cannot reach, control or conjur.

There is a desert trail that is familiar now to me. I run it after these episodes to reset my mind for the day. The dreams do not return. I hope for divine guidance, and no voice speaks to me, I have seen strangers here. Some have helped, others are just strangers. I learn only what a trail can tell you. Adjust your gait to the terrain, do not impose your will on it. Each stone requires recognition, the one you do not see is the one that will crack open your forehead, and require twenty stitches after you fall. The trail will tell you how much time you will spend on it, and who you will encounter.

A cloudless sky encourages the longer run, stretches of sand slow me to a walk, and I see two back packers, off the trail, smoking, and eavesdrop on them. The aroma is of some pot, and I turn voyeur, as one mounts the other, like desert sheep, and thrust themselves to some unity with each other and the universe. As much, as I want to leave, I await the orgasms, the after the moment smoke, and then with a smirk, head back.

The simplicity of that moment, brings me to tears, as I lope back to the trailhead. Desire, enjoyment, and accomplishment in a carnal act. Whatever else, they were about, for that friction in the desert, they were about the act, and nothing more. No mere thing, not grandiose, or of a legacy, just, of the moment. A glimpse of happiness and joy. Traits that were lost to me in this quest, which is what brought about the tears, or was it instead, that happiness and joy, where never on my life lists. More that I think, than not. Still, I let the tears flow and dry, untouched on my face. The mark burns as the tears flow, a feeling, I have not noticed, but, then, when was the last time I cried?

I end it, at the Zorro, and the front desk. Joey pulls out a plastic 7/11 bag, and tells me it was given to him by a young man, with a black hat and coat, who told him he knew me, I was his son's Godfather. He seemed benign, but Joey checked it out, fearing a bomb, finding only a book, unbound. I took it and retired to room 36, to tub, shower and dress.

THE VOYNICH CODEX

The father of the boy, I helped birth, that Chabadnik, delivered, a 240 page facsimile, of a 600 year old book, that no one can read. It was written in the 1400's by an unknown writer and illustrator. Some considered it an elaborate hoax, cryptographers saw it as the ultimate codex to unravel, and mystics, mostly Jews claimed it had a single secret to reveal that only a true tzadik could see, one of those walking the earth at all times to hold it together and encourage its improvement and renewal before God. My Chabad father seemed to hold me in such regard, and offered this rendition of the codex, with a note:

"MAC, There is an answer here, to a question only you know"

As I thumbed through it, the patterns of the text and the illustrations were not mysterious. They seemed to be clusters of items about herbs and plants; the planets and astronomy; and women, mostly naked, bathing in some undefined liquid. The text was unintelligible to me, but, I knew that recent experts had applied Artificial Intelligence programs to it, and, found that it was, to the surprise of some, Hebrew with letters contorted or turned around, and with special spaces like the Torah. Still, the AI was, only one theory, and only that.

But, some one of group, took their time to craft this. Which, seemed to my untrained eye to be a rant of a document, an unhinged, drug or fever inspired escapade to drive out demons or contain them. The figures were oddly crafted and seemed more demonic than sensual, frenzied than joyful. It had the look and feel of one of my sweated dreams, than a book of clues.

That it had survived as a document did suggest to me some mystery. It could not be read, it was unremarkable as a work of art. Its power was that it was not deciphered. A codex of an unknown writer and a language, if there was one, with secrets to reveal. And Wilfrid Voynich in 1912 had it in his collection of odd books, and then it went from library to library, until it could not be sold, but only studied.

My tattered lost book of Rebbe Nachman of Breslev had given me direction, and purpose. There was clarity to it, that was routed in God, good works, and joy. This codex had only these illustrations on ancient vellum of plants and leaves, thick bellied women, and stars, everywhere stars. Perhaps it was not the text, at all, that had my answer to the unknown question.

I drove the facsimile to Maqroll, so he and Madrid could feel it. They had intuitive instincts that far exceeded mine. I asked Madrid to focus upon the pictures and not the text. For textual help, I would contact Gonzalo Rubio, the scholar star of such ancient languages, at Penn State University. He studied the codex and was not convinced AI had unlocked the language or the code, or, if there was one to be found.

Maqroll seemed confident that these drawings had a meaning that would speak to him, but not in this reality. He would summon the help of a spirit world, with his buddies in the Sonoran desert, where they would sit in a hut, warmed by fire, and chew mescaline buds for power. Madrid would do the same with a collection of naguals, women with deep transcendent powers. But, he wanted me to be with him for that journey. I was hesitant, since my current, unassisted reality, was enough to interpret and bare. But, I agreed to attend.

He jumped off the ground, and waved the 7/11 bag in the air, and circled it and the codex copy within, around his head, and offered a few screams and hoots. Madrid looked upon him in silence, and with a smile, pulled him away from me, back into his studio with a wave.

THE COMPOUND

Polly never seemed far away. She was irrepressible on the project. I received detailed plans and construction diagrams. Her calculations on the structure size and interior, all came from biblical sources, and the renditions of many biblical historians. She saw a Temple that was 60 cubits long and 20 cubits high. The structure itself, not the outer chambers that were created for the priests, nor the grounds, had a porch, the Holy Place, and then the Holy of Holies. Boaz and Jachin columns were 53 cubits atop the outer porch.

Polly created an animation of a visual walk through the Temple, and it revealed, much of what I wondered how we would replicate any of it. The walls showed no outer stone, they were of cedar word, some carved, with almonds and flowers, all gold plated. Outer chambers surrounded the Temple. The doors to the Holy of Holies was also gold-plated wood and carved. Inside the Holy of Holies there were two cherubim 10 cubits high with ten cubit wing spans. The gold wings meeting over the Ark.

It was not intricate building the structure. It was basically a large rectangle with high walls and porches. The more difficult choice was what materials to use to replicate the actual Temple of Solomon. For Polly, this was unlike the LDS projects, where each Temple was the actual house of God and a unique and prayer filled edifice. This was between a real Temple and an attraction. And it weighed upon her.

Such a weight brought Roberto to me. Somehow, this revolutionary found his way from the W to Barcelona and now walking towards me at the compound. Looking like a starved soldier walking with swagger out of the jungle, reminiscent of Vinegar "Joe" Stillwell, after his retreat from Burma to Assam, India on foot. Roberto had a black beret, pulled over his right ear and a 30.06 carbine in his right hand. A blueprint travel tube slung over his shoulder, holding every version of the Temple plans he could gather from any source he could find.

"Shalom, MAC."

"What's with the rifle, there are no fascists around here !"

"Really ? I know your reputation, and I know of your not so friendly neighbors. I'll have it by my work table"

He got into the ATV and drove the perimeter of the inner wall, seeing that Izzy had the corners built from large stones, and that the plum lines were in place to finish the job. Then he drove me to the center of the site, and asked me to walk with him towards its center. He put me near what, he thought might be dead center of the acreage, and asked me:

"MAC I am walking away from you. I want you to find the place for the Holy of Holies"

I became silent. Two men alone in this desert space. Activity on the periphery seemed to stop, there was no sound except for a gentle wind blowing across my right ear. Yet, as I walked a faint whistle grew louder, when I retreated it grew faint again. I knew this sound, I had heard it, and dismissed it on the Temple Mount. I was walking towards it, when an Israeli soldier forced me to back away, as I venture into restricted space.

The whistle continued to increase in volume, with a whine, like the one we did as kids mocking the dropping of a WWII bomb. When the sound was at its apex, before the explosion, I stopped, as did the whistle. I looked up and found myself, not dead center, at all, but some yards away from the center. Roberto came to me, and placed a gold colored stake in the ground.

"So, MAC. This the Ark, and from here all else we will build"

BORREGO SUN OFFICE
CHRISTMAS CIRCLE

Old man Kittle had owned the only paper in this unincorporated area of San Diego county for five decades. His son was more citrus farmer, than publisher, but, he could stir up the 3500 full time residents when he felt the urge. He wore starched shirts, and suspenders most of the time, a bowtie to underline his eccentricities, and still had all his hair and the strong face of a founding WASP.

He knew a stirred pot, when he came across it. The old guard split between some old school, hotel men, their golf courses, and the farmers, had a universal dislike of me. While, I had brought actual income to the town, I had also brought people from all over, all skin colors, and all faiths. And, some thought the mayhem over water use, while exaggerated, and illegal, still was a reason to create some zoning issue or nuisance ordinance that would send me and my Temple dreams packing.

This gathering was an unofficial meeting, hosted by Kittle to have a "fair airing "of grievances. I had no patience for this, but Double A and Maqroll knew most these folks, and I had Polly and Roberto with their plans to, hopefully, show them that we had a plan that would enhance the region, and put the town on the map for a very special purpose. No one here could take a vote or railroad any of it, only the five county, supervisors in San Diego could do that, and they seemed to rarely weigh in on land use issues unless it crossed into protected land, spoiled the environment or sucked water out of the already depleted aquifer.

Double A had dated the district supervisors, communications chief, Roy Zaslov, and he was there, to defend his bosses approval of our project. Zaslov started the meeting laying out the rules of play. The land was deeded to us, it was far away from any other development. Our plans had allowed for water wells, and sustainable energy from solar panels; security was not a public expense ; and all our applications with the State, were in process, including a final environmental impact report.

Kittel raised the concerns of security that lit up the crowd. They thought our presence was a magnet for vandals of all types, anti- religious attacks, and just demonstrations. The long lines of cars through the town had changed its nature, even, if it created viable commerce and new business. These were angry men, and a few women. The type who hold their sense of the world and their place in it, firmly. Intellect and sense, evaporates as the primal scream emerges, that you are unsettling the order of things. And as an unstated theme, except for one old gal,

"who asked you Jews to come here anyway. You don't have enough places to build your synagogues... your Temples."

Nobody gasped, but Kittle smoothed it over. It wasn't about faith, it was more about turning this quiet place into a showplace, that brought strangers, new ideas, and even a, certain, reverence for God.

Polly and Roberto calmed the room with their colorful exhibits, and her physical presence and strong voice was reassuring. Roberto was quirky and funny, but also, masterful, in showing how the building would be accomplished in stages, and truck traffic and heavy gear kept to a minimum. His mastery of the process combined with Polly's background and manner, made a powerful rebuttal to the NIMBY's.

In fact, the opposition was not about any of it. It was about change. There may have been some devoted anti-Semites, some who believed I would destroy their town with violence and drugs, but most I believe were afraid of the next thing, and a future of unknowns.

I gave no speech, quietly worked the room after the presentation. Kittle seemed pleased, and would write a front page piece on the meeting. They took pictures with MAC. I came to their place, a confused middle aged, secular Jew. And I was now a transformed, man, a religious eccentric, determined to have the Temple of Solomon rise in their desert, promising the blessings of the Lord.

They believed it more than I. Neither the Temple of Zadok, nor that of his progeny ended well. How could I guarantee that this one would have a different fate?

POTAM, SONORA DESERT

Maqroll brought us here to a Yaqui village, for a cleansing and peyote trip, that, he was certain would reveal the secret of the Voynich codex or something else. This village is mostly desert dust, scrub, some outcroppings of ancient Lophhophora williamsii, with its powerful mood altering drug, mescaline. One of seven villages left, of the Yaqui, who unlike other indigenous groups have kept their rituals and rites separate from the dominant Spanish influence. It is the Cul de Sac of the broad Sonoran desert, where Anglo's have come for centuries to slip into altered states.

It is the imagined village, I saw, as a teenager reading, Carlos Castaneda, and his journey with Don Juan, the Yaqui warrior, through his own transformation into wolf and eagle. His, so called, anthropology, was more likely a carefully crafted philosophical outlook that was revealed, in part, through peyote induced trips. Yet, it is not so easy, now, to dismiss it all as fiction. Perhaps, he tapped into another stream of consciousness, that only reveals itself for certain people, on certain missions. For all he was, if fiction, elevated him and his works to a legacy status, worthy of something. When he died, in obscurity, in 1998, it is said, a Yaqui, woman nagual, who was a keeper of the shaman traditions, took his ashes out here, and a wind came and blew his ashes into the dust of the desert.

The setting seemed authentic enough. The shaman who led us into the small sweat lodge, was an unremarkable old man, who offered unintelligible utterances. The lodge routine was not a Yaqui tradition, but the village entrepreneur thought it a worthwhile addition that helped spike his fee for the afternoon and evening escapade. We entered clothed, and removed our T-shirts as the half hour exposure commenced.

Maqroll had pulled only four pages from the folio, of the Voynich codex. When he actually sorted through the package, there were 240 pages, and ten more. He could not know that all the books and copies and analysis of the Voynich had only 240 pages. The pages he pulled were random, perhaps, part of the codex, of pages that did not survive the ages, but here they were.

One had many leaves, trees, and renditions of greenery.

Another, several stout, women naked, seemingly suspended in water.

The third, a cluster of stars and many, many dots surrounding them.

And finally, A series of humps that looked liked mountains and an enormous sun.

Maqroll had them in a sealed food bag, so they wouldn't warp in the heat. I had their images fixed in my mind, as we sat an heard low murmured chants. Water was thrown on the rocks at the halfway point, discomfort began to overtake any great thoughts. All these cleansings were, of course, more about the participants, belief than anything else. Biologically there is no cleansing, toxins get out in other ways, or penetrate tissues.

Sweat is just that, sweat. Discomfort only that.

There was no opening here, just discomfort.

The shaman stood over the rocks and poured a small pail of water upon them.

They exploded.

Pieces of rocks, flew like shrapnel at all of us. Maqroll had blood on his face. I put my hand across my face to wipe off the sweat and my hand was covered in blood from facial wounds. The shaman was on his back with his hands over his eyes.

We flushed our wounds with clear water, and took a hose to the shaman's face. He could see, but he had second degree burns around his eye sockets, and one of his bushy eyebrows was gone.

He stood and put his hand on my shoulder and smiled, then turned to Maqroll and did the same, then without a word or sound, he walked away with two women, and when I turned to call them back, they were gone.

We recuperated in a wooden cabin, with a hard dirt floor. One the table between the beds, was Dos Equos, and two bowls of a rice and bean dish. And a bottle of pure grain alcohol, that we could drink or wipe on our wounds. Maqroll ate and drank hardily, as would a man relishing his adventure. I had hoped for me, and was pensive awaiting my commitment to a trip on mescaline.

The rock explosion was hardly a sign. Rocks that are not bone dry, especially those from lakebeds or rivers often do explode, when heated. This experience was more lack of preparation and vigilance than shamanic epiphany.

DESERT NIGHT

I grew up without a night sky. The city lights usually obliterated most nights, all but the most obvious and prominent constellations, but, then, how much did I seek the stars? So centered on studies, and success, and the vagaries of experiences of developing life, I was always distracted. There is an egocentric pulse that is your heartbeat. No time for faith, contemplation, and certainly not God. Whatever, your destiny is to be, seems met as you click off one accomplishment after another, attempt to avoid emotional damage, make a living, have children, and struggle with life. The night sky becomes a mere backdrop, a moon linked to a romance, a constellation tied to a memory, its brilliance more like Mona Lisa at the Louvre 'than part of a life, certainly not, your life.

Now, as I cannot sleep, I splash the grain on my face, and it stings, like my Aqua Velva, after those boyhood shaves. I walk out, into a natural planetarium. The sky so full of stars and constellations, and clusters and clouds of matter, that I finally just lay my back on a broad rock, and gaze into it. Usually, when I am out amongst the universe, I feel inept, miniscule, and my Temple dream, a useless obsession.

Yet, this night, I feel differently.

I believe it will be built, that we will find a way. I also know that I will suffer more, because I cannot let go of it. But, that is not the concern, for this is something more than the eccentric fixation of an aging Jew, with a legacy complex. As much, as I want to deny it, I am moved to do this from something outside of me, now part of me, somehow, epigenetic.

Or, is it just a type of lunacy, that some of us get. A rare form to be sure. A belief that overtook Elijah and the prophets, The Prophet, Joseph Smith, Moses and Aaron, Christ even Abraham. All merely men of no genetic rarity, who became imbued with a mission inspired by a prophet, an angel, or a voice or sign. Yet, even such lunacy, explainable by any neuroscientist, as a right brain disorder, cannot avoid the cosmic chasm between what we know and do not now about this universe and others.

What we know it is there. What I cannot see this night, astronomers can. Back 35 billion light years, they say there are 2,000, unknown planets. And is that the perimeter of what we call our universe, are there more as vast and unknown. Do they have their own one, sentient planet? A god, they believe in more so than not ? Is there some man hoping to erect some structure of meaning, lost through war and hate?

Night skies turn the mind towards all of that. But, it all fades as do the stars.

With the dawn, I see Maqroll shaking me awake, from my sleep atop the boulder.

"MAC, Boss. It is time to eat Peyote"

THE TRIP TRAILER

A Winnebago was the unexpected place for this peyote trip. A Mexican couple, in their 20's, escorted me in the RV. They spoke to me in English, and explained that this was a twelve hour trip, and I had to stay in the van or on the property. The woman taped the pictures to the wall, the table, and the main bed. They said there would be water, but, no food. And there were no utensils, and only a paper cup. After they gave me two buttons to chew, then I would drink a tea of the buttons boiled.

They said the sensations would come and go, but a vision would come by the third hour, and more after that. The buttons would be very, very bitter, but the altered state would soon rid me of all earth bound tastes and feelings. I was assured I would be safe, although my mind would most likely think I was in grave danger, if the trip turned bad. There was no way to know, but, good men had good trips, or bad trips turned good.

They would be outside in lawn chairs, watching satellite television, and Maqroll was in his truck, texting, eating, and talking to Madrid.

The women came into the trailer with a paper cup of tea. The man opened his hand, cupping three peyote buttons from the cactus. Chew these, then drink the tea. Find a place to sit, and we will get you in 12 hours.

They left. I had three buttons on the table, and the tea. I paused, long enough to form the obvious negative thought, "What the hell am I doing", but let it go.

What I remember is this.

I was feeling nausea, it faded. I grew drowsy and then dreamy.

The entire trailer dissolved into colors of tan and brown, and black, The walls poured away, as did the sink and the table, and turned into a river of color, running through my mouth and out my ass. It seemed an endless cleansing of color, and was hot. My body in the mirror was fire engine red. My eyes colorless, emitting light.

I am pulled into a cauldron of water with small women, who are unfazed by the heat of the water. I am at once boiling and dying, and then become frigid, yet erect and penetrate the ten women, eternally, only to be lost in a sea of hot semen.

I was inside a globe of greenery, and huge mouths, ringed in green lipstick, were eating the greens, and I was anxious and fearful that one mouth would chew me, for I was a lizard, green in color, and unable, as I struggled, to camouflage and change coloration. The globe exploded, into absolute dark space. There was movement, but I could not move, I screamed, but there was no sound. I screamed until a single star appeared, and it captured me, drawing me into its space. And I collapsed there.

And then, I was awake. In a vast untouched desert, dune after dune. Airborne as a grand eagle passing over enormous stretches of land, over dinosaur sized lizards, and snakes, and scorpions. Then to a flat area surrounded by caves.

I fly into a cave. Then I land on the arm of a man dressed in white linen and his head covered with a keffiyeh.

A nuclear bomb explodes and I am turned into particles, reassembled and dropped here.

What Maqroll tells me he observed.

I was in the trailer for eight hours. It was filled with vomit and excrement. The walls are spotted with semen, and my urine on the floor.

Outside, I walk for three hours, mostly in circles, throwing sand on myself. I eventually sit in a hole and chant, Hebrew prayers, then go silent. Take off all my clothes, and fall asleep.

Maqroll pays the couple. I shower, look at the small mirror, and see the same face, I saw years ago at the trailer in Borrego. I have not aged, frozen in a body of a robust 65, 13 years later, the Mark of Aaron has not faded. And what this may mean, if anything, may seem unclear.

But it is not. I know what I must do, and when. And it is not now. So, I must keep my revelations to myself.

CHAPTER XIII

❖❖❖

FROM SANHEDRIN TO SUPERIOR COURT

Izzy is agitated. She is concerned that attendance is waning at compound events as construction is about to begin. And her debate with Roberto over what the Temple outside walls will be made of, is disturbing her vow of being authentic to the actual building of Zadok. Roberto, ever, the realist and steward of every penny, wants to us steel for the superstructure, and composite material on the outer walls, and a faux stone cut in large stone motifs. Izzy wants the stones to be actually quarried, and brought here to be moved into place.

While, I would prefer the Izzy solution. It was more than expensive, it would require a number of quarries to cut the stone, and even, then, I assured her it would not possibly be authentic. God ordered and Zadok provided stones that were not touched by metal implements. Our only option would be wooden mallets, or pressurized water, acid carving, or even high intensity lasers. All not only prohibitive, but difficult to find the craftsmen.

Fran had plotted a new concert idea for gospel groups that would return bus traffic, and she also had convinced a documentary group to offer a large scale project on the Temple that would hopefully win Sundance next winter. But, her contacts continued to support this underdog project, and gave me the occasional opportunity to have a national audience, and filter more funds into the war chest.

Between the four of us, Thursday night meetings were raucous events. I demanded that I sing a few prayers, and that we ended with Adon Olam, holding hands in the back yard, at full voice, and the dogs barking along. It is short piyut, or poem. I learned the 10 line version as an Ashkenazic Jew. It is the essential statement of my faith in an eternal and present God:

To me it was always Adon (master) Olam (of the universe)

As it Begins:

The Lord of the Universe who reigned before anything was created

Adon olam, asher malach, b' terem kol y'tzir nivra

And so it Ends:

To him I commit my spirit, in the time of sleep and awakening, even if the spirit leaves

God is with me, I shall not fear.

B'yado afkid ruchi, b'et Ishan v'a'irah.

V'im ruchi g'viyati,

Adonai li v'lo ira

This night as we sing, tolerance and compromise prevailed. Roberto agreed to a foundation and first row of quarry honed granite. Izzy agreed to the faux rock, that she would supervise for look and feel. We all agreed on the steel, instead of timbers, and that all olive wood and other carvings come from actual wood carved by artisans, or machines on treated plastic molds.

This night broke the barrier of actual from replica. It would not certainly satisfy Aaron, Moses, or the current holders of jewish orthodoxy, for the house where "he would dwell", but that had never been our goal or my mission. When, it was time for the actual Third Temple to appear or be re- built neither cost nor materials will be at issue. If the prophecy's are right, when it will happen it will be done. This is not about such biblical injunctions, only mere mortals efforts to offer this to current generations, in these "between times".

TEMPLE OF THE DESERT INN

Joey was sitting with a man who had come from Tel Aviv to meet with me. His topic was not the Temple, he told Joey, but something more. I rarely took any meeting that was not precisely about the project, yet, he flew here, and Joey had vetted him as a prominent developer of high rise buildings globally, and a student of ancient Jewish history.

He was 6' 5, at least, looked like Jerry West, but larger. Joey looked small at his most military posture, and I at a measly six feet, felt very small in Issac Delek's presence. I joked about the NBA, and he admitted he played, but poorly, still he bet he could beat me a playground pick up game. I declined the challenge.

Joey ventured the actual topic of his appearance. It was, said Joey, about the Jewish super court, the Sanhedrin. I corrected him, of course. The Sanhedrin had not existed since 425 BCE, when a Roman emperor ended it, outlawed it, and also made it against the law to ordain rabbi's. It was a Court of 70, plus the chief of it called, a NASI, or President. They existed to interpret law, and even held sway over the High Priest, at least, until, the Second Temple was destroyed. And after the revolt of Simon bar Kokhba, 132 CE, the Sanhedrin was allowed by the Romans to keep the Jews in line, but, it little power beyond daily interpretations and rule making. Bar Kokhba had declared himself NASI for three years, before his revolt was crushed. In his fortress of Betar, thousand were killed, including children at their schools.

One school had over three hundred skulls stacked on a pyre, all stabbed by a soldiers spear, then wrapped with their religious books, and burned. But from one school a boy escaped the carnage.

Simeon ben Gamliel became a NASI himself, after the revolts, the President. And it was of his family through to Gamaliel V, who was the last of the line of the court of 70 men, this Grand Sanhedrin. Under the Gamliel's, through periods of austerity, persecution, and prohibition from many pursuits, they kept the faithful together, and satisfied the Roman need to manage the Jews, even as Christianity morphed from an abhorrent faith to become the faith of the Empire.

For Issac, my history lesson was a comfort. He was gratified that I was a man with awareness of my own history. Yet, he was undaunted, in his belief that a renewed Sanhedrin would help stabilize, not only Jewish history, for generations, but, also give the world hope that Judaism would survive, to allow events of prophecy to unfold. He was not touting the Revelation, nor the Second Coming, but, he did fervently want Jews around to receive the real Messiah. His fear was that without a board of men and women to steer the law, the faith, the 15 million of us, could evaporate, either from another massive wave of repression as in the twentieth century, or a more virulent attack in cyberspace from trolls and neo- Nazi's. And then, the natural dissolution from low birth rate and intermarriage.

Issac accepted my obvious reply that others have tried to bring it back. I rolled off the dates 1538,1830, 1901, attempted by Aharon Mendel HaCohen, and the after war in 1949, to coincide with the birth of Israel. All failed.

He called me on leaving out Napolean, who set up a Sanhedrin in 1806 with much fanfare. We agreed is more a ruse than actual recognition of Jews from France to Poland. It failed before his revolution and Empire unraveled at Waterloo.

To Issac there was synergy between building the Temple and heading the Sanhedrin. He saw it as secular move, more like my project, less religious. Still it would be a marker of a continuous history, uninterrupted with a body that could steer the tribes, so to speak.

Before, I could decline, he launched into more history, and transported us to 363 BCE, and Julian, the Roman. Who actually seemed devoted to rebuild the Temple, on the Temple Mount. He began it, encouraged a new Sanhedrin, then a fire started on some of his supplies and material. Small but persistent. And there also was an earthquake in Jerusalem that year. That some Jews saw as an act of YHWH. But most historians believe the Jews were happier without the Cohen Gadol, the tithes, and the Temple. As long as the Romans stopped killing and enslaving them, life was bearable. They could find a path to the Lord on their own. But, Issac, offered with a smile, that he tried.

Joey had brought wine for Issac and a cola for me to sip. It was an entertaining few hours of give and take. Yet, I had the most important fact, that would I hoped gently end his quest for me. All the NASI, were descended from Hillel, and then by King David.

I was lowly, Levi tribe, keeper of the Tabernacle and the Temple. A second level Cohanim, brother to Moses, not to be Cohen Gadol. From Zadok, not Hillel, and certainly not King David.

Issac demurred, but a committed Cohen, even a Levite, who could build this Temple, would be accepted by the worldwide Sanhedrin, that he imagined. I could not share his enthusiasm, knowing the orthodox leaders had their own very narrowly cast view of the faith, including the Sanhedrin, the Temple and everything else. In their zeal to save the faith, they were more likely to destroy it. If they could but read the sage, Maimonides, who believed that natural law and circumstances was a better guide for Judaism, than the, old school, mystics and miracle seekers. Perhaps, Issac was not wrong, that a renewed, Sanhedrin, seeped in modernity would help the faith. But I had, the compound and the project, and I had just enough fight for that mission.

Issac gave me a hug, and left for his room. Joey gave me an envelope, that Issac gave him for me, before the session. I opened it, it was a cashiers check for five million dollars. I asked him to get me a single malt.

Superior Court Los Angeles

These were halls worn by my pacing over murder cases, assaults and rapes, and predators of every type. Worn as I awaited the signal the jury had returned. Mostly, the wait was worth the angst, usually we prevailed, the hand of justice firmly around the neck of the bad guys. I thought, I would never be here again, the D.A. and her partner now retired to Belize, one Sheriff died of old age and Alzheimer's, the other fishing with his sons in Alaska, most of the judges also gone, even the boot black, before the metal detector, who called me, "Mr.C", went back home to die near his family, somewhere, in South Carolina.

Here I was again, pacing. Fran keeping the cameras away. The trials of the two shooters long gone, convicted of second degree murder, with life sentences, running concurrently. The head of the gang, Jackson Weathers, convicted of criminal conspiracy, assault with a deadly weapon. But because he cut an early deal, and fingered the killers, got 5-15 with parole. Probably out, in five.

I was here for the verdict on Jonas Stepler, of Stepler Citrus who set this all in motion to get me for taking his water and, for being a Jew, in his neighborhood.

And a big loud neighbor, with tractors, back hoes, and buses of religious folk of all kinds and colors.

His ornery nature just got the better of him one clear skied night, and he paid for the gang to destroy the compound. He did not count on two of his night raiders killing three security guards, the guards out to send more money home to their families, nothing more.

He was charged with conspiracy to commit a crime, aiding and abetting criminals, and another count for hate crime. He could get as much as 25 years. His family and friends overwhelmed the small courtroom. They were in their Sunday finest. More wealthy ranchers than citrus farmers, or land owners. They were loud talkers, and some finger pointers at that man with the white beard, and good posture. If imagined if they were let loose, they'd tar and feather me, old west style, then, write a song about ole' Jonas and sing it a campfire tonight.

The guard motioned us all in.

Judge Weingarten motioned us all to be quiet. And he proceeded:

"Considering the charges against you and the ultimate result of your actions, the law might have a more severe remedy for your thoughtless and hateful act. But, I cannot sentence you to life, because you only created the circumstances where three good men were killed. I can not sentence you solely on the destruction that ensued due to your actions, you did not destroy the property.

But, Mr. Stepler, as assuredly as if you were present, you conspired to do harm, and show no courter. Out of both anger and prejudice, and indeed hate, you took action to frighten and terrorize these people and their project to devoted to understanding biblical history and, their God.

This is a heinous act. A hateful act. And, although, you have no record of ever being outside the law, I cannot send to probation on your farm. I am sentencing you to five years of incarceration for your actions, and you will eligible for parole.

Stepler turned to his family. Some were in tears, one of his boys went to him for a reassuring hug.

In the media area, I was asked for my response and offered only that I thought the sentence was judicious and I praised the prosecution for staying with cases until justice was delivered for the three victims.

The defense offered their outrage at the sentence and felt probation was appropriate, and claimed that he was overcharged and over – sentenced.

I had long ago lost my special parking privileges, the walk through the vast concrete parking lot was hardly a victory lap. I as always felt more satisfaction over the system working than any personal victory. Our talk turned to the delivery of steel to the compound, that next week. Fran and Double A took the front seat, as I began to slide into the back.

I heard the crack of a 9mm, and turned towards the sound, not knowing I was the target, until blood dripped down my right hand and from my leg into my right sock.

I did not see the shooter, only his body frame. The EMT was with me in minutes. The wounds to the lower arm and the right leg by the soleus. This guy was a bad shot. The distance too far for accuracy. Somehow, I held my temper, until I was comfortably in a small room at the hospital. Then as I let the anger release, I heard myself, and stopped.

I was not that prosecutor anymore. I was alive. I had a mission. And all that really mattered was that I be well enough to go forward.

CHAPTER XIV

✺✺✺

FACE TO FACE WITH AARON

THE ZORRO ROOM 36

Healing wounds takes less time than adapting to loss. Overtime, the skin once parted is sealed, the clots form, crust and decay. The old scars turn a marble white, and the bones knit, enough to support what is left of you. In the mirror of this room, there are reflections: a room, filled with building plans, books, and clothes drying on every door and nook, it is a locker room of dreams, about be fulfilled, out there at the compound. But, the mirror doesn't lie.

There is a line above my left eyebrow from the rock explosion in the sweat lodge, two bullet holes, still purple, as they heal on my arm and lower leg. The face, is, otherwise unmarked, and with only the wrinkles of decades ago. And my hair is full and white, as is my beard. I have maintained the darker skin, from hours in the pursuit of the Temple, at the compound.

I have lost nothing of muscle, and the skin still only sags where it did since high school. There is a firm chin, and a neck that will stiffen after a long night of no sleep or lifting a stone, I should have left alone. In all, fit enough for any years granted now, who only sees a doctor when a bullet finds its way into the old man.

And that mark, the Mark of Aaron, has not faded. It stands as it did when discovered a small triangle below my right eye, that will not go away. This genetic blemish that sent me careening into this journey, staring back at me, all these years. At once a tattoo signifying a past, and a sign of what is to come.

160

You expect life will be about adding people, lovers, children, accomplishments, a grand staircase of progression to success or, even a share of some happiness. And, there is that, but there is loss as well. Somewhere along that path of your life, there are fewer in stride with you, not as many behind. The sounds of crying children, laughter, a nighttime sigh next to someone you love, fades. You see other things, hear other sounds, some you missed and others that were always there, drowned out by your cacophony.

Frank is gone to pancreatic cancer. Tina married to a talent agent in West Los Angeles. Most of my male colleagues are long dead from diabetes to brain cancer. There is virtually no malady that has not demolished someone I knew, counted upon, or offered me more in friendship, than I ever gave to them. Then there is son, Gabe, my parents, and every Cohen who sat with me at Passover and hoped to be in Jerusalem next year.

No more plum whiskey for Uncle Usher, or a hug of the young women for Uncle Nate.

Fanny, Tommy, Schmul, Rose, Rosa, Esther, Harry, Jacob the Older and Jacob the Younger, the Rothchild twins, Nate, Sandy, Moshe, Franny, Chas, Brian, Papa Joe, Izzy, Bruce, Rachel, Naomi, and Bunny. Yes, Bunny the card player, optometrist. And a hundred others, who would have thought me simply a lunatic for what I am doing.

I expect they are praying for me. I should say Kaddish for them all, light some candles or start a bonfire. I want to gain some solace and say that this Temple is for them, and it is, in part. But, it is more for those to come, Jew and not. A simple, direct message that there was a glorious place, built by a Jewish King for his God, and all the people. And to walk through will signify that somewhere, there is a memory, and that memory can take shape and become manifest.

There is value to imagination, and virtual experiences, but what hate and prejudice, and might, destroyed can be reformed, even by a simple old man, eccentric enough to believe it can be done.

Roberto knocks and enters, dragging me to the compound.

THE TEMPLE WALL

He wants to build the Tabernacle again, to shield visitors form the heavy work now commencing inside the inner walls. He has installed cameras so they can watch the construction from a viewing area on large screens. But, he hopes he can divert traffic by creating another Tabernacle, and enhancing the visitor experience. We walk to the location and mark off the perimeter.

He has already drawn a new plan for the Tabernacle, that is more historically accurate than our first version. And the opportunity to have his artisans rebuild the ARK and other essentials has his team excited. He can complete it in a week, and wants me to open it with a well organized gathering of builders and architects, so he can parlay that into a conclave on how he will build the Temple, and get some help on the acquisition of special materials he wants to use to improve the look of the interior.

I am driven through the inner gates and get to see the steel rising, and the slabs of stone stacked, awaiting the attachment to the outer wall. The workers are off all backgrounds, race and nationalities, but, the predominate language is Spanish. I am surprised to see that pony tail of Polly's, meeting with the chief of the steel operation. She is speaking Spanish to him, and runs over to hug me, almost knocking me over. She thinks the superstructure will be ready in another few months, and the outer shell done by Christmas.

She thinks by next August, the damn thing will be ready. And she pokes Roberto hard in his side, "if this Basque can hold up his end, that is!"

Zorro 36

Roberto drops me, and I proceed into the room, strip, and jump into the hot tub on the porch. An Eagles song is playing into the night air, from another room. I face the mountains, and stretch the muscles.

The cell phone interrupts.

"This is Uncle Jimmy, Jacob. Jacob"

Pause. I respond knowing this is from the other life.

162

"Ruth is dead Jacob. Died of a stroke, while driving on La Brea"

"OK, Jimmy, what are the arrangements.

"They just wanted you to know. The service is at Hillside Memorial. You know where its at?"

"yeah, yeah, I know, when?"

"Thursday at 1"

"thanks so much Uncle Jimmy for calling"

"just thought you should know, thought you should know"

Now what.

The woman loved and abandoned, divorced and left behind, is gone. Dare I show up at the service and face the family, what is left of it. The recriminations are obvious, and deserved, I could not speak for the hypocrisy of whatever I would say would be seen as disingenuous. My very presence a symbol of a narcissism so vile that they would wish me in the coffin.

Am I such a coward that I cannot face this, after all I have endured. There is no bullet as damaging to my body, as this decision is to my soul. If I chose the wrong path, it will haunt me to me end of days and eternally. Do I have no one who will hear me out, and offer some guidance. Can I not fall on my knees, before YHWH, the ancient one, and find direction. Have I not done enough, to prove my value, enough to answer this one, damn prayer, for forgiveness, and, more for guidance?

I pray, until, exhausted I fall asleep on the bed, with the door open, and the tub boiling.

Dawn

The tub is off. The doors pulled shut. I smell coffee.

There is someone facing the mountain, sitting at the table, drinking a trucker size 64 ounce cup.

I quietly take out my .38 from the nightstand, and walk towards him.

I ask him who to get up and lock his hands over his head. A tall slim man turns, and smiles. He is dressed in blue jeans a black T-shirt, and cowboy boots. He sports a large handlebar mustache, white in color. He is part Sam Eliot and, when he speaks, Jeff Bridges.

"Why don't you put on your pants MAC, and drop the gun, I mean you no harm"

I comply, wash and dress quickly.

"So, who the hell are you fella' a builder, a hired hand, or gun"

"Nope"

I sit across from him, pour some of his coffee into my mug. I notice under his right eye is a somewhat larger triangular mark, same as mine but a bit larger. So, I explain I have a fairly busy day ahead with some very difficult decisions, and I feel asleep looking for some guidance.

"That's why I'm here, MAC"

Not wanting to pander to this fellow or insult him I take the most direct route.

"So who are you, and what can I do for you"

"I am Aaron HaKohen. Brother of Moses and Miriam. From Goshen."

"I was anointed as the first Priest by God in the desert, tended to the Tabernacle, watched over the ARK, and tended to my younger brothers needs as we journeyed across the desert plain. I know you are troubled, so I was summoned, because you are of my line of priests. From me to my youngest Eleazar, through the centuries to Zadok, and from Zadok to you."

"Right, and I'm the King of France"

"Do you doubt me because, I do not resemble those medieval images of me? Or you are afraid to face your faith, and believe that what you have read, studied, and prayed all these years was a fraud. Why am I less real, than anything else.

Is it so unbelievable that God still speaks, that our spirits still roam the earth. Do you not hope, in your most, intimate thoughts, that you just might be one of us, one of the 36 tzadiks? And might you be the one who does something to be remembered for all time. Or be the one turn of the key of history that finally unlocks the true destiny of our people, and, praise be to God, the Messiah, even?"

"Ok, I will play along here, for a while…"

"You are troubled by loss. I know it. Nadah and Abihu, my oldest were burned alive by divine fire, because they did not properly prepare the altar, on the very day of my consecration."

"And what of your humiliation for leaving your wife, what of mine? Moses goes to Sinai and is with Hashem for many, many days. The Israelites construct the Golden Calf, and when Moses returns he smashes the covenant, and God is about to destroy every Jew for all time. Moses saves us, and I cry my only tears that day, when we are forgiven, and it leaves this mark, for all to know of my humiliation."

"My sister Miriam was struck with leprosy for my failings, only to be healed by God, after I pleaded with Moses that I was at fault, not she"

"And now, you doubt yourself and all of this. Do you think, an ordinary man, gets to do any of this without God's guidance. Moses and I grew impatient after 40 years of wandering, and hit the rock at Kadesh. It was, after all, our last year of the pilgrimage. But, no God said to talk to the rock, talk to it, he commanded. Moses hit it. And the price of that was I could not step into the promised land. What price do you pay if you do not complete this, or bury Ruth?"

"Is there a cave atop some Mount Hor for you to die in"

I was beginning to believe that this was Aaron. He knew me somehow. And our conversation became more wide raging, not about the Temple but the faith, and the hand of God. He had beautiful face, and folksy manner. He seemed the kindest of souls and an ally more than a foe. He paced the room, commenting on how he had wished to live longer than 123 years, and actually see a Temple built. But, he admitted he had no idea what it might look like. So I showed him the plans, and the videos. He was aghast at the ornate structure, more like Egypt's monuments to many deities. He thought the Temple would be closer to the people, and the entire display of Judaism, smaller and more like the desert tabernacle.

There was a tension, I could feel, he had between being the boy from Goshen and his brother of Egypt. God needed them both, but wanted neither to plan the next path for his people. He somehow knew that history had him played as the supporting actor to Charlton Heston's, Moses. Still, he spun tales with gusto of his staff, sprouting ripe almonds, the famous staff to snake trickery that impressed the Pharaoh 's priests, and the carrying of the mysterious Urim and Thummim.

"The Urim and and Thummim are stones that are translucent. When I put them in my breastplate, the one with the twelve stones of each tribe, my Hoshen, I could ask a question of law, or the covenant. And I would receive an answer. But, this was not just a Q and A like this, MAC. This was with Hashem. Once the stones were in place, two great beams of light would strike my vest and strike out from the stones towards the sky, and when I would ask, the answer would come as one light died. So I was guided by the light of the Lord."

"And the stones are ?"

"In the desert, lost after the destruction of the First Temple"

The next hour passed into two more. We discussed the Torah, the meaning of the 613 commandments, and life. Frankly, he knew more of that, it seemed than of the texts.

The wisdom of Aaron did not seem more or less unique than another scholarly man. But he was imbued with an aura of certainty that was infectious.

"So, MAC, what are you to do? The Promised land or curl up in a cave?"

"Finish it Aaron, finish it, if God gives me the will and the strength"

"Oh he will MAC, he will."

And with that he put on his black cowboy hat, and put a white stone in my hand, quoting Revelation 2:17

"To the one who is victorious, I will give some of the hidden manna. I will also give that person a white stone with a new name written on it, known only to the one who receives it."

And he was gone.

I turned the rock over in my palm

"Moses Aaron Kohen"

I showered and trimmed the beard, eyebrows, and nose hairs. Packed my best suit and tie, and called Double A to pick me up and drive me to Los Angeles for the funeral service of dear, Ruth.

CHAPTER XV

֎ ✥✥✥ ֎

3Q15

Backyard of Trailer

I have pulled on twenty clays, Lobo hardly stirring in my lap. Fran knocks 18 of twenty with that reliable,16 gauge Mossberg. Double A hits ten of ten, before Maqroll approaches with Izzy excited about something. It seems he has a chance to paint two aging women from Ash Meadows, Nevada, the site of a little shack den of iniquity in Nye County. The are old, but their bodies are wise, and he has no portraits of anyone who spent a lifetime in that profession.

He showed me the pictures, and encouraged me to come meet them. They were of Blaze Starr and Ann Corio size. Both with large hips and thighs, that befit Maqrolls portrait style. They had hailed from Winnemucca, where they started as girls of 14, and made their way to Ash Meadows, when the town turned civil, and lost its frontier spirit, the told him.

They remembered at 18, screwing some of the cast of a Hollywood film, The Reward, filmed at Rhyolite nearby. One thought she saw one of the girls service Efrem Zimbalist, and another Gilbert Roland. Yvette Mimieux sat bemused on a porch chair. Now, they were roaming the West in their RV and heard of Maqroll's place and decided they wanted to be captured in oils. Even in their 70's, they had all that Maqroll wanted to satisfy his artistic, and, still, prurient interests. He planned to paint them against a plush cathouse backdrop of velvet and lace, and turn their bodies alabaster, as if it was 1880.

He handed out the sandwiches and beer, and everyone lunched and Izzy fired off the AK, at the rabbits in the distance, hitting not a one for her 100 round burst. Then, she came to me, with that sullen, frozen face, as if, she was about to throw me, as a sacrifice, into a cenote rimmed with fire.

"We are almost there MAC, but everyone is afraid to tell you we need more cash to complete this by next August, or we wait. Polly knows, Roberto knows it. But they are afraid it will kill you, to know it."

I am about to rise, when Lobo knocks me back into my chair. I motion for Izzy to come closer, and I grab her thick neck, and bring her cheek to my lips.

"I am not angry, nor afraid. I know I will live to see it done. And I have a secret, a place revealed to me, to travel that will fulfill our needs."

Fran looks at me, as though, I am the worst actor on the planet. Certain my reassurances are empty promises designed to encourage, but without substance Usually, she can catch my true spirit. But not this time.

That peyote trip gave me little, but a wild psychic journey, except for the clearest vision of a place, I now knew I must encounter, and fueled by the blessing of Aaron that I would live to see the Temple completed, I could travel without fear of dying, at least.

I was circled by these friends, and they did not want to let me go on some useless excursion from which I would not return. Maqroll stood before me defiant:

"You will not go without me, MAC"

"I will go. And I will not be alone."

And in unison they laughed:

"Yes, God will be with you !"

QUMRAN, THE CAVES

I had this plan, from the moment after, I cleaned up after the trip in the trailer on peyote. I saw caves and miles of sand, and an Arab man standing in a cave amongst others. He was inside the entrance to cave 3. I wrote to the Israel Antiquity Authority, and they sent me to the online renditions of the Dead Sea Scrolls. But, not a single scroll had what I wanted, not the precursors of the text of the Bible, but instead the storied treasure map scroll.

It as the scroll found in the very back of cave 3 in Qumran, the 15th one discovered. But, this not by the, chance and good luck, or divine grace, of the Bedouins, but by John Marco Allegro, a Brit on the 14th of March 1952. It was two scrolls in cooper and some tin, written in a form of Hebrew, that seemed impossible to unravel, let alone decifer.

But JMA, worked with chemists and metallurgists to cut it into 23 strips. And he translated them. Returning the sheets to Jordan for eventual display. It was a curious document because it seemed to locate 63 places, where "talents" of silver and gold where buried in the desert. The location ancient, and seemingly, unknowable. Theories abounded that is was the location of the vestments, the ARK, and the treasures of the Temple of Solomon; others that is was of the Second, and pointed to the Arc Of Titus in Rome, which Romans carrying out an enormous Golden Menorah; and, others that it was just a hoax.

Allegro suffered with it all. What should have been a stunning discovery faded as, but another, unresolved biblical archeological mystery. So, he set out on his own expedition, and over two years roamed the perimeter of Qumran, and the settlements surrounding it. His theory was that 3Q15, was written by the Hebrew sect, the Essenes, who had vowed to be anti- Temple, anti hierarchy, and worshipped God through an ascetic life, and celibacy after birthing their children. He wandered with his crew with only the most primitive investigative tools of axe and shovel, and the translation to guide him.

But, even, this scholar could not make enough sense of the code to find anything but, sand and frustration, at every dig. And who could figure it out with such cryptic entries:

In the ruin that is in the valley of Acor, under the steps, with the entrance to the East, a distant of forty cubits, a strongbox of silver and its vessels, with a weight of seventeen talents. K(Z) N

Each for each panel, the same. A location, some specifics, where to dig, and a mysterious last three Greek letters. And as the years went by, no one came again. If there was an answer the desert locations were buried forever. Some, Evangelical Christian groups came to dig, one or two convinced that if the vestments, and the other Temple artifacts were found, it would signal the start of the Second Coming, since the Third Temple could now be restored. But, eventually, the inquisitive were overcome by the reality of the difficulty. Serious archeologists had much to find in the region that was treasure, merely by being unearthed, pure archaeological discovery. And the Israel Antiquities Authority stopped issuing permits for investigations and surveys of the Qumran area to search for the treasure of the Copper Scrolls.

I was not disheartened. I contacted Dafna Dudai, a rising expert on the region, and a treasure hunter. She agreed to join me in researching the manuscript for any overlooked clues, but also, to enlist the most current technology to map the region. Her close relationship with the man who issues the permits for initial exploration, they dated exclusively for a few years, got use a permit to fly drones over certain sites. And she had finally acquired the most coveted permit, for a fee, to conduct ground surveillance for three months, with she acting as the official IAA broker, if anything was found.

It an undertaking of some size, where she brought two full dig units from her research firm, and contracted with Tom Belzoni to do both the initial drone fly overs and the more intricate Lidar Laser mapping. John Allegro was the scholar, without any technology, we were amateur biblical archeologists with state of the art gear.

Dafna had circled six locations, that aerial mapping indicated had ground anomalies, and that Lidar could help close in on further. We would explore each, and only dig if all indicators gave us some indication of metal or wood below the surface. There was a high confidence level that tons of silver and gold would show up on the scans. But, the area was vast, and shifting sands each night, with searing heat during the day.

Belzoni was himself a monument. A stout 6'4". Solid like a WWE wrestler, with cannon ball shoulders, a Marine haircut, and a SEAL tattoo on his right deltoid. He carted his laser gear into place with his men. But, he spoke with a soft tone, and a distinct Baltimore/ Philadelphia accent. And he was a kid who grew up in South Philadelphia, spoke fluent Italian, and developed the laser at Drexel University, as young phenomenon.

He had helped at the excavation of a Maya site called El Zotz in Guatemala. Lidar revealed kilometers of fortifications they never noticed. It would have taken decades to find them. It uses laser light to sample densely the surface of the earth. Millions of pulses are sent to the ground, every four seconds from a plane, chopper or drone. The wavelengths are then measured with sophisticated algorithms and they, in turn, create three dimensional maps. If it can work in forests, and other landscapes, how will it do in the desert?

Dafna used both the text and the drone maps to attempt find possible targets. But try as we could, there never seemed to be a place in the text that exactly corresponded to the location, we surveyed. Forty five days and three sites, and nothing but, holes, a few leather straps or bindings, a camel saddle, and three modern pistols, circa 1920.

During a three day break, after the Sabbath, I was alone with this sturdy Israeli woman somewhere equidistant from 45- 60. A Sabra, military service, lost two cousins in conflicts, and one served now in a Mogen David rescue unit. Both parents alive one in Tel Aviv and the other a professor at Ben Gurion University in the Negev. She had spent her life roaming, searching for things, treasure, cash flow, success, and, the proverbial love. Unfound for now, and not on her list this year.

We took to short runs at dusk, and a cool tub bath, under the stars. I found I never slept better in the many years than here. I was calmed by her presence, and being in this place that seemed as if I had spent a lifetime here once before.

The fourth place, at first seemed to have promise. The scanners indicated a large perimeter below the surface. And it was to be that, fifteen days of digging a wall was revealed from a settlement of some sort, probably Bedouin, and not Hebrew. But, as we analyzed the wood, it dated to 70 BCE and the few pottery shards, earlier. This was a major find, but, not for us. Belzoni called in the find, to the IAA, and when their people arrived to verify and claim the site, we moved on.

While, I was enjoying the adventure. This one night, I was troubled. I was here to find treasure and convert some of it to cash to complete the Temple. This was not, for me, a pure expedition to prove the veracity of the Copper Scroll. I put the white stone into my hand and opened it to the glow of the full moon. The light came through the stone and into my eyes, and I saw two white Peregrine falcons, flying towards me. The light ceased, only to show two pure white birds, sitting on my right arm.

I put them on walking stick, inside the tent and fell asleep.

MORNING AT SITE FIVE

A young man dressed in white and a turban brings me tea. And offers crackers to the falcons. He says to me in perfect English:

"The white ones only come from Allah to show the way, Effende."

I explain our mission to find treasure, and the boy says he is aware of it. But that technology will not help find it here, only faith.

"If you tie this prayer to them it will bring you great luck. They will find it. But if they do they will die, Allah's blessing to them complete."

"You must decide if it is worthy of death, if so then let them go tonight, and they will find what you seek, as the sun rises."

He left me with two identical prayers:

Ache naseeb ke liye qurani amal

This Wazifa was designed to be recited by believers to ask for good fortune, but, here, if I attached to their legs, they would find the treasure, and die. I had learned through these years to toss aside my efforts to hold onto reality. Since, I could not know, what state of reality I was in, the present state, or one altered by a higher force to enable my pursuit of my objectives.

I went to the site and participated in the dig and hope that another shadow seen by Lidar would be a site of those evasive talents. By dusk, I invited Dafna to my tent and introduced her to the white falcons, and the prayer. Then, I played out the prophecy.

THE NIGHT OF THE SEVEN ORGASMS

She was not surprised but instructed me to let her prepare me for the morning, and cooked a small meal, at the conclusion of which, she tied the prayers to the falcons and kissed each on the head and released them into the moonlit night. Then she, turned to me, and asked that I not speak, nor question what she would do until morning came upon us.

Dafna disrobed and stood before me, and took off my clothes, and laid me on the floor, she had covered in towels. Then she shaved my left leg with a bowl of warm water nearby; then she brought me to an erection and orgasm.

Then she rested as did I, and she shaved my other leg, and brought me to erection and orgasm.

She shaved my left arm, and put me inside her, until I came. A pause of time. Then the other arm, and the same insertion and result.

Dafna was quiet, but humming at times, like this was making chicken soup.

She eventually rolled me on my back and shaved it. Turned me over and with her mouth, expressed me again. Then the front shave, and a joyous, rocking of me, with her atop me, to a scream, I could not contain, and a slap.

By the time, the sun begins to emerge. I am spent, but she washes me with a towel, and proceeds to cut my beard and shave it off. Then I enter her from behind, as she stands, and the seventh flow of semen, ends it.

Then, she instructs me to dress all in white. I drink an orange juice, my mouth so dry from a night of being drained, and I eat two crackers. She stands nude, like Bathsheba after her conquest of David that first night, and pulls back the curtain.

The boy is waving from a dune close by, and he lifts the two carcasses of the falcons, yelling, Effendi, Effendi.

THE SITE

Less than eight feet deep, the men have excavated three small areas. One is barren, the other yields a single silver bowl, 18 inches in diameter, with no obvious markings. The third has a small box or chest. That I am to open. There is both fear of the wrath of God, and the fear of finding nothing.

Before, I go into the excavation, I pause, look at Dafna, she nods, and I say a prayer first to myself quietly, then to everyone, with nothing else prepared, out of my mouth comes the Shema.

"Hear O Israel, the Lord our God, the Lord is One"

Sh'ma Yisrae'el YHWH (Adonai), 'eloheinu, YHWH,(Adnoai) 'ehad

Then, I sing the other versus, some sing with me.

I lower myself on one side of it, Dafna the other. I pick up the top and it falls into her hands. There is a fragment of a purple and white material, enough to see it was a garment. It is photographed and packaged. And then under it are gem stones. Ten of them, all of the same cut and size. Our minds begin to spin at the possibilities, each of us with a theory. But cheers rise as dawn comes to Qumran. We have found something, how significant we do not yet, know.

But Lidar and Belzoni, the boy and the falcons, and the mystery of this Dafna Dudai, have conspired under God's will to put these stones before us. The IAA and Dafna discuss the find, even as, she sends pictures over her phone to be registered, and sets in motion a meticulous process to determine the nature of these stones.

I am certain, they are more likely the stones representing the tribes of Israel once imbedded in the sacred breast plate of the high priest. The plate either buried elsewhere or destroyed, and only the precious stones saved. And the piece of cloth, by color, purple and white, either a part of the shroud over the altar or, even the ephod worn as a bib by the high priest. But, it is all speculation, and until something is known, it has biblical and archeological value, but there will be no cash flowing from it.

But, for Dafna and Belzoni, it means years of digging and exploring ahead of them. This area of Qumran has given up something of significance, the remnants of what maybe proof that 3Q15, was neither a hoax, nor, an errant guide to hidden riches. But, for now the millions of dollars in "talents" of silver and gold remain beneath the desert sands, as they have been for two thousand years.

There is a confidence that comes from deep beliefs, either in your Lidar lasers, the competency that comes from years of study, or just blind faith, like mine that can cough up results. This 3Q15 expedition was all of that. Belzoni has a new way to accelerate finding the lost treasures, and Dafna a lifetime of knowledge, that can be directly applied to the lost treasures of the Copper Scroll.

The media interest is hot for a two day cycle, turns tepid and then is gone. Dafna is seen everywhere, and Belzoni and his Lapir fascinates the morning news programs across the globe. They are attractive, articulate and have their hands on solving an ancient mystery. Yet, the main stream media have no long term fascination with muses about the treasures of destroyed Temples, a box of gemstones, or the fate of the Essenes. They quickly return to the conflicts of nations, politicians, and the current nude photos of some popular actor or singer.

The experience brought some needed publicity for the Temple, and the promise of 30% of the net proceeds of whatever is uncovered to the foundation. In the long term, the value was substantial. The journey, itself, was unavoidable, driven by an inner compulsion and the direction of God, and the experience of being prepared for the discovery through a test of carnal pleasures, transcendent.

CHAPTER XVI

THE DAY OF ATONEMENT COMES

UNDER A CHUPPAH
IN FRONT OF THE TABERNACLE

I stand next to Rabbi Greenberg who is ordained and can marry people. Before him, my boyhood friend Sammy "Starman", who still dressed in his bikers gear, ran the compound in my absence. By his side the bride, Doreen Culver, in tight jeans, and flowing white blouse. The both have tied their heads in Axel Rose bandanas. His is light blue, hers is white.

The stand in this, otherwise, traditional ceremony under the Chuppah, symbolic of a home they will share together.

My role is to offer a short speech about the bond of marriage and our wishes for them both. Then the actual Rabbi, concludes the ceremony. I could do it, but for all my internal feelings of my rabbinic, and patriarchal roots, to the world, I am MAC, a Jew, devoted to building a Temple, but not ordained, by anyone or things, but my own imagination or lunacy.

I say the expected, stay within the confines of the ceremony, and offer each a Buddhist prayer, sungdi, of a single strand of red fabric for him, and yellow for her. Before, climbers went to conquer Everest, they would often stop by the hut of the great Lama Geshe of Pangboche. I give them this, as a symbol of the kindness and gentleness, The Lama offered to all climbers. For as he instructed, I instructed them:

"You may think you will conquer the mountain, you will not. It will let you climb it. Your spirit and how you use it, is the power. Without it you will whither. As in marriage, you cannot command it to work, it begins with kindness, and love eternally offered, as God offers his presence in each of us."

Then the roar of the motorcycles, as they kissed. Their friends surrounding the ceremony, revved their engines in celebration. Then the Rabbi motioned for silence. And Starman crushed a wine glass. To which, everyone said, Mazel Tov.

I muttered the meaning of the glass ritual to myself, and said the prayer that fit the moment, to never forget the destruction of the Temple:

"I will not forget thee O Jerusalem, even as I consecrate this bond. I shall return to the sacred place."

The reception ensued by the outdoor amphitheater, and Joey had brought in a Gospel group from Inglewood, and the more traditional sounds of Danny Longwood and his ensemble who could kick Hava Naglia, as well as, the great American songbook.

Danny had become West LA's living scholar on the dance and the lyrics. And I suffered, an explanation, he had offered me before, when I Jacob Cohen, attending events with Ruth. It is, he intoned, A Hassidic Nigun, and came out of Palestine, during Ottoman rule. Unknown, to most Hebrew, as we know it, was not encouraged until that time, and this song became a rallying cry for Hebrew reinvention, and the outlook of Jews worldwide. When the Balfour Declaration sliced Palestine from the Turks, this niggun was a uniting force for the small Jewish community in Jerusalem. It sounded like a Ukranian ditty, and was comforting, and uplifting.

It was also curious that it was mostly seen in the post WWII years, as a secular song of joy for everyone, unmoored from its Balfour roots. Danny loved to offer the factoid that it was iconic, pioneer of civil rights for performers, Harry Bellafonte, who popularized the song, and who, by his own, admission thought it was as important to his early popularity as his standard, the Banana Boat song that made him famous.

This night Danny had conspired with the Baptist Church of Inglewood's choir to offer a unique rendition of the song. The gaiety of it, captured the moment and the rising spirits of the crowd. I was hesitant to "hora" myself, but was dragged into a spinning circle by the new bride.

There I was a link in a circle of bikers, masons, architects, laborers, and the man crushing my hand with his grip, who then took to spinning me around, "hoe down" style at we went, in and out of the inner circle of the dance. It was one long hora. I made my way back to an empty table, only to be joined by dancing partner, the father of bride, Levi Culver.

He was a man of size, a body replica of Dan Blocker, who rose to fame as Hoss Cartwright, in the television series, Bonanza. It was no surprise when he introduced himself more formally,

"Just call me Hoss, everybody always has, even my dear departed mother"

"MAC, Hoss"

This was a narrative of two boys, Hoss, and brother Buford, who everyone called, "Slim", who grew up outside of Abilene, near Cisco, their father a construction foreman. They had a few businesses, worked the fields in Midland, and fell eventually, fell in with some scientists, who had an idea about how to force liquids through pipes into rock beds to release oil and natural gas. They got to know, the big gun, George Mitchell who started what was called, "fracking" in shale beds in the Barnett Shale of north Texas. And they learned how to drill horizontal and vertically. Before long, the production of their fracking techniques began to chip away at the oil and natural gas dominance of other countries. Over time, they made billions, and more enjoyed beating back the sheiks and OPEC, than making billions. They eventually sold off their share of the business for over 4 billion. Now Hoss said, they just like to buy land, mostly Montana and Wyoming.

But, he was not chatting me up for the hell of it. He had a connection to the God of Abraham, and had a stake, he felt in what we were doing here in the desert. He was, also a pastor in a little known church, more a sect, that a church. He called it, The Assembly of Yahweh 7th Day Church. It was an amalgam of Jewish beliefs and Christian. It was a combining of the presence of Yahweh as God and a reinterpretation of early Christianity, in a pure form. Almost like the ascetic Essenses wanting to flee the hierarchial, Temple laden Priest directed life, in Qumran.

Hoss had traveled to Israel many times, and came to embrace the journey of the Jewish people, prayed at the Western Wall, cried at Yad Vashem, and believed that Christ will not return until the Third Temple is built or returns to the Temple Mount. So he wanted to be a Jew, at least partially.

He pondered this from the porch of his home, overlooking his 80,000 acre, Montana Ranch. Then it came to him, he recounted, during a particularly cold winter afternoon, as he rode a snow plow around the property. There is Yahshua, of Yahweh, and there will be a second coming. They believe in the festivals of Leviticus 23, including Passover and other festivals, and they observe the Sabbath, and keep the covenant with God given to Moses on Sinai, and blend a belief in all 66 books of the Bible, old and new testament.

But, Hoss bends to a simple creed for his church from Matthew 22:36-40

"Love Yahweh. Love your Neighbor"

This Hoss Culver was a man who found himself, even through, humble beginnings, made a fortune, and still had a yearning for something more. So, undaunted by tradition or the naysayers, he went ahead and cobbled together his own faith, and ministers to it. He thought us not so different, in our willfulness and devotion to the same God. He, however, seemed clear of any self doubts, I still had all of mine. Still, I was moving forward, the Temple only stalled by a lack of finishing funds.

Ae weddings go, the booze, cake, and energy goes flat, like the spilled champagne and beer on the table and in the sand. The place begins to smell like a honky- tonk at 4am.

Eventually everyone leaves, and Hoss and I are alone shifting from theology to this project. I walk him through the grounds from the Tabernacle, to inside the gates and walk up the stairs of the Temple, into the larger uncomplete Temple.

We walk from the inner court to the altar, to the steps and shroud that separates the Holy Of Holies, which we enter together.

"In the Temple, Hoss, the ARK would rest here. Above it two cherubims, depicted as winged creatives, plated in gold, their wings almost touching. Only the Kohen Gadol would enter. But, only on the Day of Atonement, and utter the true name of God, spend time with the Lord and exit with the covenant secure."

He seemed touched and sat with me on the steps, looking back at the unfinished building.

"What will it take, MAC. To get this done?"

"Another 80 million, and I don't have it. I will get it, overtime. I will"

"MAC, I can do that. But there are conditions"

I doubt, there would be anything he could ask, I would not grant. Still, I waited, what seemed an eternal pause for his conditions.

"You will put my daughter and her biker husband to work as managers of the operations of this place. They need a job, and she has a good spirit and head about her, and her hero husband, it not going to settle down unless you force him to be responsible."

"Two, you let me bring my church here from time to time to hold services on the grounds and celebrate some holidays here

I am feeling I am getting off easily.

"And you, MAC, God loving man, better be here to dedicate this damn thing when its done, and we cut the ribbon together"

It is a wish, I wish I could grant, I tell him. But in the end, "That Hoss, is Not in my hands"

He puts his arm around me and we walk out together into the coming dawn, the sun's rays, cracks over an Eastern mountain, and I finally have that feeling of release a man has after he has accomplished something of lasting value to him.

TRUCK GATE
EARLY SUMMER

Hoss's money accelerated our purchase of material, especially cedar logs, that Roberto and Izzy where having sliced in half and mounted on composite wall board for the interior. The truck stream was constant for the few months. The material had piled up by this drop off point, and Izzy was screaming in Spanish to the workers to off load the logs more quickly. She has everything organized but, Roberto was driven to get the logs secured, so Polly could bring her artisans and begin the work of creating a gold inlay that would mock the actual gold lining of the Temple.

After enough trips Izzy's shop stewards knew the drivers and their cargo. Most where on schedules she designed and sent to them via computer links. And every load had a stock number, and every one of those, a corresponding code to exactly where what was on the truck was going. This meticulous, woman could organize anything, whether dropping rocks in the desert for arts' sake or this project.

It was a jolt, then, when one truck came through without any authorization. And it moves erratically, with a maniacal purpose, towards us. Another alert driver backs up his Volvo rig, into the oncoming grill of the Freightliner, and ends its progression. Out of the cab, a man exits shooting two pistols.

Roberto aims his 30.06 and downs the assailant with two shots at his core. One bullet blows open his heart, the other his lungs.

He lays in his blood, with two 9mm's, by his side. His car license identifies him as Randy Stepler, the youngest son of Ralph of Stepler Citrus Farms. By the time, we read the ID, a deputy has arrived and enters the information on his computer, and sends it to the Sherriff. Apparently, his father died in prison, a week ago, and the family buried him over the weekend. It may have been just too much to bear that this Temple was rising, even as, his father had conspired to destroy it and me years ago.

There was no knowing for certain, if it was Randy who tried to assassinate me years ago. But, the deputy thought it likely. Roberto, as eccentric a character as he was, had one eccentricity that saved my life. He was a great shot.

TISHA B'AV

Nothing stopped the forward motion. Not the shooting, the media interest. Nothing.

All of our petty concerns, including eating and sleeping seemed to fade as we devoted our collective energy towards the completion and opening of the Temple.

There was a hope that before the August date commemorating the end of both Temples, we could open ours. All of the planning and frenetic activity could get us to that conclusion. Delays, a mistiming on delivery or how fast an artisan can really work were all obstacles. And, I strained, pulled myself out of the place of compassion and kindness and became a cranky old man, after a singular, narrow result.

We were all on edge.

I went for a slow lope along a trail, the heat made me feel young, in just shorts and trunks, still running near 80, now into this place. And I feel like I did when I first arrived here, and found Maqroll, and Izzy, Joey and the others, in this place that housed so much mystery and revealed a mystical realm that would alter my reality, to become MAC.

Without food that day, I had fasted for Tisha B'av to mourn the loss of the Temple. Even though, my own faith, told me as a Jew, we were all blessed that the Temples fell and with them the hierarchy of the Priests, the narrow rule of Sanhedrin law, and the restriction of the faith to be passed through an army of priests, prophets, and orthodoxy that restricted our direct path to "the ineffable ".

Still, I knew that building this Temple, this extraordinary replica, would excite the world to reconnect to their own faith, and use it as tool, so that others can believe that all faiths can have a place where they could dwell. As the old Gospel intones, "There is a place for everyone in the Temple of the Lord."

When I returned, I called everyone before me, at the main construction site. And I declared an imposed paid two week vacation. And told everyone, including the inner circle to get off site, and just close us down, until the end of August. There were cheers, and a few complaints, but eventually everyone was gone, except for me a security force.

I took the dogs from Fran and retired to the old trailer, and drifted back to the way it was twenty years ago.

YOM KIPPUR

I had planned a special service for anyone who wished to come. I was not ordained. But I was MAC, a Levite and imbued by a sense that I was part of the lineage of Aaron. So, I invited anyone, Jew or not, to see what a Yom Kippur service was like in Temple days, without the actual sacrifices, at our Temple. While the inside was only partially finished, there was enough, now, to suggest a Holy place. There was an altar, unfinished, the steps and doors to the Holy of Holies. There was enough completed to imagine what it would be like, to offer an insight into a day of atonement with a Temple.

For my preparation, I invited both a Rabbi and cantor from a small San Diego, reform congregation to bring their members, and to ensure that the traditional service would occur, and not be marred by having it presented by someone as inept at the rituals as me.

The Kohen Gadol would spend seven days preparing for the event, stay in a special room. He would practice the rituals, read scripture and review the animals readied for sacrifice.

And then at the Eastern Gate, that morning, he would review the animals, run his hands across the perfect hide of the red bull, and emerge in a white linen vestments, to begin the service called Avodah. Wherein a passage,

"Look to the Levite Aaron and his sons, robed in splendid garments, offering sacrifices, on behalf of all the people, fulfilling God's command : Cleanse me thoroughly of sin. I know my neighbor's transgressions, Can I recognize my own?"

The words, the Kohen Gadol stated to all before him:

"The world is sustained by three things: Torah, deeds of loving kindness, and the Temple Service."

I began to explain to everyone what the actual priest would do, as I stood before them, in white linen and a faux chain of gold around my neck. I would change my garments five times, each time, washing in a ritual bath. I would also bless and sacrifice animals, Yom Kippur was a blood bath at the altar.

There would be two goats. One for God and one for Azazel. Azazel, a fallen angel, with devil like qualities, who roamed the desert as a ghost spirit. The first goat is slaughtered for God, the second is given a red, wool string wrapped upon its horn, and sent into the desert. The goat wanders during the service far into the desert, until it reaches a rugged canyon, where another priest shoves to its death. This scapegoat, carries all the sins of the Israelites into that gully. And when it dies the shofar is sounded to end the day of atonement.

While at the Temple, the Kohen Gadol, kills and burns a ram, slaughters the red bull, and mixes its ashes, to be held for dedication rites for future ceremonies. Out of this blood, the Priest would enter the Holy of Holies. I walk there to demonstrate and do two things of great mystical value. First, he would sprinkle the blood of the bull eight times, one upward, and then, seven downward. And do this three times.

Second, he would go inside the chamber with the Ark, and a rope tied to his waist, and utter the actual name of God, the tetragrammaton, only uttered once a year. I say, I do not know what was said, and no one else does. It being lost. But it is uttered, and the crowd around the Temple would bow, and hope that Yahweh, offered a response of good will to his people.

The actual service continued. I said the prayers of the Kohen Gadol, as I had rehearsed them for a week with the Rabbi, in Hebrew, and then I read in English:

"May it be your will, Lord our God, and God of our fathers, to grant us, with all Your people Israel, a year of blessing, a year of corn and wine and oil, a year of prosperity, of Assembly in your Temple, a year of abundance, of happy life and a year of atonement for our sins. May he grant us wisdom of the heart. And may there be peace among us. Amen."

And then, I offered that to a disciple of God only required that you belief, in a God that is gracious and compassionate, and thus to honor him and be atoned you vow to be the same a person who is gracious, kind and compassionate.

It was a service, never explained and never seen. So, if nothing else it was glimpse into ritual, superstition, or actual revelation brought by men of faith to their God, through the existence of the Temple. To the audience it was more spectacle, I do not know it brought anyone of them closer to God or served as the best vehicle for penance.

The cantor sang the final prayer. She motioned for the shofar to sound. I came down from the steps of sanctuary and joined the Rabbi, and he motioned to me. And I stood over them, and raised my arms as did Aaron, spread my fingers, in what they all considered a Vulcan greeting from Doctor Spock, and wished them a Happy New Year.

And, as was the way of the Temple, we held a banquet for everyone to break the fast, and danced into the late evening with a jazz quartet.

It was some performance, I had offered and a look into Temple history. But, I went back to the Tabernacle, where it was quiet. I said the service, the one I did as a boy, without any histrionics. And, I prayed for forgiveness for a lifetime of sins, harshness, and anger that drove too much of life. I was still, not fully repented nor repaired.

Nor was the world. May God grant me another year in the book of Life.

CHAPTER XVII

∞ ❖❖❖ ∞

I Am That I Am

On Good Morning America
5 AM PST

I am sitting on a deck chair I front of what is a mostly completed Temple. And I am speaking to a camera lens, the other end of which is a delightful, if clueless young woman asking about what I have accomplished and why. I am not embarrassed, as I sit in my black blazer, and black turtle neck, looking like a fashion icon, or Vegas mogul.

Fran made this last public splurge happen, an all network satellite tour of crazy MAC, who after twenty years, finally did get this Temple of Solomon to rise in the sleepy, desert own of Borrego Springs. But here it was behind me. The actual Temple re – created according to the command of God in Kings and Chronicles. The struggle of fighting haters, the Jewish mainstream groups, the Neo- Nazi's, and the vandals of the desert, were behind us. And this gal was not interested in any of it. She seemed more interested in me as later day Walt Disney than a descendant of Aaron.

"So what do you have there, MAC, besides the Temple"

"We have picnic grounds, an amphitheater for concerts and services, a historic biblical history walk, gardens and fruit orchards, and even a small farm nearby where you can see and touch animals of the time of the Temple. You know burros, bulls, sheep, and rams mostly"

"Do you have a favorite spot"

"I do, it's the Tabernacle, exactly as we think it was as the Hebrews traveled through the desert on the Exodus. It is simple and direct."

"You bring this Temple to millions, was that the idea?"

"It was, always my hope that if we put it up here, that people from all faiths, and would want to experience it all"

And so the next five interviews went. Nothing probative or frightening, but more interest in the attractive than the substance. But, that did not matter to me today. They showed the grounds, one network had me stand in front of the Molten Sea, and the twelve oxen that supported it. It was for their viewers, a world they only knew through pictures and verse, now transformed into a reality they could visit. I was not that naïve anymore that this would bring some revelation or outpouring of religious feelings. It is a replica after all.

But one voice on the other end of the satellite came closest to my feelings about its value:

"MAC twenty years ago when this started, there was no peace in Israel. The Temple Mount was contested land, A Jew could not pray on the site of the Temple, and most nation's refused to agree that Jerusalem was the capital of Israel. And today"

"We have an Embassy there. The position of most governments remain anti –Israel. The conflicts through the years have further reduced peace initiatives, not expanded them, and the Temple Mount is still occupied by sacred sites to Muslims and limited access for Jews."

"So any closer to a actual Third Temple?"

"No, and only God knows, when the will be right for it to be built. So I am blessed that we stayed with this long enough to offer it to the world"

"But, it is still a source of controversy"

"Yes, it remains a debate among the orthodox of my faith, and among the traditional leadership whether I should have done this. But now, I hope they will if not embrace it, at least grow silent."

And the interviews ended.

The entire complex was full of people. The parking areas crowded with visitors, and buses lined the transportation center. The pure Temple appeared white against the morning sun. The shuttles hurried to get everyone to the front of the Temple for the ribbon cutting.

It would be streamed live on our www.templeofthedesert.com, so the world could experience the moment. I stood next to Hoss, and his daughter and husband, Polly was at my left hand with Roberto, and Izzy. I had asked a color guard from Camp Pendleton to present the flag, and to play the national anthem of the United States. This was a Temple of Israel, but it is the freedom I was guaranteed here that allowed me to become MAC and create it on our soil. It was not a time for Hatikvah,, but for America, and I wanted it branded, as such, indelible in the minds of the assembled.

And as the last note soared, Hoss and I put our hands on the Red, White and Blue sash, and cut it with an oversized pair of scissors.

Then the tours began. Polly leading the media through the site, and Roberto hosting the foreign press.

Fran came to me, and offered a goodbye hug, and bringing me Lobo, on a leash. Red now long ago passed. She was ready to head back to Los Angeles, and take her RV back to some beach, and still attend a red carpet from time to time.

"You have grown attached to each other MAC, he is your guardian angel, isn't he?"

And she left, I made the rounds after a few more hours, and exhausted drove my old ATV back to the trailer.

To celebrate, I took a sip of a single malt on the porch, and loaded a few clays, and blew them into pieces, the sound of it like a desert lullaby, and Lobo barked.

UCLA REAGAN MEDICAL CENTER
NOON
TWENTY YEARS BEFORE

Maqroll has just awakened me. I am in a wheel chair, awaiting his car.

"You were out for a few weeks Jacob. The family asked me to bring you home"

The car arrives, I walk into the passenger seat. Maqroll pulls behind the wheel

"Where to Boss? In and Out? Home?"

"No amigo, your place, the desert!"

"Whatever you say"

"It's been a long sleep"

"Indeed, my friend, as we say, "LA VIDA ES SUENO

"A dream, indeed, Verdad !"

Printed in the United States
By Bookmasters